AC NW
WOLVES
BOYS OF
RICHLAND
XXXX
THE
SAVAGE

Copyright © 2022 Daniela Romero

All Rights Reserved, including the rights to reproduce, distribute, or transmit in any form by any means. For information regarding subsidiary rights, please contact the author.

This book is a work of fiction; all characters, names, places, incidents, and events are the product of the authors imagination and either fictitious or used fictitiously. Any resemblance to actual events or persons, living or dead, is coincidental.

TRIGGER WARNING

The Savage is recommended for mature readers 17+
If you don't have any triggers, turn the page and enjoy.
If you do, check out the list below and make sure this book
is a good fit for you!

The Savage deals with sensitive subject matter including
but not limited to suicide, suicidal thoughts, grief, and the
aftermath of sexual assault.

Please read responsibly.

The Savage is not a standalone novel. Gabriel and Cecilia's
story will continue in The Striker, available now.

PART ONE
THREE MONTHS
EARLIER

1
CECILIA

wake to a dry mouth, a sluggish brain, and a pounding headache. God, how much did I have to drink last night? Just turning to the side, my face still mashed against the pillow, sends a spear of agony stabbing into my skull.

I let out a pain filled groan and a wave of nausea slams into me. Fuck. I think I'm going to be sick. Sightlessly, I reach out to get my bearings and fumble to get myself in a seated position so I can make a run for the bathroom. Or walk. I swallow the lump in my throat. Right now, I'll settle for a crawl.

My fingers cling to the sheets beneath me and I shove up.

Wait a minute. I clench and unclench the material beneath my hands. That's not right. It's thick. Flannel. But that can't be right. My sheets are cotton. Light and thin because I hate waking up in the middle of the night overheated.

This isn't my bed.

Forcing my sticky eyelids open, I push the long tangled strands of my dark brown hair out of my face and take in my surroundings. Blinking hard against the hazy light that filters in through the window, I stare down at the very blue fabric beneath me. Definitely not mine.

Where the hell am I?

I scan the room. It's decidedly a boy's. Posters of half-naked girls leaning against muscle cars decorate the walls, intermixed with athletic trophies and sports paraphernalia.

Classy.

Swinging my legs over the side of the bed, I scoot to the end, but have to pause when the room spins and everything along the edges of my vision blurs.

I've been hungover before, but never like this, where my entire body aches and I can't remember why I'm in someone else's bed. Slowly, so as not to black out, I glance over my shoulder and exhale a breath of relief. Not my bed, but whoever's it is, they're thankfully not in it with me. That's something, at least.

I turn back around with a sigh of relief but it's short lived when I look down and notice the state of my dress. It's torn down the front, my chest spilling out of the ruined satin and lace. I clutch at the material, bringing it together, but it's no use.

Something hard pokes me under my arm and I fumble around inside my dress, finding the edges of my bra.

Untwisting the damn thing, I bring the front clasp together, satisfied at least that my boobs are no longer on display.

That's when I see the bruises. I haven't let myself think beyond the pounding in my head and the nausea twisting my gut, but now, holding my hands out in front of me, I take in the dark purple smudges that circle both of my wrists and forearms.

What the hell happened to me?

I stare at them in abject horror, rotating my arm to see all the way around. Are those... finger marks? I don't like the scenarios my mind conjures up. The numerous ways I could have gotten bruises like this. None of them are good.

This is the stuff you see in movies. Not real life. Not to someone like me.

I need... I — it hits me and my chest heaves, breath seesawing in and out. This isn't real. It's a dream. A bad, bad dream.

I squeeze my eyes closed and clutch my hands to my chest. I remember going out with Kim and Joelle. The Zeta Pi party. Austin.

Bile climbs up my throat and I cover my mouth with my hand. Thick, oily dread settles into my veins. I really am going to be sick. I stumble to my feet but my legs give out beneath me and I crash to the hardwood floor. My knees smart and tears pool in my eyes, but it's not the pain that causes my emotions to well up inside me.

It's memories of last night assaulting my mind that do that for me.

He... he... I squeeze my eyes closed. No! Tears spill over my cheeks and track down my face. When I open them again, I spot a waste bin beside the bedside table and lunge for it, barely making it before my stomach empties itself.

This isn't happening.

Cool air hits the backs of my thighs, informing me that my chest isn't the only part of me exposed.

I vomit again.

Please be a nightmare. A sick and twisted figment of my imagination. But it isn't, and knowing that has a keening sound slipping past my lips. This is real. It's sick and not okay, but what happened to me, it's real.

My stomach is empty now, but I continue to dry heave. It's like my body revolts against the revelation of what's transpired.

Gut wrenching sobs wrack my body and I try my damndest to muffle them. I don't know if anyone else is here. If Austin is still around.

What will he do if he finds me? I can't wait to find out.

Wiping my mouth with the back of my hand, I begin the frantic search for my shoes. I don't see them anyway, but manage to spot my phone.

On shaking limbs, I force myself to get up and retrieve it. My entire body is sore, like one big bruise has taken up residence on every inch of skin I possess. Grabbing my cell, I swipe my thumb over the screen. Nothing. I do it again.

Dammit. It's dead.

Voices in the hall freeze me where I stand. I strain my ears. More than one and all male by the sounds of it. Every muscle in me locks up.

Footsteps move closer to the door. Shit. My fingers tighten around my phone, clenching it as if it's my last lifeline.

What do I do?

I scan the room, searching for something, anything, I can use as a weapon but there's nothing.

Footsteps pause on the other side of the door. The knob twists. I watch in horror as it turns three quarters of the way before stopping, almost like whoever stands on the other side knows I'm waiting.

On silent hinges, the door swings open to reveal Austin Holt. PacNorth's star soccer player. Head of Zeta Pi fraternity. And the man I know will soon haunt my nightmares.

"You're up." His blue eyes take in my disheveled appearance, and he smirks. "We need to talk."

2
GABRIEL

"**M**amá? Pops?" I call out, stepping through the door.

No answer, not that it surprises me. I ignore the lack of response and step further into my childhood home. The house is quiet. Still. But I don't let it deter me.

There's this oppressive sense of loss that hangs heavy in the air and settles on my shoulders like a physical weight. One I've learned I cannot escape so long as I am here.

I hate it.

This used to be home. My haven. Now, it's nothing more than the tomb that holds a collection of broken memories. Ones I am desperate to forget.

Being here makes my muscles tighten in anticipation. Like another bomb is about to drop. Only this time, I have some measure of warning. Too bad knowing what's coming doesn't make it hurt any less. If anything, it makes matters worse. They know exactly what they're doing and have made it clear, they don't care.

Pictures line the walls, an eclectic collage my mother put together over the years while I was growing up, but more striking than the images themselves are the gaps interspersed throughout them. The faded shapes where picture frames once stood but have long since been removed.

My fingers trail over one particular gap. My brother's and my first steps. We were just under a year old and stood in our front yard, excited grins on our faces at what we'd just accomplished. Even with it gone, I can see the image in my head as though Mom never took it down.

I drag my hand further along the wall, trailing around the frames that still hold photographs of friends and relatives through the years until I reach the spot in the center that once served as the focal point of our family gallery. It held my parents' wedding photo but now it's empty, the paint darker here having been protected from the sun. I shake my head. It's been like this for months, but I still can't get used to it. It's like the soul of the house died. Right along with any love our family had for one another.

There are more empty spots than there are filled. Anything with Carlos was removed after his death. Family portraits. His school pictures. Following that, Mom took down pictures of me. Seeing my face became too much for her. A constant reminder of the son she lost. I used to wish we didn't share a face. That he'd never been my twin.

Now, I just don't care.

She should have taken all the photographs down. It'd look less... I don't know, depressing, maybe, if she had.

I drop my helmet on the entryway table, ready to get this over with, and cut through the foyer on my way to the kitchen. Despite not getting an answer when I first arrived, I know my parents are home. They're the ones who scheduled this bullshit meeting today, after all.

Dad's leaning against the kitchen counter when I step into the room, a glass of amber liquid in his hand. No surprise there. The man hasn't been sober in months.

Mom sits at the dining room table, claiming the seat furthest from him with a glass of wine in front of her. Wonderful.

They knew their son was showing up and both decided alcohol was the best way to deal with it.

Neither of them looks at the other and only Dad bothers to acknowledge me, offering a small nod of his head before he indicates the thick envelope resting atop the kitchen island, my name written in thick black marker across the top of it.

Tension sits heavily in the room. I've only just walked in and already it threatens to suffocate me. How long have they been sitting here like this?

"This everything?" The sooner we get this over with, the sooner I can leave.

Mom doesn't look at me, but she does take a heavy drink from her wine glass. Why is she even here? She hasn't spoken to me in months. Neither of them has. I'm surprised they didn't ask me to mail in the papers and save everyone the trouble of being here right now.

"It is," my dad says. "We just need your signature and then we..." he trails off, but I don't need him to finish. Like the two of them, I'm aware of why we're here.

Swallowing past the lump in my throat, I tear open the packet and make quick work signing my name on all the lines their attorney's bothered to highlight in yellow. I don't waste time reading over the documents. This benefits me more than it does them. The sooner we get this over with, the better.

My grandparents set up a trust for my brother and I when we were kids. Nothing crazy, but education has always been a big deal in our family and they wanted to make sure my brother and I had the means to go to college.

If my grandparents were still around, I think they'd be proud to learn I earned a full ride to PacNorth to play soccer. I don't need their money for school. Not that it makes it any less mine.

When Carlos passed away, his portion became mine as well. Something about it being a joint account. With one brother gone, the rest falls to the other.

There are stipulations on the account. Carlos and I both gained access when we turned eighteen, but only for expenses directly related to college and each withdrawal requires my parents' consent. Carlos never had the chance to spend so much as a penny and I've never touched a dime.

I never needed to. Since I don't need the money for school, I shouldn't have access to the account until after my twenty-fifth birthday. But that's three years from now and for my parents, it's three years of being tied to me, too many.

They've decided to sign over the account early. A few signatures here and there and I no longer need their consent to access any of it. I'll have more money than I could need as a senior in college, and they'll have no reason to see me again.

For them, it's a win-win.

Sometimes I wish I saw it that way.

Closing the packet, I shove the papers back into the envelope and drop it down on the countertop.

"Anything else?"

Dad shakes his head. I turn to Mom, silently begging her to say something, anything. Fuck, I'd be happy if she'd just acknowledged my fucking existence, but she still won't look at me. She sits there, quietly drinking her wine like she can't be bothered. I shouldn't have expected anything less. Mom checked out of my life years ago. I rub the ache in my chest, hating that after all this time, her indifference still affects me. I don't get it. You'd think after losing one kid, they'd fight harder for the other, but instead, they throw me away. It's hard to believe they ever cared about me at all.

"You know..." I shake my head and suck on my teeth. I should drop it. Let this shit go and move on with my life.

My eyes bore into her. I can't, though. This is fucked up. I don't deserve to be treated like this. No one does.

"It's not my fault we share the same face."

Mom flinches but doesn't turn my way. Her throat bobs as she swallows another mouthful of wine, probably wishing I'd hurry up and leave already, but why should I? It's not my problem, she's uncomfortable. That the very site of me, her own fucking son, makes her ill. How does she think it is for me? Waking up and seeing his face every fucking day?

She'll get what she wants soon enough. Once I walk out that door, she can go back to pretending she never had kids. That I'm not her son. That she didn't abandon me when my world was already falling apart. And that making me sign these papers isn't her way of stabbing the knife already buried deeper into my chest.

"Just like it's not my fault he's gone."

Silence.

"It's not my fault he was selfish. Or that he fucked our family over."

"Gabriel—" My father's voice is soft, pleading with me not to fight this. Not to make a scene.

I turn to look at him. "None of this is my fault!" I remind him. "Yet you two are so fucking intent on punishing me for Carlos's sins, anyway."

He hangs his head but says nothing and I don't bother to stick around. All it does is lead to more disappointment.

Grabbing my helmet from the hall, I slam the door behind me, the sound reverberating against my back. I give my childhood home one last look as I climb on my bike.

Fuck them. I didn't need my brother. I sure as hell don't need them.

3
CECILIA

In case you were wondering, talk is code word for threaten, blackmail, and basically, go out of your way to ruin my life. I should have seen this coming.

"Hey." I wave.

It's lame, but I'm not sure what else to do here. My heart races in my chest as I look from Austin to the door. "I, uh, actually need to leave. I'm sure Joelle and Kim are worried sick that I never came back to the dorms last night."

He either doesn't hear me or, more accurately, doesn't care. And what he does next drops a ball of dread, like a heavy stone, into the pit of my stomach. Austin smiles. It's charming and attractive. Or it would be on anyone else but him. Not after learning what he's capable of.

He steps further into the room and closes the door behind him, locking me inside.

I swallow hard and try not to panic.

Shaking fingers hold the torn front of my dress together as Austin stands there with that stupid smile on his face. He eyes me up and down, like he's remembering what's hidden beneath my dress.

Bile rises from my stomach, coating the back of my throat. I wrap my arms around myself in a desperate attempt at modesty. Like it changes anything.

"What do you want to talk about?" My grip on my phone tightens. I wish the stupid thing wasn't dead. That I could call for help. Before he came in here, he was talking to somebody in the hall, which means we aren't alone.

If I scream, will anybody come help me? Does anybody even know that I'm still here? I think about it. Seriously think about it, because at this point, what have I got to lose?

Austin doesn't look worried, though. He's confident. Hell, relaxed even.

This is a man without a care in the world. Not about me screaming, at least.

"Did you have fun last night?" he asks, breaking the silence.

"Sure. Loads." Lie. I most definitely did not have fun. Being assaulted is not fun. Being forced — I drop that train of thought. Hold it together, Cecilia. Now is not the time or the place. Right now, you need to get the hell out of here. The rest can wait until you're home. Until you're safe.

I force myself to smile. To relax. "But, like I said, I need to get going."

"I get it." Austin casually leans against the door. "Just want to make sure everyone is on the same page. You know how it is. One small misunderstanding can fuel the rumor mill and all of a sudden, a night of fun turns into a bunch of bullshit in the media. Your dad is up for reelection this year, right?" The way he asks, with that curious glint in his eyes, it sets me immediately on edge.

"Why does that— "

He cuts me off. "My parents contributed. To his campaign, I mean. Did you know that?"

I shake my head, not understanding why any of this is relevant to me. My dad is running for Mayor again. Lots of people contribute to his campaign.

"I don't like to brag…"

I barely manage to contain my snort. He's rich, in the Zeta Pi fraternity, on the PacNorth soccer team, and good looking. His ego is bigger than this bedroom and he's one of those guys that likes hearing the sound of his own voice, so he definitely does, in fact, like to brag.

"But my family is a big deal here in Richland." Good for him. "We own Holt & Associates. The law firm down on Twenty-Second Street."

That rock in the pit of my stomach turns into a boulder, and a barely audible gasp slips past my lips.

He hears it, and his smile grows even wider. Holt & Associates is one of my dad's campaign contributors. But more concerning is the fact that they're one of the best known law firms in the state. Hell, maybe even the country. They like high-profile cases. The controversial ones that get their firm on the news, which means more often than not, they represent problematic people. Criminals. And they do a really good job getting them off clean.

"Recognize the name?" He chuckles. "I thought you might. Last I heard, they're one of Russo's largest donors. Your parents and mine are probably good friends." He winks. "Like the two of us."

Indignation floods through me. Friends? Is he serious right now? We are not friends, and I see what he's doing now. "Fuck you."

His eyes flash in surprise. "Excuse me?"

My cheeks heat and I mash my lips together as I bite back my words, but screw it. Screw him. "I know what you're doing." I'm not stupid. I can read just fine between the lines he's so clearly drawing out for me.

Austin quirks a blond brow. "Do you, now?" His tone is condescending. If I was at all confused before, I'm not now.

Nausea sweeps through me when I nod my head, the motion making the room spin, but I manage to hold myself together. "You..." I swallow past the lump in my throat. "You raped— "

"Woah, woah." He holds both hands up in the air. "See. That's what I'm talking about." He makes a tsking sound and shakes his head. "You and I need to get on the same page here, Cece. That sort of accusation can ruin someone's reputation."

My upper lip curls. "Are you screwing with me?"

His eyes are hooded. "I think we did a good amount of that last night, but if you're looking for round two— "

"This isn't a joke." I swing my arm and hurl my phone at his head with every ounce of strength in me. It narrowly misses him, thudding against the wooden door as he jerks out of the way.

Meanwhile, I crash into the dresser beside me as I lose my footing, but I manage to stay on my feet, barely, nails digging into the dresser top.

I bare my teeth. "I'll die before I let you touch me again," I seethe. "Stay the hell away from me."

Austin looks momentarily at a loss for words as he looks from me to my phone and back again before his expression hardens.

"You're not feeling like yourself," he tells me, bending down to retrieve my phone, "so I'm going to make myself clear. What happened last night was— "

"Rape."

He continues on, ignoring me. "A few friends having a good time. We had some drinks. Things got a little out of control."

I'd shake my head if I wasn't so worried I was going to pass out.

"You... you—" I can barely get the words out, but I force myself to say them. "You held me down. You held my hands behind my back while—"

"While my buddies fucked your face," he finishes with a smirk. "Yeah. I did. And you liked it." The look on his face is one of complete satisfaction. He's proud of himself. He makes me sick.

"No. I didn't!" What the hell is wrong with him? How could he possibly think I enjoyed any part of what he did? "You helped your friends assault me and then you—" My brows pinch together. Parts of last night are still a little hazy.

It was late. I was drunk. I wanted to find Kim and Joelle and leave. I remember being tired and when Austin offered to help me find my friends, I took him up on it.

I thought it was kinda sweet. I didn't know him that well, but Kim's had a secret crush on him since freshman year. Having his help was an easy way to introduce the two of them. Give her an in. I talked her up, even. Told him how great my friends were. How Kim was probably his type, and he seemed interested at the time. But it was all just a game to him.

He checked the yard while I checked downstairs, but no luck. When he suggested we check the bedrooms on the second level, I dismissed the idea. No way would either of them hook up with some random at a party. But Austin thought we should look, anyway.

He led me upstairs. I remember thinking it was weird when he bypassed the first two doors. Like he was heading for a specific room. And looking back, it's clear he was.

There were two guys waiting inside, and when I apologized for disturbing them and turned around to leave, Austin blocked my escape. He used his size to press me further into the room, forcing me to stumble back before closing and locking the door behind him.

He planned it. All of it.

"You had it all worked out," I whisper to myself. "The room. The drugs." He drugged me. I remember that now. That must be why my head is so foggy. After he helped his friends, he forced his fingers into my mouth and rubbed something on my gums. A powder of some sort. It tasted awful, but after that, everything starts to fade.

"What was it?" I ask.

"What was what?"

"The drug. Whatever it was you made me take."

He doesn't even bother to deny it. "Ketamine. And don't give me that look. It helped, didn't it? You were more relaxed."

My hands curl into fists. "I didn't want to relax!" I scream. "I wanted to leave. I wanted to get the hell away from you."

He takes a menacing step toward me. "You got what you wanted last night, Cece. Stop deluding yourself. You came to a party dressed like that." He points to my dress. "What did you think was going to happen?"

My mouth hangs open. "No girl wants what you did," I tell him. "Wearing a dress and going to a party isn't asking anyone for what you did."

He snorts. "Stop making this bigger than it needs to be. You gave some good head and got laid. Get that stick out of your ass and move on."

Laid. My mind clings to that word. There were three of him. Did they all—did anyone else —

"Did all three of you rape me?" I can't believe I'm asking him, but I have to know. The last thing I remember after being drugged is Austin laying me on the bed. His hands groping my body. His fingers between my thighs and him climbing on top of me. But after that... nothing.

He glowers at me in silence.

"Answer me," I beg. "Please."

He huffs out a breath and rolls his eyes. "Benson and Chambers fucked your mouth. Only I fucked your cunt. Happy? Can we move this show along now?" He glances at the watch on his wrist. "I have practice to get to."

The way he's so blasé about everything baffles me. He admits to drugging me. To raping me. And yet, he's more worried about getting to practice on time.

"You're not going to get away with this."

He sighs. "Yes, I am. The sooner you realize that, the easier things will get for you."

The horrible thing is, he believes the words coming out of his mouth.

"I'm trying to help you, Cece. Get the two of us on the same page. The right page."

"Don't call me that."

Austin rolls his eyes again. "If you walk out of here and make up stories, it isn't going to end well. Not for you. Be smart."

"Get out."

"Cece—"

"Out!"

He sighs. "Look at the video I texted you." He places my phone on the nearby desk. "I'll send it to your email in case this little outburst of yours broke your cell. Make sure to watch it. You'll reconsider things after you do."

4
GABRIEL

The instant my ass hits the seat, I'm out of there without so much as a glance over my shoulder. I head to the Pier knowing my boys are waiting for me. They offered to come with me, help me deal with my shit. But I declined the offer.

We grew up together. Know each other inside and out. They know what things were like for me after Carlos died. And they know the bullshit my parents pulled today.

But as much as I love my friends and know they'll always have my back, their pity is the last thing I want or need. Which is what I'd get if they were there. If they saw the indifference on my mother's face. The rejection in my father's eyes.

It's bad enough I had to see it. I don't need it taking up space in anyone else's memories beside mine.

It took some convincing, but we all agreed to meet up at Pier 39 instead.

Julio and Felix's bikes are parked near the boardwalk when I arrive, along with an unfamiliar car that is way too expensive to be here. *And who might you belong to?*

My brows furrow as I pull up beside it, and before removing my helmet, I take a quick look through the windows. I wouldn't say we're on the wrong side of town per se, but this sure as shit isn't the ride side where you expect to find rides like this.

For being so nice on the outside—a sleek silver Audi RS 5 —the inside is a disaster. Clothes, coffee cups, and random shit like a hairbrush and a crap ton of books litter the inside. It's like a bomb went off in there, letting me know this is a chick's car for sure.

Removing my helmet and dropping it on my seat, I head down to the Pier, keeping my eyes peeled for whoever the Audi belongs to. We don't own the boardwalk, but it's been abandoned for so long that just the idea of outsiders being here makes my shoulders stiffen.

I shouldn't have been worried. As soon as I turn the first corner, I spot Julio and Felix, and standing beside them is one person I didn't expect to see. "Alejandra!" I call out and she turns, a wide grin on her face, and she jogs toward me. I should have known the car belonged to her.

She throws herself into my arms and I spin her in a circle. She laughs before I put her down, brushing strands of dark brown hair out of her face.

"What are you doing here?"

She mock punches me in the shoulder. "That's a stupid question," she tells me. "Where else would I be on a day like today?"

The reminder makes my smile dim, but not for long.

"None of that," she admonishes. "I drove four hours to hang with you three. Today we're going to have fun."

Felix chuckles, coming up behind her and throwing an arm around her shoulder. "I'm surprised Roman let you escape," he jokes.

Her lips press together and she gives him a conspiratorial look. "He might not know I left."

This time it's Julio who barks out a laugh. "Please tell me you're kidding?"

She shakes her head. "You know how busy he is. It's preseason and they're doing two-a-days." She shrugs. "He won't even notice I'm missing."

Julio shakes his head and pulls out his phone. Brave man. He's not wrong to call Roman. Not after what went down a few years ago. He has reason to worry about her. We all do. But Allie's got a knack for revenge pranks and no way am I looking to put myself in her line of fire.

Allie gasps, reaching for the phone, but Julio holds it up in the air high above his head.

"You wouldn't?"

He smirks. "Yeah, baby girl. I would. You know how he worries."

Before she can make a grab for the phone again, I pull her into my arms, her back to my front, and wrap my arms around her, locking her arms across her chest.

She tilts her head to glower at me, and I meet her sour look with a grin. "He's just looking out for you," I remind her, resting my chin on her head. "It's what *familia* does."

She softens at my words, relaxing into the embrace, and I give her one last squeeze before releasing her, confident she'll let Julio make the call she knows she should have already. There was a time when we couldn't touch Allie like this. When casual contact was met with a flinch or a sharp inhale of breath. She's better now, thanks a lot to her overprotective boyfriend—Roman.

It's a debt the three of us can never repay him for. Bringing her back to us. Making her whole.

"Fine," she grumbles. "But if you're snitching, you three owe me— "

"Way ahead of you," Felix interrupts, pulling out a handful of mini *obleas con cajeta* from his pocket.

Allie snags two from his hand, quickly unwrapping the candy and biting into the sticky caramel with a groan. "So good!" she says around a mouthful of sweets.

Julio pats his shoulder in thanks and walks off to make his call, leaving me to frown at my best friend. "Where do you even hide all these?"

His mouth twists into a mischievous grin. "I have sisters,"
he says. "I make it a point to always be prepared."

PART TWO
PRESENT DAY

5
CECILIA

I'm one of the lucky ones. Or so I've been told. I sure as hell don't feel lucky. But according to my parents, my therapist, and the doctor who bandaged me up, I am.

Lucky, that is.

Why?

Because I didn't die.

I should have. That was the plan. It was a well thought out one, too. Thoroughly researched. All of my i's dotted. My t's crossed. Yet, I somehow failed. And believe me, it wasn't for lack of trying.

I didn't consider that the location I chose for my farewell wasn't nearly remote enough for things to go off without a hitch.

Had the cut been deeper, had I bled out faster, maybe it could've worked. It should have. I put in some serious thought and effort here.

The campus pool closes at seven every night. The locker rooms are empty by seven-thirty. I planned everything out perfectly. I'm not kidding. I was diligent in my research. I even tracked the custodian's schedule to make sure everything was going to line up.

But what I didn't plan, what I couldn't possibly anticipate, was *him*. He was a variable I never could have seen coming. The nameless boy who had to go and ruin everything.

It took so much nerve to make that first cut. I wince thinking about it. And it took even more to make the second.

Do you know how stressful it is to slit your own wrists? I had to Google how to do it. I watched videos online that explained how long and how deep to drag the blade along my wrists. I made sure the razor blade was clean and sharp. Not that I was worried about an infection or anything, but I wanted to do it *right,* ya know?

I was positive it would all work out. I've always been a model student. I follow directions and I usually get things right the first time around, but that day, I messed up.

I take that back. I didn't mess up anything. He did. He wasn't supposed to be there.

No one was supposed to find me until morning when the custodian re-opened the pool. But *he* was there, and *he* was the one who found me. It'd only been minutes since I'd made the cut. And thanks to his intervention, I'm still here, hanging out in the land of the living.

I huff out a breath. I'm so freaking tired. I just want to close my eyes and not wake up again. Is that really too much to ask?

I don't know if or when I'll try again. A part of me feels like it's inevitable. I made the first attempt when I realized there was no other way out. Nothing has changed since.

Well, some things have, but none of them for the better. It's not like I have a million reasons to want to stick around.

My parents watch me more, as if I'm a ticking time bomb seconds away from going off. Lucky me. If I thought I wanted more attention from my parents before, I sure as hell don't now.

I go to therapy now, too. Twice a week. Not that it helps. I understand the reasoning behind seeing a shrink. In theory, if I open up, it's supposed to help. At least, that's what Dr. Walker, my therapist, tells me each time I see her. But to be frank, it's a load of bull.

I don't need to talk about what happened. Not my trauma and not my attempted suicide. I know what happened to me. I know what I did. I'm not in denial. I am very cognizant of everything I've been through.

I'm a realist, and talking about it won't change anything. It still happened. I still can't do anything about it. No one believed me before and they sure as hell aren't going to now that we've added nutcase to my resume. Case closed. Time to move on.

What would really help is if everyone left me the hell alone.

It's been a month since he-who-has-no-name came to my unrequested rescue, and in that month, I moved out of my dorm room and back home with my parents.

Not by choice, I might add, but it's better than the alternative. Better than being committed for thirty days to make sure I'm no longer a danger to myself. I shudder at the thought. A seventy-two-hour hold was long enough to know I wouldn't survive being locked up in there.

The psychiatrist tried to medicate me. They forced me to take mood stabilizers and antidepressants. I hated them. They made me numb, which might sound like a good thing given what I have to deal with, but it isn't. They slowed everything down. My thoughts. My feelings. It was like walking through quicksand. I don't really know how else to describe it.

But when I did feel, when my memories of what happened this past summer crept up on me, I couldn't get away from them. The drugs trapped me inside my own head and I'd sink into my thoughts, unable to escape. It was like reliving my rape all over again.

I promised the 'rents I'd stay home for one semester. Long enough for them to assure themselves I'm okay, and I'll stick to that. I hate liars, and despite everything that's happened, I refuse to become one. But, when the semester is up, all bets are off.

If life is better by then, great. Not that I'm counting on it. But if it is, cool. I'll roll with it. It's not like I want to die.

But every day, it gets a little bit harder to breathe. And a new piece of me I don't even realize exists until it's too late withers away and dies inside me.

But, I made a promise. One semester. I can give my parents that much at least.

They didn't ask for a head-case daughter. They're good parents. The best I could have asked for, to be honest. Mom was a stay-at-home mom when I was younger, and growing up as an only child, I received all the love and attention a kid could possibly need.

Dad works a ton, but he's always made time for me. He'd go to the high school football games just to watch me cheer.

They really are the best.

But they have no idea what happened this summer. And they can't even begin to understand why I tried to kill myself.

After seeing how hard they took my first attempt, I don't have it in me to tell them. Not now. Probably not ever. I don't think any of us can handle that conversation.

If I try again to end it all, I have to make it to the other side. None of us can deal with this emotional rollercoaster again. The doctors. The therapists. The worry and uncertainty. I sure as hell can't.

I tug on the strap of my messenger bag and turn the corner, heading for my first class of the day. It's been a month, and yeah, I know I said it already, but reminding myself I've made it an entire month makes surviving the day seem a little more possible.

It's time to pretend everything is back to normal, which means going back to school and acting like I give a shit about my classes.

Pretending I still want to get a degree in public relations and marketing. That I want to make something of myself. Maybe help Dad on future campaigns. Who the hell knows.

My head is down, my chestnut-colored hair creating a curtain around my face that hides me from the sea of bodies all around me. I try not to think about everyone here. The people I don't know. The guys who walk past me who are bigger and stronger than I am.

I suck in a breath. Come on Cecilia. You're doing great. I remind myself I'm safe. There aren't any bedrooms around for people to drag me into. There isn't any loud music to cover up my cries for help.

I'm so busy staring at my feet and talking myself down as I make my way to class that I run smack dab into a hard, unyielding body.

"Sorry." The apology falls from my lips before I even realize who it is I've run into. But as soon as I do, it's like a bucket of ice water is poured over me.

Austin Holt stands before me, an annoyed look on his face before our eyes meet and recognition flares in his gaze.

This is the boy who lives to haunt my nightmares.

I stumble back, but he catches my shoulders in a firm grip, taking a step closer and leering down at me. I freeze, my entire body locking in place as I wait to see what he's going to do.

I glance from side to side, desperate for someone to step in, but everyone around us goes about their business, ignorant of the panic that squeezes my chest.

"Hey, CeCe," Austin says, keeping his tone even, like we're old friends.

A slow smile spreads across his face, but it isn't a nice one. His smile is twisted and cruel. A mask that hides how sick and depraved he really is. I can't believe I never saw it before. There was a time when I actually found him attractive. Between his blue eyes and sandy blonde hair, Austin has that whole American Eagle model vibe going for him.

But what I missed before was how empty his eyes are. The color is so striking. A clear blue that would be beautiful on anyone else. But when you stare into them, you realize that his eyes are dead. Flat. Lifeless. They say a person's eyes are the portal into their soul, but if you ask me, Austin Holt doesn't have one.

"Let me pass," I bite out.

I can't show any sign of weakness in front of him. I know what he's capable of. My shoulders are tight and my hands tremble but I hide them in my pockets, refusing to let him see how much he unnerves me.

"Heard you tried to kill yourself," he says, not moving out of my way.

His gaze travels up and down my body like he's undressing me with his gaze. It makes my skin crawl, but I hold myself still as he looks his fill before his eyes settle on my wrists. The long sleeves of my sweater hide the scars we both know are there, but I tug them down further anyway.

"Obviously, you didn't try hard enough." He makes a tsking sound. "Better luck next time."

I swallow hard, shrinking in on myself before I remember I can't let him get to me.

"Move," I try again, adding a bite to my voice. I edge around him but he sidesteps, blocking my way.

"You're keeping your mouth shut like we agreed, right babe?" I ignore the endearment and manage a nod, keeping my lips pressed together so I don't scream.

I tried to get help after what he did to me. I went to the school board and told them everything that happened that night. Gave them the names of everyone involved.

It was a mistake. One I won't make again.

"Good. Wouldn't want that video to get out. Imagine what dear old Dad would think?"

It's all I've thought about. It's why I later tried to kill myself.

People say there is a light at the end of every tunnel, you just have to look hard enough. But all I see at the end of mine is never-ending darkness. If that video gets out, it will ruin me. Ruin my family. Dad is up for re- election, and his daughter being gangbanged is a scandal he can't afford.

I haven't seen all of it and there isn't a single part of me that wants to. Austin sent me a clip and then his parents played parts of it for the board when I came forward. Proof of their son's innocence, they claimed.

Just thinking about it, knowing close to a dozen strangers saw me at my most vulnerable moment, it makes me sick.

I was not a willing participant. I know it. Austin knows it. Everyone in that goddamn room knows it.

But that's not how it looks on video. You don't see a college girl begging the three guys in the room to let her out. You don't hear Austin tell me to shut up. Or threaten to hurt me if I don't give them what they want.

You don't see the moment his fist connects with my face, making me nearly black out because I refuse to give in and spread my legs for him. And you don't see the drugs he forced me to swallow to make me compliant.

What you see is a girl on her knees and two guys naked in front of her. That's when the recording starts. Austin holds my hands behind my back while his friends fuck my face one after the other. But he keeps himself out of the frame so all you see are their dicks and my face.

You don't see Austin's grip on the back of my head or how he pushes me forward, forcing me to take them deep until they hit the back of my throat.

The video he taunts me with looks like a cheap porno. A girl willingly sucking two guys off.

I have to give it to the sick bastard. He thought of everything.

When the drugs kick in and they don't need to hold me down anymore, Austin takes what he wanted from me all along while his friends watch, recording every humiliating second of it.

I haven't watched that part. I don't need to. I've replayed it in my mind often enough.

I couldn't move. Trapped in my own body, my limbs unwilling to respond to my mental commands.

Austin isn't stupid. The asshole planned everything out down to the smallest detail which means he's done it before. He made it look like I wanted it. Like I was a whore begging for their attention. And the next morning, when he swore things would get harder for me if I came forward, when he promised no-one would believe me over him, he was right. And I was the idiot to ever think otherwise.

So, he has nothing to worry about. I won't go to the police. Not after the way the school handled things. I'm too much of a realist to think justice will ever be served.

If I go to the cops, Austin's made it clear he'll leak the video. And even if someone does believe me, even if they see what really happened, that I was drugged and raped, I still lose.

Because then, it's out there for the world to see. I'll never be able to escape it. It'll be all over social media, probably uploaded to porn sites, and God knows where else, because Austin is that much of an asshole. Every time someone Googles my name, that will be the first thing they see. Every guy I meet. Every employer I try to get a job with. There's no way to get around it.

Austin won't let me escape unscathed. Like he hasn't done enough damage already. After going to the school board, he made it his personal mission over summer break to make my life a living hell. He turned my friends against me—even dated one of them for a bit. I still can't believe Kim fell for his bullshit. That she chose him over me.

And if that wasn't enough, he and his buddies would send lewd and threatening messages to my phone at all hours of the day. Sometimes they included pictures of me. Screenshots from the video recording they have. They handed my number out too and I'd get random phone calls from creeps saying they got my number from a friend who said I could offer them a *good time*.

I've had to change my phone number three times in less than three months.

Austin even convinced his family to withdraw their support from my father's campaign. Not that he had to try very hard. They were involved as soon as I came forward and stood by his side, happy to say my claims were baseless and that I was just an opportunistic slut, looking for an easy payday.

Just thinking about what they said, the way they looked at me, makes bile rise in the back of my throat.

The school dismissed my allegations in less than seventy-two hours. And the Holt family made it clear that if I pursued things further, they'd destroy not only my reputation but my family's, and judging by the looks on their faces, they'd enjoy every second of it. It's easy to see where Austin gets his psycho behavior from.

Austin being dragged through court is a blip on the radar. I know how these things work. He's an all-American soccer player. Good-looking. Comes from a reputable family. I'll be lucky if they give him a slap on the wrist.

The more likely outcome is he gets a public apology from the DA's office for his troubles—just like the Dean of PacNorth gave him. Meanwhile, I'm dragged through the mud. Disgraced. My family humiliated.

Back in 2016, Brock Turner got six months for raping an unconscious woman. He was released after three months and that's without both of his parents being practicing attorneys like Austin's.

Austin thinks he's untouchable. And in a way, he is.

I hate him. More than I hate the other two boys involved—Parker Benson and Gregory Chambers. I hate Austin the most. I don't know how he does it. How he smiles and nods without a care in the world while he tears me in two.

A new voice draws his attention and Austin's grip on me loosens.

"Holt, what's up, man?"

I recognize the voice immediately and shrink down a little more. It's *him*.

"Gabe, how've you been?"

Gabe. That's his name. I taste it on my tongue, rolling the name around in my head with what I know of him. It fits. He looks like a Gabriel. A guardian angel. Though I wish he found someone else to save. Anyone else but me.

The two give each other a fist bump and Gabriel's honey-colored gaze turns to me. His eyes widen for a split second before he covers up his surprise.

"I don't think we've met," he says with a small quirk of his lips.

It's a lie. We've met, but only the one time when I was on the locker room floor, a pool of blood all around me. But I appreciate that he pretends otherwise.

"I'm Gabriel, but everyone calls me Gabe."

"Ah, you haven't met my girl, CeCe?" Austin throws his arm around my shoulder.

I flinch at the contact and Gabriel notices, his eyes narrowing, but he doesn't acknowledge it. Great. Leave it to me to react like a domestic-abuse survivor.

Hah.

I wish.

And isn't that a sad thought? That I actually wish I suffered that form of abuse instead of rape. I'm seriously messed up in the head right now.

"Nah. I haven't. Should I have?" he asks, a curious tilt to his head.

Gabriel is just like I remember, only somehow *more*. He's taller. Broader. Everything was hazy then, so I didn't catch that he has white, perfectly straight teeth or that his skin is a sun-kissed bronze.

He's Hispanic, I think. Though he could be Italian like I am. Maybe even a mix. His hair is a dark, nearly black shade of brown. But it's his eyes that throw me off. They're a honey-gold color that's surprisingly light for his complexion. Not quite hazel. There's more yellow in them than green.

Austin laughs, jerking my attention away. I hunch my shoulders and pray the two get lost in conversation long enough to forget I'm even here. Maybe then I can slip out from under Austin's arm and scurry away.

"Yeah, man. You should. A lot of us got to know CeCe *real good* over summer break. Isn't that right, babe?" He turns a knowing smirk my way and I force myself not to scream or cry or to do any of the things I want to do right now.

I didn't want to get to know him or any of his frat brothers the way he's insinuating. Not one of them gave me a choice.

Tears prick the corners of my eyes and I blink them away. I will not give him the satisfaction of seeing me cry. He'd enjoy it too much. Just like he did then.

I slip out from underneath Austin's arm and this time he lets me escape as I move to step around the two of them, flicking one last look in Gabriel's direction.

Of course my would-be guardian angel is one of them. A devil in disguise. I don't know why I assumed otherwise. It's the beautiful ones who hide their rotting centers best.

If he knew who I was, what his friend did to me, maybe he'd have left me there on the floor and I wouldn't have to suffer through this hell of a life anymore.

Austin certainly would have.

Actually, Austin would have watched. He would've enjoyed seeing my life slip on by, and then, like the sick bastard he is, he probably would've raped my corpse.

I begin to walk away, letting my hair fall back around my face when *his* voice stops me.

"CeCe?" There's a frown in his voice.

I hate that nickname. Only Austin and his buddies call me that, and even though I know I should keep walking, I hesitate.

"It's Cecilia," I correct.

Austin says something else to him and as soon as he looks away, I turn the corner and make a hasty retreat.

I don't want anything to do with any of the guys at PacNorth University, least of all anyone associated with Austin Holt and Zeta Pi.

I made the mistake of letting myself fall victim to them before. I won't let it happen again.

6

GABRIEL

Seeing her again is a shock to my system. When I found her lying on the floor of the girl's locker room, blood all around her, I thought she was a goner for sure. She was pale. Lifeless. But seeing her now, she's none of those things.

She has color in her skin. A healthy tan that compliments her dark brown hair and equally dark brown eyes. And she's definitely not lifeless, though I don't think panic stricken and terrified are what she should be after.

Is she worried I'll tell Holt how we know each other? I wouldn't do that. I figured she'd catch on after I played it off like we hadn't met. I was hoping she'd stick around for a minute so we could talk to her.

I've worried about her. And seeing her now, it looks like I still have reason to worry. Shit's still eating at her, that much is sure.

She was small then. She's even smaller now. I remember how little she weighed when I lifted her in my arms and ran to my car. How limp she'd been as I'd hauled her into the waiting room of the PacNorth emergency clinic.

I don't think I've ever been that freaked out in my life. Not since Carlos, and back then, I knew it was too late. The dread was the same. That all-consuming feeling of *hell no* and *why* mixed with a few *fuck you's* directed to the big man upstairs.

But unlike Carlos, she was breathing. She had a chance to pull through, even if it was a slim one.

Knowing that is what put the panic in place because calling 911 wasn't an option. Richland is a small town. The closest hospital is close to forty minutes away and the nearest fire station is even further. Paramedics never would've made it in time.

Thankfully, the campus clinic is well staffed with doctors and med students. They had everything they needed to give the girl a fighting chance. Only it doesn't look like she's doing much fighting. She's lost weight she couldn't afford to lose, and her dark brown eyes are dull. Haunted.

I keep my gaze trained on her retreating form as she turns the corner, barely listening to Austin as he goes on about some party happening this weekend. I have zero plans of going, so I don't bother to listen as he rattles off a time and directions to some dude's house that I've never heard of or met.

Austin knows I don't do the party scene. And I don't kick it with outsiders. So I don't know why he bothers to tell me about any of this, but I pretend to give a shit anyway. For his benefit, at least.

Austin is one of those guys. You know the type. Comes from too much money, born with too much privilege. He kicks it with me and my boys sometimes because he plays soccer with us, but he isn't one of us.

He's a Greek. Something no one in my crew would ever think twice about being a part of.

Fraternities are for boys still struggling to become men. They think they're part of some cool kid club when really, they're just the assholes hanging on to the memory of high school, where popularity makes them feel like a special fucking snowflake.

They haven't realized that none of that shit matters in the real world. No one cares who you're dating or where you buy your clothes. If you're rocking Skechers instead of Adidas or higher priced shit.

But guys like Austin live for the attention. Dressed up in his Abercrombie & Fitch polo with blue plaid shorts. He's even got the puka shell necklace that the early two thousands called and want back.

I swear the dude has more gel in his hair today than I use in an entire month. But despite all that, he's not all bad once you get used to him.

He has a killer elastico on the field and he works hard. Puts in his time at practice even though he's not trying to go pro.

Soccer is just a game for him. A way to pass the time until he gets his degree and follows Daddy's footsteps with the family business.

He's pre-law. Not that I think he'll make it to graduation, let alone go on to law school. The guy isn't the sharpest crayon in the box, if you know what I mean.

Rumor has it his Pops pays some of his teachers off. Austin's joked about it on more than one occasion so it wouldn't surprise me if it were true.

"Yo, what's her deal, man?" I ask, interrupting whatever it is he's saying, not that he seems to mind.

Austin looks over his shoulder as if he expects to catch a glimpse of her even though she's long gone.

"CeCe?" he asks.

I nod, remembering she corrected me. Cecilia. That's what she wants to be called. It fits. Pretty name. Pretty girl.

"No clue. She's a hot piece of ass. Me and a few of my brothers sampled her over the summer." My eyes narrow, but Austin doesn't seem to notice. "She's a good lay, but too much drama, if you ask me." He shrugs and the fact that he talks about her like that, like she's a piece of meat to try and throw away without any thought or consideration, it makes my blood boil.

Does he know what she's been through? That she tried to kill herself? If he knew, no way would he talk about her like that.

I bite my tongue and remind myself Austin isn't the only guy at PacNorth who acts like a dickhead. Most of the jocks behave the same way.

It's a big part of why Julio, Felix, and I keep to ourselves. Our mothers raised us never to disrespect a woman like that, and we don't need to lose our spot on the team because some asshole runs his mouth where he shouldn't. Coach has a strict no fighting policy. He'll turn a blind eye to drinking, and he's been known to overlook the occasional recreational drug use as long as it doesn't affect anyone's performance. But fighting, that's where the old bastard draws the line.

"She seeing anyone?" I ask just to keep him talking. Austin's got that look in his eyes. The one that says he's spinning his wares. He's a slippery fucker and I know he's not telling me everything.

"Nah. I think she's still torn up over this summer." He gives me a knowing smirk. "She knew the score when we hooked up. Guess her feelings got hurt or whatever when no one wanted a relationship after the lay. You know how it is."

I frown and mull over his words.

"She doesn't seem like your usual type."

Austin likes slutty, and there is nothing about Cecilia that gives off the *I'm easy* vibe Austin usually gravitates to.

He snorts. "She isn't now. But she was back then." He licks his lips, and dude has no idea it makes him look like a straight-up creeper. "She used to party with Zeta Pi a lot.

She was on the cheer squad, too. Always came to the house in her uniform, and fuck me sideways," he bites his fist, "it showed off all her assets, if you know what I mean." He winks. "Didn't take long for her to get a reputation for being easy. Guess she didn't like it. She pulled a complete one-eighty out of nowhere." He shakes his head. "It's a damn shame."

Huh. That seems ... odd. I wonder if —

"She tried to kill herself a month ago," he adds.

It's like the fucker can read my mind.

"Yeah?" I play dumb as if I wasn't the one who found her. I don't know her. Don't owe her any loyalties. But a voice in the back of my head tells me to keep my mouth shut on the matter, and that voice has never steered me wrong before.

"Yeah. Guess all the rumors and slut-shaming got to be too much for her." He shrugs again. "It's too bad. If she wasn't fucking crazy, I'd tap that again," He chuckles. "Get enough booze in me and I still might. She's fine as fuck. You never know. A few shots and shit might happen."

"Right." I work my jaw as an uneasy feeling settles in my gut.

"But, seriously, man. Take my advice and steer clear of that one. She's got some serious damage. You do not want any part of that."

Austin's going out of his way to steer me away from her. Is he just looking out or is there something I'm missing here?

My phone buzzes in my pocket and I pull it out, silencing the alarm. "I gotta head out. It was good catching up," I tell him and turn to leave.

Austin falls into step beside me.

"Don't you have a class to get to?" I ask.

"I can be a few minutes late. Besides, you seem interested in CeCe, and I think you need the whole story on that chick." He drops the cocky persona, his face suddenly solemn. I slow my steps and wait for him to fill me in.

He doesn't take long.

"Over the summer she cried rape to get a bunch of guys expelled." He shakes his head. "It was fucked up, man. She could have ruined a lot of people's lives with that accusation."

My eyes snap to him. *The fuck?* "Was she raped?" That would explain ... a lot.

"Nah, man. It wasn't like that. I was there. She threw herself at me and some of my boys. Everyone was drunk. Things escalated. It shouldn't have happened the way it did, but I can tell you for a fact that no one made her do anything she didn't want to." His jaw tightens. "She was just pissed off that no one wanted her afterward." He snorts. "She thought she was clever, but there's a video—" He catches my expression and holds his hands out in front of him. "I didn't record it," he rushes to add. "One of my Zeta Pi brothers did. And yeah, it was fucked up. But it's a good thing he did."

I force myself to unclench my jaw. Did the fucker even have her consent for it?

"It was the proof we needed after she went to the school board and tried to get us all expelled."

I stop in the middle of the hall, hardly believing what I'm hearing right now. She—

I shake my head. Fuck.

"She cried foul but the whole thing was dropped by the school. It's not a problem for me or any of my boys, but it leaves a bad taste in your mouth. I'm just giving you a warning. Shit with us was dropped because we had that video and we had witnesses. The whole damn house knew her game, but you're one guy. I'd hate to see her try and flip the script on you. I'd stay far away from her if I was you."

I nod. Yeah. Fuck. I don't have time for that kind of drama. But if she really did all that—"Why were you talking to her, then? If she cried rape, I'd think you'd want to avoid the chick at all costs." Not cozy up to her and shit. Who does that? Something's fishy here.

"I don't know, man. I guess I feel bad for the girl. I mean, she's got issues, but I don't want to feel responsible for her offing herself. I'm not heartless."

When he puts it like that, it makes sense.

"Anyway, I gotta go, man. Good catching up. And the party this Friday, you'll be there?"

"I'll see what I can do," I say, giving a non-committal response.

He accepts it with a grin even though we both know I won't be there. "That's my man. I'll catch you later."

He leaves and I head to my first class of the day.

An uneasy feeling lingers in the pit of my stomach. I try to ignore it. Cecilia isn't my problem. And if what Austin said is true, she isn't a chick I want to risk being around either.

I'm here on scholarship and all it takes is one accusation, even a false one, to put my place at PacNorth University in jeopardy.

It shouldn't matter if a part of me wants to check in on her. Make sure she's okay. It's not a risk I can afford to take. Right?

I suck on my front teeth as I step into my class and drop my bag beside me. I close my eyes, recalling Cecilia's wide eyes and stricken expression from the hallway.

Fuck.

Wrong. So fucking wrong.

7
CECILIA

For a nobody at school, I'm getting a lot of attention. Zeta Pi must have spread some garbage about me already, because even before everything happened this past summer, when I was still on the University cheer squad, I was never on the receiving end of this many whispers and pointed looks.

It should bother me. On some minuscule level, I think it does. But for the most part, I can't find it in me to care. No one here matters.

They're not my friends.

My family.

They're nobody to me.

Who cares if they know I tried to kill myself? Twelve percent of college kids attempt suicide at some point during their first four years. I know because I Googled that too.

A lot of them have probably been in the same place I was... *am*. Albeit for different reasons, but this doesn't make me some weirdo. It means I was hurting. I'm still hurting. So, screw them. If they want to stop and stare, that's on them.

In the grand scheme of all the things that are fucked up in my life right now, being the center of campus gossip registers pretty low on my give-a-shit meter.

I head for the parking lot after my last class of the day, ignoring the looks as I make a beeline for my Jeep. I'm parked near the soccer field, and would you look at that, my guardian angel steps out onto the field, shirtless and looking very much like his namesake.

Sunlight glistens off his tan skin, droplets of sweat sliding down his muscular abs. He has the coveted V at his hips all the girls lust after, and without even trying I spot at least a dozen girls drooling over him from the sidelines.

A flash of interest stirs inside of me, but I immediately squash it. I'm not interested in any guys, least of all one who associates with Austin Holt.

I shake my head and right as I'm about to look away, Gabriel's head lifts, his eyes somehow finding mine. He tilts his head to the side, a silent question in his gaze, but for the life of me, I'm not sure what he's asking.

He lifts one hand in the air, offering me a small wave.

I frown and look around. Did he mean to wave at me, or is that for someone else? I glance around, not spotting anyone else nearby and his eyes stare straight at me.

A few girls near the field follow his line of sight, their expressions hardening when they see I'm the one holding his attention.

I bite my bottom lip, but don't bother to wave back. He has to know I won't return the gesture.

But his smile never dims, and from where I'm standing it almost looks like my lack of response amuses him. Is he messing with me? He has to be.

That thought alone infuriates me, and is enough to push me into motion.

I turn on my heel and unlock my Jeep, ignoring the heat that's now creeping up my skin. Why did he do that? Single me out the way he did?

Asshole.

I don't spare him another look as I put my car in reverse and get the hell out of there. I'm so ready for the day to be over.

The end of the day should bring with it some measure of relief, but pulling up to my childhood home does the exact opposite, and I find myself sitting in my car, my stomach churning with dread as I stave off the inevitable.

I moved out when I started at PacNorth as a freshman. My parents live close enough for me to commute, but I wanted to live on campus. Really embrace the college scene.

Joelle and I shared a dorm room and Kim lived across the hall from us in the same building. And for two years, it was perfect.

Until it wasn't.

I can't believe everything went to hell like it did.

Moving back home feels like I failed. Like I couldn't hack it on my own.

Mom's Land Rover is in the driveway right beside Dad's F-two-fifty truck. They're both home, even though Dad shouldn't be here until well after five and Mom usually stays late at the office on Mondays.

Lucky me.

I turn off the ignition and plaster a smile on my face before stepping inside.

It's as if they've been waiting all day for me to walk in the door. Mom jumps from her perch on the sofa and rushes forward to give me a hug, and Dad is there, right behind her.

"How was your first day back at school?" Mom coos, running her hands over my shoulders and tucking my dark hair behind my ears.

I pull away from her, not missing the flash of hurt, but she's quick to hide it.

My chest squeezes and I force myself to stop, to stay in the entryway a few seconds longer than I'd like to to make up for it. I don't mean to hurt her. Or make her worry. I just hate all of her hovering. If she wants things to go back to normal, she has to stop treating me like I'm made of glass.

"It was fine," I tell her and wait, knowing we're about to play a twisted round of twenty questions all to make sure Cecilia isn't at risk of killing herself again.

"Did you see your friends? Do you have any classes together?"

I shrug. "I don't really hang out with the same people anymore," I remind her.

Before this summer, I hung out with the cheerleaders and the Greeks. But I don't want anything to do with Greek row, and as far as I'm concerned, my former squad can rot. Kim and Joelle were my best friends. Ride or die, or so I thought.

Kim's always had this massive crush on Austin. Ever since freshman year. And Austin Holt is smart. So fucking smart.

That morning, before I even made it back to my dorm, he arranged a date with her for the very same day. And when I blew up her phone, freaking out like a crazy person because hello, she was on a date with my rapist, he used the time to convince her I was jealous. Claiming he asked me about her at the party and that I threw myself at him.

He seriously got her to believe I'd say and do just about anything to get between them. That I was desperate to ruin their shot at happiness. So when I came clean and told her what happened to me, she didn't believe me. Not even for a second.

She called me a liar. Said I broke girl code by going after the guy I knew she wanted.

I tried to explain. I told her I said no. Repeatedly. That there was no way I would sleep with Austin willingly, let alone screw around with Parker Benson and Gregory Chambers at the same time, but she didn't believe me. *Like anyone would ever reject an advance from Austin Holt.* That's seriously what she said to me.

For a second there, I thought Joelle was on my side. That she believed me. She knows I've never been into Austin. The clean-cut, preppy-guy look isn't my type, and I'd never date a guy in a frat or have a three some. It just isn't me.

They're players and I'm not the kind of girl who gets around. I'm not claiming to be a saint, but I don't do one-night stands or friends with benefits. And I sure as hell don't do threesomes.

I'm a relationship kind of girl. Every guy I've slept with, all two of them—not counting what happened this summer—I was in an actual relationship with. Kim and Joelle know that. They know me. And Joelle saw the bruises with her own eyes. She was the one who suggested I go to the school board first.

But whether she believes me now or not is irrelevant because Kim called me a liar, and Joelle doesn't have the backbone to go against her, which means I'm on the outs.

Leaving the squad was easy once it was clear they weren't going to change their minds. I loved cheerleading, but more than that, I loved being a part of a team. Belonging and having people I cared about beside me. Take that away and there isn't anything left worth sticking around for.

"How about new friends? Did you meet anyone you clicked with in any of your classes?" She's so damn hopeful. I don't want to steal her joy, not after everything I've put her through, so I offer her a little white lie, hoping she'll drop the subject after that.

"Yeah. One," I tell her. "His name is Gabriel."

"Ooo, a boy." Mom's eyes spark with interest, but I don't miss Dad's frown. Probably should have expected that. Even when I was more outgoing, and had friends, he always encouraged me not to hangout with boys.

I'd like to say he's just your typical overprotective father type. But I'm not naive. Dad's the Mayor of Richland and I'm well aware that what I do and who I spend time with is always up for scrutiny.

"Is that a good idea—"

"Hush, Joe," Mom says and smacks him lightheartedly on the chest. "Our daughter is making new friends. Be supportive."

He mashes his lips together and grunts, but otherwise doesn't comment.

I peek at him through the curtain of my hair and give him a wink, letting him know it's not a boy he needs to worry about. Seeing the gesture he nods and steps back, leaving Mom to do enough hovering for the both of them.

"I'll let you catch up with your mother. You can find me in my study if either of you need me."

"Alright, dear. Let me know if you need anything." Mom doesn't take her eyes off me. I know she's about to grill me for any and all details she can manage about Gabriel, but before she dives in, I head her off.

"I was actually just popping in to drop off my school books. I made plans tonight, so I'm going to head back out after I change real quick."

"Oh." Mom's brows pitch forward, and she plays with the strand of pearls around her neck. A nervous gesture I've grown used to seeing more and more often these days. "Are you—"

"I'll be fine, mom. New friends. Remember?"

She perks back up and slaps on a too-bright smile. "Yes. Of course. You'll call if you need anything?"

I wave my phone in her direction. "Will do."

"And ..." She hesitates. No one likes to talk about the elephant in the room. It's that nameless phantom that's just waiting to strike again. Seeing the masked worry on her face makes me want to scream or maybe even snarl a bit. But I hold it back. It's better to pretend. That seems to be our family's new M.O.

Mom thinks I'm struggling with depression, and sure, maybe. But that's not why I did it. She'd know that if she ever worked up the nerve to ask me why. No one has. Not her. Not my dad. Not even my therapist. Everyone just assumes I have some sort of mental illness. I almost wish that were true.

If Mom wants to know what I'm dealing with, the signs are all there. I don't wear revealing clothes anymore. I don't party. Alcohol and I aren't on good terms, and I don't hang out with any of my former friends. I spend my weekends reading in my room or swimming laps in our pool and I don't smile anywhere near as often as I used to.

I'm almost angry she's never asked. That she's never even suspected what happened to me. One in four women are sexually assaulted while in college. Google told me that too. Gotta love the magic of the internet. You learn all sorts of things.

Hell, she could have typed my shift in behavior right into the search bar and I'm betting it'd give her the correct answer. So, it's not a far leap when wondering why your daughter tried to off herself, right? She should know. And I hate that she doesn't because I'll never have the nerve to tell her.

She's my mom. She's supposed to know.

I exhale a breath. I'm getting worked up and it's not going to help anything. "I'll check in, okay?" I tell her, brushing past as I head up the stairs to my bedroom.

"Okay, honey. I love you."

"Love you, too."

Once I'm safely tucked inside my room, I drop my bag and lean against the door, letting my feet slide out from beneath me until my butt hits the carpet. There's one small problem with what I told Mom. I don't actually have any plans. But

I'm not about to stay here and be on the receiving end of her tenth degree either. So without a plan, I ditch my long-sleeved, purple shirt and jeans for a short sleeved-maxi dress and slip a thick bangle on one wrist and a velvet scrunchie over the other. I hate having my arms exposed, but this way, when Mom sees me slip back out, she'll believe the lie that I'm meeting people. Someone I'd bother to dress up for.

Slipping my feet into a pair of sandals, I quietly slip down the stairs and out the front door, grateful she's not hovering like a wraith in the hallway.

I exhale a relieved breath and take a few minutes to consider what I'm doing before starting my Jeep. My swimsuit in the backseat catches my eye, and not letting myself think too much about it, I head back toward campus. Back to where it all happened.

I haven't gone to the campus pool since that day, but it's the only place I can think of going where I'll be left alone.

Where I can just be *me*.

8
CECILIA

When I was little, Dad used to tease me that if I spent any more time in the water than I had already, I'd sprout gills and become a fish. The taunt never stopped me. If anything, it made me swim more, hell bent on becoming a mermaid, and ever since, swimming pools have been my oasis.

The outside world can't reach me here. Not when my head is beneath the water, all outside sounds and smells muted.

Whenever I need to get away, I swim.

It doesn't matter if it's in a pool, a lake, or the ocean. The urge to swim is just as strong as my urge to breathe.

The way the water feels as my body glides through it. The weightlessness of floating. There's something about cutting through the surface with each stroke that helps me wipe my mind and push reality away. For a little while, at least.

I'm hoping I can find that same peace here today, despite my not-so-distant memories. I'm not off to a great start, but I'm not about to tuck tail and run either.

My hands shake as I tuck my clothes into an empty locker and slip on my modest one-piece swimsuit. When I turn, the pink stained grout in the corner pulls my attention, but only for a moment before I force myself to look away. I pull my hair into a high ponytail, deciding not to bother with a swim cap, and grab my goggles before closing the locker door. My ears pound and I glance at the corner once more before making myself move for the door.

Swim season is still a few months away, so the pool is relatively empty.

There are two swimmers in the pool to the far right, regulars who train in the off season judging by their form. Their strokes appear effortless, the ripples in the water nearly nonexistent as they propel themselves forward.

PacNorth boasts three Olympic-length swimming pools matching the three Olympic medals former alumni have brought home. The first two are your standard fifty meters in length, with nine lanes measuring three meters deep on both ends. The third includes a high dive and boasts a five-meter depth, but I'm not a diver, so it isn't a pool I've bothered dipping into.

I thought about going out for the swim team last year. I'm good enough to make the team. Cate Carrington is their lead female swimmer in the fifty-meter freestyle. Her average time is around twenty-eight seconds. It's a decent time, but she'll need to shave at least four seconds off to qualify for the Olympics two years from now. Doable, but not an easy feat.

My average time is twenty-four point six seconds. I already meet the minimum time to qualify, but I haven't been able to convince myself to take the plunge and try out.

Swimming is where I go to get away, and I'm reluctant to turn my safe space into a competitive occupation, because that's what training for the Olympics is. There are no half measures.

It's a daily grind both in and out of the pool, and I'm realistic enough to know I'm not in a good head space for the level of focus it would require. It's always nice to dream about, though.

Climbing down the ladder, I slide into the water, forcing my body to relax as I roll my shoulders back and slip my goggles over my eyes. The cool temperature wipes some of my nerves away and I push off from the edge, starting with a sidestroke as I warm up my muscles.

I don't bother to count my laps. I'm not here to race the clock. I'm here to breathe.

I let myself get lost in the motions. Stroke. Stroke. Breathe. Stroke. Stroke. Breathe. I keep up the pattern, kicking with my legs to propel myself forward. When my fingertips graze the pool wall, I do a flip turn and keep going, increasing my speed on each revolution until I'm sprinting the length of the pool as fast as my body will allow.

I tear through the water, letting all thought drop away until my shoulders burn and my left leg starts to cramp. And even then, I push harder. When I'm here, I feel strong. Powerful. No one can touch me in the water.

I don't know how much time passes when fatigue starts to worm its way under my skin. There's a voice in my head that urges me to keep going, but it's the same voice that sometimes tells me it's okay to slip away and it's not, so I ignore it and instead listen to my body.

I come to a stop mid lap and swim to the ladder, pulling myself up and over the edge. My chest heaves and I tear my goggles off my face, dropping them beside me as I take stock of myself.

My thigh spasms, the muscle contracting in a painful way. I massage the muscle with one hand and use the time to catch my breath and survey my surroundings. The two swimmers who were here when I started are long gone.

The clock on the wall reads ten after four. I've been swimming for forty minutes. Weird. It feels like it's maybe been half that time.

A movement on my left pulls my attention and I turn to find a familiar face sitting on one of the benches, watching me.

I freeze.

Gabriel's brows are drawn, his jaw tight. He looks at me like he's trying to solve a complicated puzzle. Almost like he's convinced if he stares at me long enough, all my secrets will suddenly spill out.

I don't like it.

I'm not sure what to make of him, but as each second passes, the coil of tension inside me winds tighter. Our eyes are locked on one another, neither of us blinking. For some strange reason, I can't seem to tear my gaze away even though I want to.

He shifts in his seat, like he's readying himself to stand, and that's all I need for a sudden flood of panic to spear me in the chest.

I massage the muscle in my thigh a little hard.

What if he walks over here?

What if he tries to talk to me?

Hard pass.

I flex my calves and roll my ankles. It's as good as it's going to get.

Slipping back into the pool, I don't bother with my goggles this time before I dive right back into my swim, switching it up with a back stroke so I can keep track of his movements. I don't like that it's only the two of us here. He's not even swimming, so what is he doing here?

It's a question I don't have the balls to ask him.

Gabriel stays in his spot, never moving, not even to get comfortable. It's unnerving, to say the least. This time around, I count my laps as a distraction. Ten turns into twenty and twenty turns into thirty-three.

One mile.

If I had to guess, I did two miles before.

I figured he'd take off at some point. Get bored watching me and give up on whatever it is he's waiting to say, but he never does. With another twenty minutes under my belt and my body screaming for relief, I admit defeat and drag myself back up the swim ladder and out of the pool.

Tension pulls at my shoulders, tightening the muscles in my lower back.

I'll have to hear him out or risk drowning. Not as unappealing as you'd think, but what puts a real damper on that thought is knowing he'll try, and likely succeed, in rescuing me all over again.

Yay me.

Have I mentioned how much I hate having my own guardian angel?

Not wasting any time, Gabriel pushes from his seat and walks straight for me. But when he gets close, a frantic urge to run consumes me and I slip back into the pool to tread water in the middle of my lane. *Shit.*

Something flickers in his eyes.

My left leg cramps and I swallow hard, desperate to keep the grimace of pain from my face. *Don't show any signs of weakness.* Guys will jump on it. He'll use it to his advantage to hurt me. I won't let him hurt me.

My throat tightens just thinking about what he could do to me. Here, alone, with nobody else around.

He hovers a few feet away from the pool's edge, his frown deepening.

"I thought you were done?" He shoves his hands into his pockets and rocks back on his heels.

I try to take him in. To get my mind off what ifs and onto the here and now.

He's not in the same clothes he wore earlier. He's wearing a tight white shirt that hugs his muscular frame and he's traded in his low-slung jeans for a pair of black athletic pants that are as revealing as they are modest.

Gray sweatpants have nothing on these when Gabriel shifts his stance, angling his body to the side.

I squeeze my eyes closed for a second and shake my head. *Do not stare at his dick.*

"I am." My words come out garbled. I swallow hard and try again. "Done, I mean." My left leg seizes again, and I have to use my arms to keep myself afloat. He's standing right in front of the ladder, effectively blocking my escape.

I don't like the idea of getting out when we're alone, let alone when he's this close. It's one thing to be in a crowded hallway, which is moderately safe, thanks to the sea of potential witnesses if anyone was to step out of line.

But it's a whole other story to be alone in a room with a guy I don't know anything about, wearing nothing but a swimsuit.

I'm smarter than this.

Confusion is written all over his face. "If you're done, why did you jump back in the pool?"

I hesitate and try not to let him see how much he unnerves me.

Squaring my shoulders as best I can while treading water, I lift my chin and push the tremor from my voice. "Because you all but lunged for me. Call me crazy, but I'd rather be safe than sorry."

"Safe? From what?"

From you. I scream in my head, but don't bother to say it out loud. It doesn't take a genius to put two and two together, and given that he's an athlete and that PacNorth requires all players to maintain a 3.0 GPA minimum, he can't be this stupid.

"You think I'll hurt you?"

And there it is. I knew he'd get there on his own.

I try to shrug, but the effect isn't the same when you're struggling to stay afloat in nine feet of water. No such thing as a shallow end in a lap pool.

"I don't know you," I remind him. "I have no way to judge whether you're capable or hurting me or not." Though let's be honest, I can tell by just one look that he is very much capable.

Some weird little voice in the back of my head wants to believe he isn't. Or at the very least, wants to believe that he wouldn't try to. He did save my life, after all. But that doesn't matter. At the end of the day, the potential to hurt me is there. He has the physical strength and ability to overpower me, and that's reason enough to be leery.

"I saved you," he snaps, indignation clear in his tone.

His honey-colored eyes darken, taking on an amber hue. My stomach does a flip and I jerk my gaze away.

Don't look at the pretty boy with pretty eyes.

Come on, Cecilia, get it together.

"Yeah. Thanks for that." Sarcasm drips from my words. "Look, can you just say or ask whatever it is you need to and go away? I'd like to get out of here sometime this century." I try for haughty annoyance, but I'm not sure he's buying it.

He surprises me when, without argument, he walks himself back, not stopping until his shoulders press against the far wall, leaving a good fifteen feet between him and the ladder now.

"I just want to talk. See how you're holding up." He nods to the ladder. "You can get out now. I'll stay right here."

I consider him for a moment, searching for the lie, but before I can come to a decision, my leg spasms again and I dip below the surface, taking in a mouthful of water. That makes the decision for me.

Pushing myself forward, I climb up the ladder, careful to keep him in my line of sight as I inch further away from him around the edge of the pool. My legs shake and I know he doesn't miss it.

Grabbing my towel from a nearby chair, I wrap it around me, but I don't bother to take a seat no matter how fatigued I am.

If this conversation goes south, I need to be on my feet, ready to bolt if I have to.

"You know I won't try anything, right? I'm not like that. I don't hurt women."

"Sure," I say to placate him.

He curses under his breath, in Spanish I think. But I don't know the words. His harsh tone and expression are enough to convey his meaning, though. He's not happy. Guess what? Neither am I.

"What's your damage?" he demands in a clipped tone. "You're acting like I'm the enemy or some shit when all I did was carry you out of here when you needed help."

"I never asked for your help," I remind him. Is he expecting a thank you? I hope not, because he won't be getting one from me. If that's why he's here, I hope he's prepared to leave sorely disappointed.

Gabriel's mouth drops open, eyes flashing in indignation. "Are you fucking with me right now?"

I shake my head. "No. I didn't ask for your help." I wait, expecting him to tell me I'm stupid or to storm off in a huff, but he doesn't do either of those things.

His eyes bore into mine, like he's trying to peel back my layers to see what's hiding underneath. His penetrating stare leaves me exposed, but it's his words that grip me, making my veins fill with ice as guilt and shame surge through me.

"You're going to do it again." He barks out a humorless laugh. "Aren't you?!" His loud voice booms through the empty room and I barely manage to keep myself from staggering back.

His eyes are unwavering. I know he wants to step forward. To crowd me. I can see it in the veins that stand out on his arms. In the tension lining his neck. He's holding himself in place, not allowing himself to take a single step closer. But he doesn't look away.

The hairs on my arms stand on end.

The way he says it, like it's a statement. A fact. He doesn't need me to answer because he already knows.

I cross my arms over my chest and chew on my bottom lip. How does he *see* me? See the things everyone else misses?

No one else has bothered asking me that. I'm sure they think it, but no one says it. Not out loud.

But Gabriel seems intent on driving his point home. "It might not be today. Might not even be this week or this month. But the thought is still in your head, right?"

I don't answer.

"RIGHT?" He mutters another foreign curse and hangs his head. His chest heaves as he sucks in a deep breath. *"Fuck!"*

A sinking feeling hits me and I try to decipher where it's coming from, but draw a blank.

"Answer me!" He straightens and takes a single step forward.

I ball my hands into fists. "Why do you even care?" He doesn't know me. We're not friends. Why does any of this matter to him?

A stark expression crosses his face, but it's only there for a second before a new emotion covers it up. Anger. Vivid and raw.

"Do you have any idea how fucking selfish you are?" He pushes from the wall and stalks toward me. "Does it even register for you the kind of damage that little stunt of yours caused?"

My pulse races and a chill climbs up my spine.

He doesn't pause to let me answer. "I saw your parents that day. After they were called to the clinic." His lip curls in disgust. "They were wrecked. And you want to do that shit to them all over again?"

My heart pounds in my chest. My mind short-circuiting at his words.

"You're a real piece of work, you know that?"

Words jam up in my throat. I don't know what to say to that. Or if saying anything will make any of this better. More likely, it'll just make things worse, so I keep my mouth closed and ignore the sting of tears behind my eyes. Gabriel's expression bleeds with emotion. Anger and anguish warring with one another. My shock at his words begins to wear off the longer he stands there and I realize he's only a few inches away. My throat constricts. He's close. Too close.

My feet are frozen in place. My breath trapped in my lungs.

A shuddering exhale hisses through my teeth and it takes everything inside of me not to mentally shut down. To curl in on myself as I wait for whatever comes next. He's just so angry.

Hot tears threaten to spill over, but I refuse to give him the satisfaction. He has no idea what I've been through.

"You don't get to do shit like that."

My feet finally move, but I've only retreated two steps before my back hits the wall

Gabriel follows suit and braces his hands on either side of my head, caging me in.

"You're not a child. No one is going to excuse your behavior. Whatever the hell your issue is, grow the fuck up and get over it. Life moves on."

My jaw tightens.

"And don't for a second think it's okay to do what you did to them. I don't give a fuck what your damage is. Shit like that doesn't go away for the people you leave behind."

He barks out a humorless laugh.

"What am I thinking? You don't care. You don't give a fuck if you scar your loved ones. If you fucking break them."

My head snaps up.

"For the record, you will. You'll destroy them when you succeed with your little getaway plan."

Frustration crashes over me and my lips press together in a tight line. No one else talks to me like this. Not about what happened. What I did. Mom and Dad coddle me. My therapist tries to understand me. But no one blames me like Gabriel is doing right now. No one else says this is my fault.

He watches me intently, searching for the cracks in my exterior he can latch on to.

"Do you have any idea what will happen once you're gone? The level of destruction that'll be a direct result of your actions?" He pauses for me to answer, but I have no words. None. They're trapped in my throat, making it ache and burn. I want to deny what he's saying but I can't.

His eyes bore right into me, seeking out my vulnerable parts and demanding that I listen. That I acknowledge the role I've played.

"Your parents will be beside themselves with grief, and all grief needs an outlet." His gaze is like a physical weight pressing down on me, and there's a bitter edge to his words. He's no longer speculating. He's speaking from experience. His own experience. "They'll wonder what they could have done. What signs or signals they missed." His jaw clenches. "Did they tell you they loved you enough? Did they try hard enough to make you stay?"

I turn to look away but Gabriel won't have it. His arm drops from the wall and he captures my chin, forcing my gaze back to his. His fingers dig into my cheek, his thumb anchoring along my jaw.

"Asking those questions won't make them feel better, so they'll move on to the blame game." His smile is cruel as he glares down at me. "They'll blame each other for your death. They have to blame someone. Anyone. But they sure as shit can't blame you. Even though it's your goddamn fault. They can't think of it that way." He tsks.

I try to pull away but Gabriel's grip on my face tightens. His other hand lowers to settle on my hip, fingers digging into my skin. There's no escape. I should be freaking out right now, fighting to get away from him.

But he isn't finished.

I need to hear what he has to say.

"They'll remember you as the perfect child who never made a single mistake. They'll forget all the bad things in their grief. All the times you fucked up. All the therapy and hospital stints. The sleepless nights. None of it exists, so blaming you, putting any shred of responsibility on your shoulders, is wrong."

He releases my face and stabs a finger into my chest, looming over me like an avenging angel. "But it's not wrong. Them being fucked up over what you did *is* your fault. *You're* the one who deserves the blame. It'll be your fault when they get a divorce because the sight of one another is a constant reminder of the kid they lost. And it'll be your fault when your mom gives into depression and gets hooked on painkillers. When your dad turns to alcohol so he can forget his kid killed herself and that he lost his wife to her pain. All of that shit will be *your fucking fault!*"

I wilt under the onslaught of his words. Each one hits me hard, like a knife in the chest, leaving me to bleed out on the cold stone floor.

"I ... I didn't think—"

"Clearly." His chest presses against mine, heaving with each ragged breath. The muscles in his neck are pulled tight, tendons straining. I don't know what to say. There's this crazy, irrational part of me that wants to comfort him. He's like me in a way. Broken. Hurting.

"Who did you lose?" My voice is hoarse, throat thick with emotion.

His warm, heavy breaths fan over my face and his fingers flex around my hip. Our eyes are still locked together and I see anguish flicker across his face, but as quickly as it appears, it's gone.

Gabriel touches his forehead to mine, the moment all of a sudden intimate. I squeeze my eyes tight and place my hand to his chest. His heart races beneath my palm, eager for escape. Mine does that too. Sometimes I wonder if it beats fast enough, loud enough, if it can succeed in running away, and finally put an end to all my suffering.

He presses his lips to my temple and we just stand there, drinking in one another's pain. Seconds pass turning into minutes, and I realize having him this close doesn't terrify me like it should. My heart races but for an entirely new reason

He squeezes my hip once more before pulling back, and before I even meet his eyes, I know the moment is gone.

I peer up at him through my lashes, taking in the thin line of his lips. His flat, emotionless eyes. He's shutting down. Withdrawing into himself in a way I've seen myself do time and time again.

"I lost my brother." There's zero inflection in his voice. "My twin."

I gasp, fingers covering my mouth. "I'm so sor—"

"Don't."

I snap my mouth closed, unable to imagine what that sense of loss feels like. I want to ask more questions. How did it happen? When did it happen? Is there anything I can do? But I keep my lips firmly together. He doesn't owe me his secrets. Not when I'm unwilling to offer him mine.

Gabriel steps back and runs his hands through his hair, tugging at the dark strands with an irritated huff. "I don't know why I told you that."

He shakes his head and looks away, giving me an up close and personal look at the cut of his jawline. Sharp and unyielding.

Then, without another word, he shifts on his feet and heads for the door.

I stare at his back, reeling. My mouth opens and closes like a fish out of water. I'm tempted to call out for him, but what would I say?

I'm sorry for your loss.

I wish I could help.

You can talk to me. None of that makes any of this better.

His pain permeates the air around him. I don't know how I didn't notice it before. It's there in the hard set of his shoulders. The aggression in his steps. Even now, as he walks away from me, I know the muscles in his back are tight. The strain in his body close to snapping.

He doesn't want pretty words of comfort.

He doesn't want anything.

Not from me.

And for some strange reason, it bothers me.

9

GABRIEL

The muscles in my arms burn as I shove the bar up from my chest. I hold it there for a few seconds, before lowering it back down. My breath hisses through my teeth, and my arms shake, muscles straining to keep the weight up.

I adjust my legs, widening my stance, and pressing down on my heels to give me a more solid base as I repeat the motion.

Up. Down. Up. Down.

A muscle jumps in my bicep. I ignore it and do another rep.

Again.

Come on.

My biceps scream out for relief. Jaw tight, I glare at the bar nestled between my fists and struggle through it.

Fuck.

A sharp stab of pain spears into my shoulders. *Almost there.* Arching my back off the bench, I bare my teeth and shove up until the pain becomes unbearable. My lips peel back from my teeth in a feral grin.

What I'm feeling now is the reason I came here. I love lifting. The strain and agony it puts my body through. The sheer effort and determination it demands from me.

Pressing up again, I know I won't be able to bench press another round, so I tilt my wrists back and set the bar on the rack. Metal clanks against metal and I grunt, swinging myself into a sitting position. Fatigue sweeps through me. *So close.* Another twenty minutes in the gym and I'll wear myself out enough to crash as soon as my face hits my pillow. And then, bliss.

"Damn, bro. What are you benching?"

Using the front of my shirt to wipe the sweat from my brow, I look back at the bar and shrug. "I don't know," I tell Felix. "Didn't bother to count." There's a small bite of pain working its way down my spine and I consider ignoring it. All I want to do right now is catch my breath and then go at it some more.

I close my eyes and sink into the pain, eager to feel something physical. I'm damn near desperate for the distraction. Most of the time, hitting the gym is enough to take my mind off things. It's always been there to clear my head. But the shit storm brewing in my mind refuses to go away.

"You didn't count?"

I shake my head. "Nah."

After leaving Cecilia at the pool, I came straight here to the gym on campus. I needed to work off some steam. Didn't really care how I did it. So, when I sat down to bench, I threw on my usual plates and started, but it wasn't enough. Three reps in, I needed more, so I added them. A few reps after that, I added another plate.

I benched and added, and benched and added, until it hurt. Until I could stop thinking about the pain in my chest and could focus on the ache in my muscles instead.

Felix cants his head to the side, his lips moving as he wordlessly counts. "Savage, man. You've got two-twenty racked up."

I shrug. It could have been three hundred and I wouldn't care. I'm not here to show off or to get any sort of praise. In fact, I'd be a hell of a lot happier right now if I were alone, but one look at Felix lets me know that isn't going to happen. He's still staring at the bar, a somber expression on his face. I don't have time for him to read into my shit, so I grab the water bottle I left beside my gym bag and chug half its contents while I try to come up with a reason to get him out of here.

"Any particular reason you're here when it's not one of our scheduled training days?"

"Nope."

His brows furrow and he peers over at me. "Alright. Wanna explain why you're being an idiot and maxing out weights without anyone to spot you?"

"Not particularly."

I tug off my shirt and use it to wipe the sweat from my neck and shoulders.

Felix sighs solemnly. "Is this about Carlos?"

I throw my shirt in his face and shove to my feet. "I'll catch you later."

Of course, escaping my best friend isn't that easy. Felix is hot on my heels as I storm out of the gym. "We made a deal, asshole," he calls out behind me. I ignore him. This isn't the same thing.

Felix runs to catch up and stops in front of me, shoving me back before stabbing his finger into my chest. "We have an agreement, *cabrón*." *Fucker.* "You can't just all of a sudden decide to go back on it. That's not how family works."

I bark out a laugh. "Fuck you, Felix."

He pulls back like I hit him. "What the hell is your deal, man?"

My mouth fills with acid. *Fuck!* Felix doesn't deserve my anger. I know he's only looking out, but I can't deal with this shit right now.

"Nothing," I brush past him, my shoulder knocking into his. "Forget what I said. I gotta go."

Felix makes no move to follow me, and I exhale a breath of relief as I cut across the parking lot to where I left my bike. I throw my leg over my CBR1000 and reach for my helmet when Felix calls out, "Your ass better be going straight to the Pier."

I glance in his direction, shielding my face from the sun as I shake my head.

He walks toward me. I consider throwing on my helmet and just getting the hell out of there, but I know how Felix operates, and his bike is parked only a few spots away. He'll chase my ass and tail me around town until I give up and stop running. His persistence is one of the fuckers best qualities. It's also what makes him so damn frustrating to deal with sometimes.

"I'll meet up with you later," I say, but judging by the look on his face, he's not having it.

"Not good enough. Bad shit is going on in that head of yours. I already messaged Julio—"

"Dammit."

"—and he's on his way. You know the deal."

I tilt my head back and stare up at the sky, ignoring the blinding sun as I silently curse the universe for giving me good fucking friends. Felix stands there and waits, knowing I'll give in and do what he's asking. That was the deal we made. When shit gets hard, we meet at the Pier. Nothing and no one can touch us there.

We stumbled upon it one day when we were kids, out riding our bikes. I think we were maybe twelve at the time, and back then we thought it was the coolest place on the planet.

It's not anything special. An oversized dock with rickety planks that juts out from shore. There used to be restaurants, shopping, and even an arcade, but all of the businesses are boarded up now. And have been since long before we found it. It's Richland's very own mini ghost town. But for us, it's a sanctuary.

Only this time is different.

I don't need a heart-to-heart with my boys about a break-up. Or advice about how to navigate my parents' divorce.

What I need right now is to be alone. Not at the Pier. Not working through my feelings. I want to figure out how to stop feeling like this. Like my heart is seconds away from tearing a hole in my chest.

It's pure fucking agony.

This feeling consumes every viable part of me. Shredding my skin. Eviscerating my soul. I can't deal with it right now. And I sure as shit don't want to talk about it.

All I can think about is finding my brother. About losing my other fucking half. He killed a part of me too that day, and I'm drowning in the loss all over again. Relieving the days that led up to his death. The fights. The secrets. The vile words we threw at one another.

I didn't realize the shit he was going through. I thought he was being stupid. Reckless. He never opened up. He was like a fucking tornado that entire last year. Blowing in and out however he pleased, uncaring of the destruction he left in his wake.

But when he needed me, when he all but begged me for help, I didn't hear him. I ignored the signs. I knew shit was bad. But there was no way to know what he was going to do.

But I should have. I knew Carlos better than anyone else. I should have seen it. Should have known he was steps away from walking off the cliff.

Between the drugs and the parties, it was obvious he was spiraling. But we all assumed he'd bounce back. Sooner or later, he'd hit rock bottom. And I told myself when he did, I'd be there to help him up. He was my brother. I had his back. Always. No matter what.

Until I fucking didn't.

My hands clench around the helmet in my hands. I'm so pissed at him for what he did. He left. Took the coward's way out without so much as a backwards glance.

But I miss him. And I'm furious with myself for not finding a way to make him stay.

"Gabe—" Felix's expression softens.

Shit. How long have I been in my own head?

"Twenty-minutes. That's all we're giving you."

I stare at my friend in confusion. Did I ask that out loud?

"Ride. Blow off some steam. But if you're not there in twenty, we're coming after you."

I huff out a breath and give in before my composure has a chance to slip any further. "Fine." A cold breeze blows around me, but I barely register it despite my naked chest. Throwing on my helmet, I kick up my kickstand and start the engine. Felix takes a few steps back, giving me room to maneuver the bike before I clamp down on the clutch, hit the gas, and tear out of there.

Wind slams into me and I hunch my shoulders forward, hugging the gas tank between my thighs as I weave through traffic, searching for the exit that will take me on the outer loop of town.

As soon as I've escaped the highway, I gun the gas and fly forward, everything around me morphing into a blur. I don't want to think about shit with my brother, but now Cecilia is here and I'm drowning all over again.

I don't know if I can help her. And it's pretty clear she doesn't want me to. But, I think I owe it to my brother to try.

10

CECILIA

I don't see Gabriel the rest of the week. If I had to guess, it's intentional on his part. He's avoiding me. Not that I let myself dwell on it, or on his words from Monday at the pool.

I just ... can't. Not when I'm barely keeping my shit together.

I'm losing time. It's happened before, but this time it's worse.

One second, I'm changing back into my clothes in the women's locker room, and the next I'm home, lying in my bed.

I don't remember the drive. Or getting home and walking up the stairs to my room. I don't remember any of it.

I lost over an hour that day. But what's more concerning are the days after. There's something wrong with me. It's like I'm in a haze. I don't recall attending my classes last week. I have notes so I was there, and I must have paid attention. But, I don't *remember* any of it. Not the lectures. The assignments. Nothing.

I eat little and I sleep even less. Neither of which are new. Not since … well, you know. But this seems worse. I barely remember last week and the weekend is little more than a blur. I'm pretty sure I stayed in my room for most of it, not bothering to venture out for even a swim.

I think Mom talked to me at some point, but I have no clue what about.

Rationally, I know I should tell someone. I do. But I know what comes next and it's not something I want to deal with right now. I'm still trying to find a sense of normalcy, and I can't handle the freak out that will ensue if I tell my parents what's going on with me. They worry enough as it is.

Better to just add this to my already long list of things I'm choosing to ignore. I'm aware it's not healthy, but it's life. Sometimes you just suck it up to survive.

Sighing, I grab my bag and cut across the parking lot to my first class of the day. I've been walking into the communications building each day in an exhausted state of paranoia, just waiting for Austin to jump out at me.

We don't have any classes together. *Thank god.* But we both have morning classes in this building, making him virtually impossible to avoid.

Holding my breath, my gaze darts around the hallway, but there's no sign of him. Not taking any chances, I dart through the halls, careful to keep my head down.

Foreboding niggles at me with each step I take and as I turn the first corner I catch sight of Austin. Shit.

"CeCe," he calls out, immediately spotting me.

I force my feet into motion, increasing my pace.

"Aww, don't be like that." Austin falls into step beside me, hands tucked into his pockets.

Speed walking now, I try to out-pace him, but he easily keeps up thanks to his long-legged stride.

"I'm digging this hobo vibe you've got going on." He flicks the collar of my shirt and I rear back, my skin crawling.

"Don't touch me."

Anger flashes in his eyes and Austin does more than touch me when he spins me around and slams me back against the wall. I suck in a pained gasp and my eyes dart left to right, waiting for someone to notice what he did.

But no one does. Everybody here is too worried about getting to their own classes on time to bother paying attention to anything we're doing.

"Austin?" The plea in my tone is evident, though I'm not sure what I'm asking for.

He steps close to me, bracing his hands on the wall behind me as he cages me in. "Are we going to have a problem, Cece?"

My face heats up at the reality of being cornered like this. Why does no one say anything?

"No." I shake my head. Tugging on the open lapels of my flannel, I cross my arms and hug the material around my chest, as if the added layer of fabric can ward him off.

I'm eye level with Austin's jaw and I watch through my peripheral as a muscle ticks.

I haven't looked at his face and I can tell it bothers him. Austin isn't used to being ignored. As one of PacNorth's star athletes and a member of Zeta Pi—the largest fraternity on campus—he's used to women fawning over him, desperate for any crumb of his attention.

Sucks for him because he'll never get that sort of reception from me.

Dropping his hands from the wall, he places one on my hip, fingers digging into my flesh in warning.

I flinch, barely managing to keep myself still. Panic rises in my chest.

Auston chuckles, seeing my reaction and leans into me. "See that we don't." His breath fans across my neck and ear like he's sharing a secret. I fight back a shudder and wait for him to move now that he's terrorized me for the day. Mission accomplished. Only he doesn't step away.

His fingers flex on my hip again.

"Austin," I warn.

His lips ghost across my neck. It's a move intended to remind me of my place. That he can do whatever he wants, whenever he wants to, and I can't stop him.

This time, I do shudder.

He chuckles, enjoying my reaction.

"You might pretend you're not interested but I remember the way your body responded to mine."

I hold myself perfectly still, praying he'll step back and release me. Of course, it's never that easy. This is how he gets his kicks. Posturing. Intimidation. A proverbial game of cat and mouse.

"You liked me touching you, didn't you?"

Swallowing hard, I shake my head and tears prick the corners of my eyes. No. I very much did not like him touching me. Just thinking about it makes my skin crawl.

I want to give voice to my denial, but more than that, I want to get the hell away from him, and keeping my mouth shut is the quickest path to that outcome.

I turn my head, desperate for someone, anyone to intervene when I catch sight of a familiar face. Kim. She stands a few class doors down from us but her attention is focused solely on me. Her lip curls in disgust, like Austin pinning me to the wall somehow confirms her original doubts.

I shake my head, my gaze pleading with her to understand it's not like that. I don't want him.

Austin looks over his shoulder, following my gaze. "She was fun," he says. "But she's served her purpose. Time to move on."

I choke on my own spit and he turns his attention back to me.

"Look at me," he demands.

I take a deep breath before shaking my head. At my refusal, Austin cups my jaw, and forcefully tilts my chin up to meet his gaze. To anyone else, the action would look sweet. Two lovers sharing a moment. He strokes the side of my face and offers me a cruel smile, enjoying how uncomfortable his touch makes me.

The glint in his eyes wreaks havoc on my nerves, but he gets whatever reaction he's looking for because he finally steps away, giving me space to breathe.

"Better run before I get any ideas," he laughs.

Not giving him the chance to change his mind, I bolt for my class, ignoring Kim's furious expression as I all but run past her. That I'm doing exactly what he said, running, makes no difference. I just want to get away.

Austin's loud laugh echoes behind me and I rub my arms as goosebumps break out over my skin.

Not seeing him over the last part of summer break has left me ill-equipped for the reality of facing my attacker every single day. Especially when he enjoys cornering me at every opportunity.

PacNorth boasts over thirteen thousand students. I don't know or even recognize the good majority of the people going here, yet I still can't seem to escape him.

Fate is a fickle bitch, and I swear she likes to screw with me.

Even now, what should be a beautiful day is tainted by only one interaction. I chance a glance over my shoulder. He's right where I left him, a wide smile on his too handsome face like he was just waiting for me to look his way. Austin doesn't have a care in the world, and I hate it. Hate him.

Sliding into class, I take a seat toward the back of the room before checking to see how much time I have before class begins. Five minutes.

My classmates filter into the room, taking their time as they loiter with friends. My cell phone buzzes in my pocket and a quick glance at the screen shows me I have two new messages. The first is from my mom.

Mom: Have a wonderful day! Maybe after your classes we can do lunch!

I sigh and ignore it.

Mom hovers a lot. She hides it under the guise of bonding, but if she's not working or otherwise occupied, her favorite place to be is glued to my hip. I'm letting it be for now, pretending I believe her when she says she wants my opinion on a dress so I need to go shopping with her. Or when she says my father refuses to watch a particular rom com with her and would I please hang out in the living room so she isn't forced to watch it alone.

For the record, my father has never said no to a thing that woman has ever asked for. My dad loves my mom. It can be gag-inducing at times, just how much they love each other, so I know when she uses lines like that, that Dad refused her some random inconvenient thing, that she's full of crap.

But I pretend to be offended on her behalf and sit beside her while she munches on popcorn and fake cries at all the lovey-dovey parts. She probably thinks spending time together helps me.

It doesn't.

The second message is an unwelcome surprise. I didn't even know she had my new number.

Kim: We've barely broken up and already you're moving in on him? Get a life, Cecilia!

My blood heats but before I can decide how to respond, a hush falls over the classroom, and I look up in time to see Gabriel walk in. Our eyes meet and he doesn't look at all surprised to see me. In fact, without missing a beat, he heads straight for me, stopping beside the empty seat on my left.

"This seat taken?" he asks.

Not giving me a chance to reply, he drops down into the chair and my heart chooses that moment to kick start into action, punching me in the ribs as it pounds inside my chest.

He slips his backpack off his shoulder, setting it down beside him before he props his feet on the back of the chair in front of him as he settles in. My brows furrow. Is he lost? Gabriel isn't in this class, but with the way he's relaxing, it seems like he thinks he is.

Chewing my bottom lip, I take him in through my peripheral, too proud to turn my full attention toward him. Why is he here? The question rolls around in my head. After being cornered by Austin in the hall, something about this feels wrong. Did he send his friend in here to terrorize me? Is that why he's here?

Gabriel doesn't say anything. Just sits there, looking like he does. Which is hot, by the way. I may have zero interest in guys as a whole, and even less in someone who associates with the likes of Austin Holt, but I'm not blind. Gabriel Herrera is overwhelmingly attractive. He has the whole tall, dark, and handsome thing going for him.

Around six four with tan skin, dark brown hair, and light honey-colored eyes, it's easy to see why the other girls in class are suddenly staring. He keeps his face shaved. His hair loosely styled in a way that says, *I care, but not so much that I'll waste unnecessary time.* His jaw is chiseled, and the corners of his mouth curl on their own, giving him the smallest resting smile.

He's like a Hispanic Thomas Doherty. It's devastating in a way. Again, not because I'm interested. I just have eyes.

Today he wears ripped jeans and a long-sleeved, gray shirt. The sleeves are pushed up to his elbows, exposing his muscular forearms and the thick leather cuff he wears on his left wrist. It's a simple design. Dark brown leather with a wolf embossed on the side. PacNorth's mascot is a wolf. Probably a symbol of school pride or something.

I can feel the heat of his gaze. I don't need to look at him to know he's studying me as intently as I am him, only he's being obvious about it which has me squirming in my seat.

"Like what you see?"

I roll my eyes and ignore the question.

Gabriel drops his legs to the floor and faces me. I don't acknowledge him. A few guys call his name, waving him over to the empty seats beside them. He gives them a tight smile and a nod in greeting but doesn't get up to join them. He keeps his gaze trained on me, like he's worried I might disappear if he looks away.

If only it was that easy. Gabriel ignores their repeated attempts to persuade him, and I just ignore him entirely, refusing to fall into whatever trap this is.

"Cat got your tongue?" His voice lowers, but then his mouth curves to one side. He's testing me. Seeing how I react.

I give him nothing. I'm not interested in whatever game he wants to play.

He clucks his tongue and reaches his hand out across the gap between our desks. Instinctively, I flinch back. Gabriel freezes, his eyes sharpening on me.

His hand hovers only inches away, not pulling back, but also not moving forward. I chance a look in his direction, giving up on my attempts at being discreet.

His eyes are dark, but he's not looking at my face, it's like he's staring off into space, his gaze focused on the surface of my desk.

I give myself three seconds to take in his expression. His thick brows are furrowed and his jaw is locked. My eyes drop to his arm that still hovers between us and he shifts into motion, swiping the pen from my desk.

"Mind if I borrow this?" His voice is casual, any confusion or tension wiped clean from his face as if the last few seconds never happened.

A delayed gasp passes my lips and I stare mutely at him as he rolls my pen between his thumb and forefinger. What just happened?

Gabriel leans back in his seat, getting comfortable again as my mind struggles to form the words to his question, and for some strange reason, I blurt out the first stupid thing that pops into my head.

"Why don't you have hair on your arms?" I realize how rude that is as soon as I say it, but it's too late to take them back so I push on. "And no. You can't have my pen."

I reach out to grab it, but he drops it into his other hand, keeping it out of reach.

I huff out a breath and hold my hand out in silent demand.

He quirks a brow, a small smile curling the edge of his lips. "What was that?"

"My pen. Give it back."

He shakes his head. "Before that. You asked ..."

He trails off and my cheeks heat with embarrassment. I know what I asked but I didn't mean to ask it. Not really. I'm not even sure why it jumped out at me, but now, it looks like he expects an answer.

I dip my chin down, indicating his forearm. "Your arms. You don't have any hair."

"I know." The way he says it, like it's the most normal thing, and I mean, it's not, right? I know not all guys have chest hair. And some struggle to grow a beard. But last I checked, arm hair was pretty universal even for girls.

I exhale a small huff. "Whatever. Just give me back my pen."

"I shave it, in case you were wondering."

What? "Why?"

He shrugs, still not returning my pen. "I play soccer." Like that answers anything.

"That doesn't make any sense," I tell him. "Swimmers and cyclists shave their bodies, but there are studies that prove it can increase performance. What reasons do soccer players have to shave theirs?" Too late, I realize he's drawn me into a conversation I never intended to have, and he still hasn't given me my pen back.

I like that pen. It's my favorite pen. Not too thick and not too thin. Its base is metal, not that cheap plastic crap, and it has this sort of mermaid ombre effect where the bottom is green and as you move up it transitions to blue, and then from blue to pink, and pink to purple until you reach the top. And it has a stylus tip. I don't use it, but I like that it's there. Dammit. Why won't he give me my pen?

"I don't shave my entire body."

"Lovely." I keep my tone casual, not at all envisioning Gabriel's naked body. My cheeks heat and I chew my bottom lip. Turning in my seat, I fold my arms over my chest, determined to ignore his existence, but he continues like I haven't spoken at all as he idly plays with *my* pen.

"Mostly my arms and legs."

"Mostly?" My mind catches on the word and I mutter a curse. He continues drawing me into talking to him. Urgh. *Ignore him, Cecilia.* Only now my mind wants to know what else he shaves. If he mostly shaves his arms and legs, that means he shaves somewhere else too, right?

My gaze flicks over him and he watches me, granting me his full, undivided attention.

Okay, so arms and legs he admits to. Face is a given. His neck is bare, though, naturally, I would assume. I don't see any chest hair peeking out of his shirt, not that that is overtly telling. *Why am I even thinking about this?*

My eyes dip lower.

Gabriel chuckles, and too late I realize I just looked at his crotch and he totally caught me. Oh my god. My face flames with embarrassment.

"Not that," he says with a smirk. "I trim. All dudes should. But I'm not bare as a baby down there."

My face and neck burn and I glance around the room, looking anywhere but at him when he laughs out loud again.

"Sorry, that was rude," I mutter.

"Nah, we're good."

I meet his gaze briefly and give him a small nod. "Thanks."

"But—" he draws out the word. "It's only fair we even the score, don't you think? I told you mine. You tell me yours?"

My eyes narrow. "If I do, will you finally return my pen?"

His eyes light up with mischief. "Sure. Answer my questions and—" He holds out my pen and I move to grab it, but he pulls back at the last second. "Then you can have your pen."

"Fine."

His smile widens and he quirks a single brow before asking, "Arms?"

I shake my head. "No." If I swam competitively I would, but I don't see that happening in this lifetime so why bother?

"Legs?"

I nod. That one is a given.

"Underarms?"

I snort and follow it up with another nod. There's anything wrong with girls who don't shave their pits. If that's your stick or if you're one of the Ra-Ra female empowerment types, good for you. But, I've formed no attachment to my underarm hair and prefer it to be gone.

"Pussy?" he asks, not bothering to keep his voice down.

I choke on a breath and glance around to see if anyone else heard before exhaling a breath of relief. Looks like the rest of the class is too distracted with their own conversations to pay any attention to ours. Thank god.

"Shhh," I hiss, giving him a *what the hell?* glare. The least he could do is keep his voice down when he says something like that.

Gabriel rolls his eyes. "Relax. No one here cares," he says. When all I do is glare at him, he asks, "Want me to repeat the question?"

"No."

"No, you don't shave your pussy? Or no, I don't need to repeat the question?"

My eyes flare in annoyance. "Keep your voice down."

"Why? Our professor isn't here yet and I'm pretty sure no one in the room is offended by the word pussy."

I cover my face with my hands and groan. He's infuriating.

Gabriel coughs to clear his throat and I snap my gaze toward him with a glare. He shifts uncomfortably in his seat.

"What?"

"That noise—" He shakes his head. "Don't make noises like that."

My brows draw tight. "What?"

He coughs again, but whatever point he's trying to make must not be important because after a curt, "just don't," he drops it and changes directions. "Are you going to answer me or do I get to keep this spiffy pen?" He twirls it between his thumb and index finger. "Bare, all natural, or groomed?"

I give him a withering glare, not that he seems affected by it, before I mutter a single word under my breath. "Bare."

He leans toward me, hand cupping his ear. "What was that?"

I bite my lower lip as heat crawls up my neck. "Bare," I repeat, this time a little louder.

"Huh? Still didn't hear you."

People are looking now and I want nothing more than to reach across the gap and punch him square in the jaw. But, I can tell he isn't going to let up. "Bare," I grind out for the third and final time as I try and fail to ignore the curious stares in our direction.

Gabriel smiles and tosses my pen onto my desk. Snatching it from the surface, I drop it into the front zipper pouch on my bag and trade it for a different one I like considerably less. Just in case he gets any ideas again.

"Was that so hard?"

"You are incorrigible," I tell him. "And you still never explained why you shave." I fold my arms over my chest and slink lower in my seat. That was the point of this little Q&A, right?

"You wanna do this again? I tell you mine and you tell me yours?"

I know without needing a mirror that my neck and cheeks are a mottled mess of crimson, and I'd like to save myself from further embarrassment so I shake my head.

"Pass."

He chuckles and answers me anyway.

"I shave for three reasons." He holds up three fingers and ticks them off one by one. "I tape my ankles and wrists during games. The tape pulls your hair out when you remove it and no lie, that shit hurts like a bitch."

Reasonable, though shaving your entire arm seems a bit extreme in that case.

"Sometimes, an opposing player is an asshole who likes to rip on your hair to get a rise out of you. Instigate a fight so you throw hands and earn a penalty. That's reason number two."

Alright. That one seems more practical.

"And third, injuries happen in any sport, but muscle strain is pretty common in soccer. We have a massage therapist on staff for the team who helps us out and it's just easier this way. Reduces friction." He shrugs. "No one wants their hair pulled on when they're already in pain."

That makes sense.

"Okay, one more question." I flick my eyes to the clock. Class should have started already which means our professor is running behind, but even late, there's no way he'll miss Gabriel in his classroom.

And I sincerely doubt Mr. Arndt will appreciate him interloping. He's a no-nonsense, by-the-book kind of professor, and it's no secret that he isn't a fan of athletes on campus.

During more than one lecture, he's reminded the class no one receives preferential treatment from him. Any quizzes or assignments missed due to games or training will still have to be made up and for each day work is submitted late, he'll dock points.

He doesn't believe in excusing tests or assignments on the basis of being an athlete. It's actually one of the things that makes me like him as an instructor.

"Why are you here? You're not in this class." My words come out accusatory which isn't what I intended, but

Gabriel doesn't seem bothered by it.

"I transferred in."

My mouth drops open.

"I'm in your next class, too," he adds.

"Excuse me?"

He smirks.

"You don't even know what my next class is."

"Diversity and Historical Oppression."

Okay, that's freaky. "How do you know my schedule, and why are you suddenly in two of my classes?" I don't bother to hide the accusation in my tone, not that he's the least bit phased by it.

"I asked my counselor to look you up." He says it so casually, like it's a completely normal thing to do. News flash. It is not. "And I had her place me in the two classes you're in that still fulfill some of my degree requirements. Took a few days for the professors to sign off on everything, but we're good now."

A flurry of strange and uncomfortable feelings wrap invisible fingers around my chest, but the one that sticks out the most is anger. No scratch that. Rage.

Who does this? And more importantly, why would he even want to?

Gabriel doesn't actually want to be in this class. If he did, that would make this just some sort of coincidence and significantly less creepy. But it's not a coincidence. This is intentional and beyond inappropriate. I mean, there are rules against this, right?

He got an administrator to look up my schedule. Had himself specifically placed into my classes. Mine. That's insane. Hell, it's borderline stalker-ish.

"What could possibly possess you to do that?" I thought he hated me? At the very least, he made it clear when we last spoke that he didn't like me. So, why go to all this trouble?

Gabriel's previous carefree smile is gone, wiped away and replaced with a look of unbridled determination.

"A lot of things, but most important is the fact I couldn't save my brother." Our professor steps into the room but Gabriel doesn't miss a beat. "Not him or my parents. My family. None of it. But..." he lets his words trail off and I wait on bated breath for him to finish. My heart leaps into my throat, thumping widely. "I can and will save you."

Spine stiffening, a cold feeling twists inside me and my heart plummets from my throat to the pit of my stomach. *What?*

The anger from Monday is back. That edge in his voice that tells me this isn't a game for him. Well, newsflash. It's not a game to me either. Who does he think he is?

"I am not some charity case. I don't want or need you—or anyone else for that matter—to save me."

His eyes bore into mine, unblinking. "Too bad."

"Excuse me?"

Our professor starts to call out names, taking attendance, but I tune him out, refusing to let this slide. Gabriel doesn't get to insert himself in my life like this. It's not okay.

"You're welcome to hate it. Hell, you can even hate me. Tell yourself I'm an asshole. I don't care." He doesn't. Looking at him now, I know my opinion on the matter means absolutely nothing to him. "At the end of the day, no matter your feelings or what you say, you can't stop me."

I bite the inside of my cheek until I taste blood. "You're insane."

"Maybe," he agrees, not sounding at all concerned.

"Cecilia Russo," Professor Arndt calls out.

I raise my hand, not looking away. He moves on to the next name on his list.

"I don't need to be saved," I grind out between clenched teeth.

Gabriel shrugs and turns in his chair until he's once again facing the front of the room. "Maybe. Maybe not. I guess we'll find out. But like it or not, I'm here to stay. Just call me your personal guardian angel."

I grind my molars together. I already call him that in my head, though not with the satisfaction he so obviously feels when saying it.

I get the feeling admitting that to him will only make the smug look on his face grow, so I keep it to myself.

"Oh, before I forget. I have practice today at three." He says it like it should mean something to me. It doesn't so I don't bother with a response.

"I checked in with your parents. Told them you're hanging with me today, so you don't have to worry about checking in. They know the deal."

I wrap my hands around the edges of my desk to keep from throwing them in the air. "You spoke to my parents?" I hiss, barely able to control myself.

He doesn't look at me. "You can catch up on homework or read a book while you wait for me to finish. Your mom says you like to read."

"I am not going to your practice." Is this some sort of sick game to him? "We are not hanging out." I stab my finger down on my desk. "After this conversation, I don't want anything to do with you. Ever."

He smirks, apparently finding my outrage funny.

"We'll see."

GABRIEL

Cecilia spends all of class glaring at me. Then glares more when we get to her next one. She manages to avoid sitting by me, claiming a seat between two girls in the class just to ensure I can't sit beside her.

She thinks she's won until I claim the seat directly in front of her. I thought about taking the seat behind her, but where is the fun in that? This way, she's forced to look at me for the entire period.

I can all but feel her eyes burning holes into the back of my skull, and I can't help but grin.

She's angry in a pissed-off kitten sort of way. Feisty and furious, but overall, harmless. If I had a heart, I'd humor her and pretend to care. Maybe apologize for what I know is a complete and utter invasion of her privacy. Problem is, I don't care. Not about her feelings, and not about the lines I crossed to put myself in this seat.

After Felix pulled his bullshit with the Pier, I got to thinking. That fucker strongarmed me into dealing with my shit. There's no reason I can't do the same with Cecilia.

Force her to face her problems head on. To deal with them, so she can get over whatever pushed her into becoming suicidal. It's not a perfect plan, but it's a start, and it's all I've got so I'm running with it.

I pulled out every card in the book. And to hell with anyone who thinks I should be sorry about it. This is do or die, and I have zero fucks to give.

I don't know why she matters to me so much. I don't know her. She's just the girl I carried to the clinic. Weeks earlier, she was nothing more than a broken, nameless face.

But now she has a name. Cecilia Russo. And she has a face. It's been pinched into an adorable scowl for the last hour, but it's there. She is a living, breathing person with a life, and people who care about her. Knowing that changes things. It makes her real.

Finding her a month ago on the locker room floor never should have happened. I had no clue what I'd be walking in on, and trust me when I say there is no way you can prepare for that shit.

I froze. Stood there like a goddamn tree for a full three seconds before reality kicked me in the face and flipped a switch inside me. After that, adrenaline slammed into me and instinct took over.

I grabbed gauze from the first aid kit, wrapped her wrists as tight as I could manage to stem off the bleeding, and rushed her ass to a doctor.

I did what was needed for her to have the best shot at living to see tomorrow.

My decision was swift, but calculated. I didn't overthink it or even allow myself to see her as a person. She was broken. An object in need of fixing, and the doctors were the ones who could do that—fix her.

I couldn't let emotions get in the way, so I closed myself off. Ignored the fact that just over a year prior, I'd been the one to find my brother in a similar position. Difference was, Carlos was a determined fucker who gave everything his all on the first go every single time.

He'd always been like that. Balls to the wall. There were no half measures, not even when taking his own life.

Carlos slit his wrists across the vein, then dragged the blade vertically up his forearms until he met the hollow of his elbow. He cut through muscle and tendon. Tore open veins and exposed nerve endings. The amount of pain he put himself through to achieve his goal had to be insurmountable.

I knew he was gone the second I walked in the room, but it didn't matter. I still dragged his heavy ass out of the bathtub. Wrapped towels around his arms—as if they did a damn thing—and pounded on his chest until the paramedics arrived. It didn't make a difference.

The EMTs didn't even turn the sirens on when they took him out on the stretcher.

He was DOA—dead on arrival.

I found out later, after the autopsy, that before climbing into the bathtub, Carlos swallowed an entire month's supply of antidepressants. He followed that up with a fifth of tequila. Every single drop. Then he went through with the cutting.

Like I said, no half measures. Not where my brother was concerned. He needed help that he never received. Cecilia needs that, too. Help. I see that clear as fucking day.

Talking to her at the pool and realizing she still wants out... it lit something in me. Something I won't allow myself to second-guess.

I couldn't help my brother. But I'll be damned if I'm not going to help her. Like it or not. Her opinion is irrelevant on the matter.

People don't know what they need. And if she's anything like Carlos, she's living in denial. Pretending the shit in her head is manageable. She might know she has a problem. Might even want to get better. But you don't get better without help. It doesn't work like that. She's going to have to put her pride aside and suck it up.

I don't know what her damage is. Maybe there's some truth to what Holt said. Chicks can take it hard when their feelings aren't reciprocated. Maybe this is all about a breakup or unrequited love. Suicide seems like an extreme response, and Cecilia seems levelheaded—suicide attempt notwithstanding—but what do I know?

Bullying could've played a part. Austin mentioned there was some of that. *Slut-shaming.* People can be cruel. Maybe it just all added up.

Whatever her reasons, I'll figure it out. Once I make a decision, I'm all in. Failure isn't an option.

It took me four fucking days to get here. Three days too many, if you ask me. But I can be patient—when I have to be—and I'm damn resourceful.

My counselor flat-out refused my initial request to be transferred into Cecilia's classes. She wouldn't even pull up her schedule to see if any of them lined up with my degree program. You should've seen the look on her face when I asked. Complete and utter shock followed by swift disappointment.

That's when the reprimands started. She scolded me for a full five minutes, like I was a ten-year-old boy with a schoolyard crush who just wanted to hang out with my girlfriend.

Yeah, no.

When she finally stopped laying into me, just long enough to take a breath, I explained the situation. I told her about Cecilia's suicide attempt. Most of the faculty know what happened this summer since it took place on campus. They just don't know the who.

Another line I ran right the fuck over. Zero hesitation. I don't make it a habit to share other people's shit. It's not my style. But I needed the woman on my side. To understand why this was more than a simple request. It was goddamn necessary. Life and death shit.

Cecilia can't be trusted. She's a flight risk intent on making it to the other side.

But did saying all that do me a shred of good? Nope.

My counselor was calm. Understanding. She placated me with comments like, "That's very considerate of you," and "Cecilia is lucky to have you in her corner."

What a joke. She said all the right things, almost had me convinced she was on my side, until the moment she shut me down, spouting some bullshit about privacy policies and respecting boundaries. It's like the woman didn't hear a damn thing I said.

That's when I looked up her parents. It was easy enough. There aren't a lot of Russos in Richland. None actually, aside from Alessandro and Valentina Russo and their daughter.

They seem nice. Happily married. The mom works part time at a veterinary clinic. The dad is our city mayor. Go figure. I've seen the guy on T.V. a few times and he seems decent. No scandals on record. He's a moderate. One of those, *let's all get along* types.

Both were a little wary when I showed up on their doorstep the other day. But once I mentioned Cecilia and explained I was the one to find her, any hesitation in talking to me went right out the window.

Her mom hugged me. Then she broke down and cried on my shoulder, smearing tears and snot all over my shirt. The dad had to literally pry her off me and wrap her in his arms to keep her from lunging for me again. She was so damn grateful. Wouldn't stop thanking me for saving her baby girl. To say I was uncomfortable would be putting it mildly, but if I wasn't already committed, their reaction cinched it.

Once Mrs. Russo calmed down, I told them my plan. She was quick to jump on board. Cecilia's dad was more reserved, but nodded his agreement by the end.

Mrs. Russo contacted my counselor, letting her know she supported my decision to transfer into her daughter's classes. She knows her daughter's schedule, so if my counselor had objected a third time, Plan B was to get a new one and make the request without letting slip why I wanted the transfer.

Lucky for me, I didn't have to go that route.

The problem is, seeing Cecilia for two hours a day isn't enough to pull her out of herself. She needs to get out more. Go and do things. See people.

She needs to remember what it's like to live her life again.

From what her parents tell me, she hides in her room all day, isolating herself from her peers. She's been a hermit since they picked her up from the clinic, and that shit isn't healthy.

It was a good call on their part, making her move home. But I don't get the impression her parents are going to push her. Cecilia broke once. They're worried she'll break again.

That if they push too hard or too fast, it'll tip her over the ledge and they'll lose her, this time for good.

I understand their concern, but it doesn't make them right. It makes them scared.

Someone needs to push her. Pull her. Shake her for all it's worth. Something to make her snap out of it. Coddling her only adds to the problem.

Cecilia doesn't want help. She's made that abundantly clear. So yes, by all means, let's tiptoe around her and let her wallow in her misery some more. That sounds like a fan-fucking-tastic idea.

The stupid that runs through people's heads never ceases to amaze me.

If she'd been an introvert before, maybe I'd buy into the homebody act and believe it was good for her. That she needed the time alone to get her feet under her.

But I did some digging, looked up her socials and even talked to a few people tagged in old pictures.

She was an entirely different person a few months ago. Happy and outgoing. On the university cheer squad her freshman and sophomore years. She was supposed to be on the team this year too, but according to her coach, she just pulled out. Stopped showing up to practice with no explanation. When her coach finally got a hold of her on the phone, she just quit. Said she didn't have time to be on the squad anymore.

Something happened. I can feel it in my gut.

She was active on social media leading into July. Her last post was on the fourteenth. A selfie with a crowd of friends that says, *Life is a party #ZetaPi.*

Then all of a sudden, radio silence. No more updates. No new pictures.

One girl I talked to said Cecilia was the life of the party. A *total* social butterfly. Her words, not mine. She had friends. Guys lined up for her attention.

No surprise there. She's gorgeous even in the oversized sweater and baggy jeans that engulf her small frame. It makes you wonder what she's hiding under there. Not that *I'm* wondering about that. My interest is strictly platonic.

I only want to help. But I can see why dudes would be interested. Her face is bare. Not a lick of makeup to be found and trust me when I say, she doesn't need it. She's got this girl next door vibe going for her. It's insanely attractive.

But she stopped returning people's calls and texts. Stopped going out with her friends. No more parties. No more anything. It's like she's been body-snatched and a new alien life form has taken up residence in her head.

Holt made her out to be a slut, but no one I talked to said anything of the sort. In fact, not one person had anything bad to say about her at all, which makes her sudden and complete withdrawal even more of a mystery.

One I have every intention of solving.

Cecilia will kick it with me most days after school. I haven't explained that to my boys yet, but it won't be a problem. They told me to handle my shit so I am.

We have practice during the week, but I can talk with our assistant coach—Jameia— if I need to miss a day or two. It all depends on whether or not Cecilia decides to be difficult.

We can hang at her place on weekends, though, eventually, I want to get her out. Maybe hit up the lake. Get some sun while the weather allows it. I'm not sure what she's into, but I'll figure it out.

The bell rings, announcing the end of class, and Cecilia bolts for the door. She thinks she can run away from me. It's sorta cute.

I know where she's parked, so at a more leisurely pace I follow behind her as she heads for the parking lot. She glances behind her more than once, and I have to smother my laugh at the look of determination on her face as she increases her steps.

She actually thinks she's leaving.

We're outside when she starts to dig in her bag, searching for the keys currently tucked inside my back pocket. I slow my steps, but continue to walk toward her.

She curses, dropping her bag on the ground before crouching down to give her search a real effort. She has one of those off-the-shoulder messenger bags that works as both a purse and a backpack, though from where I'm standing, it resembles a bottomless pit.

I don't know how she finds anything in there.

"Looking for something?" I come to a stop beside her and lean against the driver's side door of her Jeep.

"My keys," she mutters.

Her frustration is all the more apparent when, with an exasperated breath, she dumps the entire contents of her bag on the pavement, only to realize what I already know.

Her keys aren't in there.

She shoves everything back in her bag and with a frown, stares off in the direction we came from. She bites her bottom lip, abusing the tender flesh with her teeth and the insane urge to tug it free washes over me but I get the feeling she wouldn't appreciate me acting on that little impulse.

"Maybe I left them in class but...." She trails off, not sounding convinced.

Saving her the trouble of walking back inside to look, I pull her keys from my pocket and dangle them between us.

"Nah. You didn't leave them anywhere. I've got them for safekeeping."

Her eyes laser in on the keys, then snap to my face.

"Give those back." Her face is pinched in this adorable frown and I realize I like riling her up like this. It might just become my new favorite pastime. I toss the keys in the air a few times and her eyes track the movement, but not once does she try to grab them.

"I'm good. You don't need them yet anyway. Practice starts in fifteen." I look at my non-existent watch. "You've got an hour and a half before you need your keys. I'll just hang onto them until then."

Her nostrils flare, and the look on her face has my dick jumping to attention.

Fuck, I like that look. Yeah, it's a little messed up, but when she's like this, pissed off and ready to wage war, she's alive. Being attracted to Cecilia Russo was not in the plans but I can't say I'm all too upset by it. If I'm going to spend damn near every waking moment with the girl, I might as well have fun while doing it. A little innocent flirting never hurt anyone.

"I'm not going to your stupid practice."

I tuck her keys back in my pocket and shrug. "Unless you feel like taking a nice long walk, you are."

Her eyes narrow, and she takes a menacing step toward me. That's right, show me how tough you are. "Give. Me. My. Keys." She holds her hand out. Sorry babe, no way am I making it that easy.

"No."

"Yes."

"No."

"Gabriel!" She stomps her foot. Literally stomps it like a five year old child. Fucking adorable.

"Want me to say it in Spanish? *No.*" Quoting teen wolf isn't something I should necessarily be proud of but, I'm a little disappointed when she doesn't pick up on the pop culture reference.

"Urgh! You're being unreasonable!" Cecilia goes for my pocket, but I twist out of reach. "Just give them to me." She lunges for me again, her fingers grazing over my cock. I don't think she notices, but I sure as hell do. I let it slide the first time, but I'm fully erect after the second and that shit is bound to be noticed.

She fights me, trying to get to her keys. Her hair is a mess around her face, and each time she reaches for me, I swat her hand away or jerk to the side at the last possible second.

Hmm. This is fun.

At one point I race around her car and she surprises me by giving chase. I love it. Riling her up like this. Her face is flushed, eyes bright.

She manages to hook one arm around my waist from behind, not that it'll do her much good. I let her blindly search for the seam of my pocket—and she again rubs her hand over my dick. With a muffled groan, I twist around and pin her in place against her Jeep.

My arms cage her in on either side, offering no chance of escape even though I'd been the one running.

Thrown by the move, her eyes widen, pupils dilating until black all but consumes every trace of brown that'd been there before.

Her breathing picks up speed and a look of fear flashes over her face.

I hesitate. She shouldn't be afraid. Not of me.

Who hurt you? I want to ask, but I know she won't tell me. Not yet. I reach out and tuck a strand of hair behind her ear, hoping she'll calm down if I give her a moment but instead she sucks in a sharp breath.

She wants me to back off. She's all but screaming it out loud with the rigid set of her shoulders. The lines bracketing her mouth. I could make this easy on her. Step away without her having to ask. That'd be the gentlemanly thing to do.

It's too bad I'm not in a hospitable mood.

Never in my life has someone mistaken me for a gentleman. Which isn't to say I'm a bad guy. I'm just not known for going out of my way for outsiders. And, unless you're *familia* or on my team, you're an outsider. Only maybe *she* isn't. Or at least, she doesn't have to be. Hmm. Something to think about, not that it changes things today.

Nothing about living life is easy. It's hard and messy and sometimes you experience uncomfortable shit.

Cecilia needs to find a way to cope. To get a handle on wherever this fear is coming from.

I won't be like everyone else in her life and step back at the first signs of her discomfort. It doesn't look like anyone else is going to push her, so I will.

Somebody has to.

Seconds tick by as I wait her out, holding myself impossibly still. Only a few inches of space separate us, and when the wind rustles her hair, I can't help but breathe in the coconut scent of her shampoo. My mouth waters.

Licking my lips, I hold her gaze and lift one brow, daring her to make a move.

Her eyes flick to my mouth and back, and a pretty blush warms her cheeks.

She can push me away anytime. She can use her words. Demand that I take a step back. If she does, I will. This isn't one of those gray areas I make a habit of crossing into. If a girl doesn't want me to touch her, I don't. End of story. If she was anyone else, I would have backed off by now and given her some space.

But with Cecilia, I need words or physical contact if she wants me to back away. I need more than body language.

She's gotta take control. Make some demands.

The longer I stare into her eyes, the quicker her emotions flint across her face. Some are easy to recognize. Apprehension. Curiosity. A touch of fear. But then a new emotion bleeds into her gaze. One I not only recognize, but respond to.

Want mixed with more than a little *need*.

She bites her lip—we really need to work on that habit of hers—and my eyes, drawn by the action, drop to her mouth.

Her body sways toward me. I doubt she's aware of the motion. If she was, I'm almost certain she'd jerk away. Put distance between us.

The thought alone adds a sour taste in my mouth.

Before she has a chance to second guess herself, I respond in kind, leaning closer and making my interest clear. I'll get shit from my boys for this later. Hell, I'll give myself shit for this because it sure as fuck was not part of my plans. I don't really care, though. I'm curious to see where this goes.

One of my hands slides down to settle on her hip. My thumb pushes beneath the hem of her sweater, finding bare skin to stroke. She's warm. Soft. I push her shirt up further, just enough for my palm to settle against her skin.

Cecilia sucks in a breath, but that's her only reaction. She doesn't tell me to back off, or shove me away.

We're still good here.

Pressing forward, I eliminate the scant few inches of space between us until her front is pressed right up against my chest.

A hitch in her breathing is followed by a hard swallow.

I'm playing with fire here. *Platonic*, I remind myself. I'm supposed to keep shit platonic. I remind myself why pursuing anything romantic with this girl is a bad idea. Problem is, none of the reasons I come up with sound good enough.

I want to see how far she'll let this go. I realize this is impulsive and short sighted. But knowing that does nothing to stop me. My heart lurches in my chest, freefalling as I flip our positions. Keeping her against me with a firm hold on her waist, this new position has my back leaning on the Jeep and her standing, nestled between my legs.

My cock hardens against her stomach. There's no way to hide it, but she doesn't pull away, despite the fact I've made it that much easier for her to do so.

She's as intrigued as I am.

Alarm bells blare inside my head. Dating during soccer season, even casually flirting, is something I generally avoided. And for good reason. So, what the hell am I doing right now?

It's obvious Cecilia isn't in a place to start anything with someone. Least of all a guy like me. Not that I'm trying to start anything. At least I don't think I am. Having her this close makes it difficult to concentrate. But, I know myself well. All I have to offer are a few great fucks. Anything more often leads to feelings and complications. Drama I don't have the time or inclination to deal with.

But knowing that, repeating the words like a goddamn mantra in my head, doesn't stop me from pulling her closer. From leaning in. The desire in her gaze begs me for a response. Who am I to deny her?

Kissing her might be a mistake. A big-ass complication neither of us needs. But right now, I don't give a shit even though I should. I'll deal with the consequences later.

Dipping my head, I give her every opportunity to tell me no or to turn away, but she doesn't. Her lips part. Her tongue peeks out to moisten them, and her face tilts up to meet mine. A silent invitation. It's all I need to know she wants this as much as I do.

Mouth dropping to hers, I press against her soft lips. *Fuck, she's soft.* It takes every ounce of restraint in me not to devour her.

Cecilia sighs into the kiss, some of the tension in her body dissipating.

I hold myself in check, keeping the kiss light. I'm careful to move at her pace. I want to make sure I'm not misreading any signals here. She's fragile. I need to remember that.

Her palms slide up my stomach, small hands clinging to the fabric of my shirt. My shoulders go rigid, expecting her to push me away and I brace myself for her rejection. But it never comes. Instead, she tugs me closer, her body straining against mine.

Yes.

I nip at her bottom lip, drawing a ragged breath from her mouth before my control snaps and I give in to my desire to deepen the kiss.

Pushing my tongue into her mouth, I cradle the back of her head and draw her impossibly close.

Her small body quakes but her tongue meets mine stroke for stroke. Tiny hands release my shirt to slide up over my chest, then over my shoulders, before settling around my neck. I groan and a strange, possessive urge to claim her slams into me.

I try and fail to reign myself in. To put a stop to this before it goes too far. But then she pushes up on tiptoe, silently begging for more, and I can't help but grin against her lips. How could anyone refuse her?

Cecilia is shy at first, almost hesitant as she explores my mouth with her own. But she gets bolder with each minute that passes.

She tastes like the cherry cola I saw her drink earlier today, and I swear it might be my new favorite flavor.

I dip lower to better accommodate her small frame—she's so damn tiny—and tilt her head just enough to achieve a better angle. Her tongue brushes against mine, fingers weaving into my hair. Fuck. *Es un sueña.* She's a dream.

There's a considerable height difference between us. She's maybe five one to my six four. We'll need to fix that, not that I can complain given she's currently climbing me like a flagpole.

Praying she doesn't freak out, I drop lower and wrap my hands around the backs of her thighs before lifting her in my arms.

She lets out a small squeak, but her legs obediently wrap around my waist and her lips stay locked on mine. Fucking perfect.

A satisfied grunt escapes me. Turning, I set her on the hood of her Jeep and nestle myself between her thighs.

Better.

My mouth wanders to trail kisses along her jawline. Down her neck.

She sighs and her head falls back on her shoulders, granting me unhindered access. I can't help but smirk at the look of contentment on her face. I need to take advantage of this moment.

"You coming to practice with me?" I ask, peppering her with more kisses to keep her like this. Soft. Pliant.

Some of the fog lifts from her gaze, but she's still floating in a heady space of desire when she nods her head. "Fine. I'll go."

Good.

I kiss her one last time. A hard and quick press of lips before forcing my feet to take a step back. I want nothing more than to grind my dick into her jean clad pussy right here on the hood of her car, but even I know that's taking things too far. Just like I know if I don't walk away right now, I'm going to do it anyway.

"You. Bleachers." I tap her on the nose. "I'm gonna go change and when I come out, I better see your fine ass in the stands as I step out on the field."

Her face is flushed as she rolls her eyes and gives me an annoyed smile. But it's a smile nonetheless.

"Fine. Go." She shoos me away. "I'll be there. You still have my keys, remember?"

I pat my pocket to be sure she didn't lift them off me while I was distracted.

Nope. Still good to go.

"Five minutes, woman."

"Yeah, yeah. Go away already," she says, and I can see some of that earlier shyness creeping in as she averts her gaze.

A stupid grin spreads across my face and I walk backwards toward the field, aiming for the locker room just off to the left. Her eyes stay trained on me and my smile widens into this goofy ass grin, but I don't care. She returns my smile, throwing in a wave to rush me along.

"You're going to be late," she hollers, cupping her hands around her mouth.

I stop, getting an idea. *To hell with it.* I jog back to her, watching her eyes widen as I near, and before she can react, I slam my mouth against hers once more in a hard and fast kiss, stealing her breath away.

"Worth it," I say, drawing back.

Her fingers jump up to touch her lips, so I kiss those too before making myself turn away, and this time, I go straight to the locker room.

Getting involved with Cecilia Russo is going to bite me in the ass. I can already feel it. But, I won't waste time regretting that kiss. There's not an ounce of remorse inside me. Not even when I catch sight of Holt loitering just outside the locker room door.

He frowns when he sees me, his eyes flicking over my shoulder to where I know Cecilia still is.

Right away, I know he saw us kissing, and judging by the look on his face, he isn't happy about it. I try and fail to find it in me to care.

Don't get me wrong, I like the guy. Sort of. But Holt's problems are his. Not mine. Just because he had issues with Cecilia before, doesn't mean I will. I don't make a habit of taking on other people's petty drama so if this is going to be an issue for him, he'll have to find a way to get over it.

Besides, the more and more I think about things, the more his story doesn't add up. I get the feeling he's leaving something out, chasing me off her for his own reasons and not because of some bullshit story about looking out for a friend. He made it clear he's attracted to her. And I wouldn't put it past him to lie. Make up some bullshit story just to make sure I don't get in his way.

I'm going to follow my gut here. If Cecilia is trouble, I'll figure it out on my own. I grin. And, I will enjoy myself while doing it.

GABRIEL

"**B**ro, what the fuck?" Austin storms after me, but I ignore him.

I'm riding a high and I sure as shit don't need him souring my good mood. I find my boys, Julio and Felix, inside. Both have already changed into their practice gear and are lacing up their cleats before heading outside.

Knowing the two of them, they've taken their time, waiting for me so we can step out on the field like a unit, the way we always do. Doesn't matter if it's a game or practice. We always show up together.

It wasn't intentional at first, but it didn't take long for us to realize that moving as one draws a certain kind of attention. It also demands a level of respect from our teammates, because together, we're lethal on the field.

I drop my bag beside them and open my locker as I make quick work of tearing off my shirt. I pull out a pair of shorts and a sleeveless practice tee, doing my best to ignore Holt when he steps up beside me. This isn't going to end well. The fucker needs to get his ass on the field, not waste time' harassing me over a chick he thinks screwed him over.

"What the hell, man? You were all over her."

I don't spare him a glance, but I know Felix and Julio's interest is piqued when both stop what they're doing to give Austin their full attention. They're not even slick about it. Nosy bastards.

I pull out my cleats and shove my backpack in my locker before slamming it closed.

"What's your issue, Holt?" I lean down, doing up the laces on my shoes.

"You know what my fucking issue is," he sneers, stepping up on me.

Fuck that. Who does he think he is right now? I shove his chest, forcing him back a step. "No, man. I don't. You two aren't together. You have no claim. None of this is your business, so back off before you piss me off."

"Bullshit. It is my business. You know we fucked—"

"So what?"Anger surges through me. I don't need the reminder, but there it is. "You fucked, what? One time? Is that supposed to mean something to me? Dude, you fuck everyone."

Felix snickers. Everyone knows Holt gets around. If he doesn't want that reputation, then the fucker should stop bragging so much about his conquests in the lockerroom.

"Where the hell is your loyalty, man?"

I snort. Is he kidding right now? "Holt, don't pretend you haven't gone after my sloppy seconds. I'm not stupid. I know you fucked my ex—"

"That's different."

I spread my hands wide. "How?" I wait but Austin says nothing. "How is you fucking my ex, a chick I dated for six months, different than me hanging out with one of your one-night stands? Someone you—" I stab my finger in his direction, "yourself said was only a one-time thing? You didn't want a repeat. Isn't that what you told me?"

His nostrils flare.

"Don't pretend to be torn up that Cecilia's moving on. You never wanted her to begin with. And don't pull that loyalty bullshit on me. You don't get to act surprised when you've done nothing to earn mine."

His jaw flexes. "You're a dick, you know that?" He storms out of the room and onto the field.

Fuck him. Things don't have to be like this. He's the one making it an issue.

I turn and meet Julio's amused expression, not liking the glimmer in his eyes.

"He's not wrong," he says.

Felix chuckles beside him, clearly in agreement.

"About what?"

"You are a dick." Julio grins.

"Asshole," I retort, though without any real heat.

"Yeah, yeah. But you love me."

I throw my shirt at him. "You're lucky I do."

The guys make jokes at Holt's expense as I make quick work of changing. I know they have questions. My no-dating rule during the on season isn't mine alone. Julio and Felix abide by it too, so I'm grateful when both let it drop without asking any questions.

It's temporary. It always is with these two. We know one another inside and out. Share all our fucking secrets like teenage girls at a slumber party. But since shit last week was heavy, they'll give me a day, maybe two, to fill them in before they bombard my ass for information.

I love these two assholes. They're family.

I catch sight of Cecilia, ass in the stands like I asked her to be. She's got her nose in a book, pretending to be fully engrossed in whatever she's reading, but I don't buy it. This is her saving face. Acting like the kiss between us was no big deal.

That's fine. I'll let her have the next hour to regroup, but when I'm done, I'm going to remind her what a big fucking deal shit really is between us.

I've never been like this over a chick. I've barely gotten to know her, but my thoughts are already consumed by her. She makes me impulsive. Possessive. Crazy. It doesn't help that Holt decided to be an asshole, egging me on like that, but I'm willing to throw my friendship with Holt down the drain to keep her—not that it was much of one to begin with but, that's not like me.

There's something about Cecilia Russo that calls to that primal part of me. The part currently insisting she's *mine*.

I shake myself out, doing my best to keep my head in the game and my eyes off the girl in the stands. The first thirty minutes of practice are normal. Coach puts us through the regular gauntlet of drills. Nothing out of the ordinary. But things take a turn when we line up to scrimmage.

We split into two teams; my group plays shirts. The other half of the team plays skins. I'm an attacking midfielder, my usual position, so it's not uncommon for me to take the occasional hit in a game from an opposing defensive player.

Sometimes it's an accident. Usually it's intentional. But it's all part of the game. I don't really think about it too much.

What *is* unusual is when your own teammate takes cheap shots every chance he gets, which is what Holt does now.

I take an elbow to the ribs. A jab to my side. He slices my shin with his cleat, tearing through skin. The asshole isn't pulling any punches.

Blood spills down my leg, and a quick glance confirms it's bad. Coach shoots me a concerned look from the sidelines, spotting the blood, and I know he wants to signal me off field. But that's not going to happen. Holt is gonna get his first.

On the next play, I get the ball and dribble up field, dodging the offensive players as Holt hangs back, his steps mirroring mine. He's supposed to be their striker, so he shouldn't be hanging back, waiting for my approach. Matching my moves. His ass should be on the other side of the field, keeping open until he can either steal the ball or someone passes it to him to score.

He's so fucking obvious about it, which only pisses me off. When only a few feet separate us, I pick up speed and slam into him. I don't even bother to make it look like an accident. I lay his ass out and score before he gets back on his feet.

I'm fouled. No surprise there. The shot doesn't count, but what do I care? Seeing Holt on his back like that—wincing as he climbs to his feet—makes it worth it.

The fucker should back off now if he knows what's good for him, but instead, the asshole jams a thumb between my ribs when Coach isn't looking. I let loose a string of curses and lose the ball to another player, but not before I rear back, slamming my elbow into his nose.

"Goddammit," Austin shouts, cupping his hands over his nose. Blood oozes between his fingers. "That was on purpose."

I lift my shirt to wipe the sweat from my brow. "Sorry, man. You know how it is when you're laser-focused. Didn't even realize you were there." I shrug. "Kinda like when you got me in the ribs. And kicked me in the shin."

His eyes darken, but he doesn't say anything else as he storms off the field heading for our assistant coach, Jameia.

I'm pretty sure I broke his nose. And I'm not upset about it.

Felix jogs up beside me, Julio hot on his heels, and both boys watch me with varying expressions as I eyeball Holt's back.

"What's his deal?" Felix asks, rolling his neck from side to side like he's gearing up for a fight. "I saw what he did to your leg. Was all that shit on purpose?"

I shrug. "I can't prove it. But yeah. He's taken cheap shots since we started."

Their eyes narrow. "Because of her?" Julio tilts his head up to the stands. "He's going to all the trouble over a girl?"

I nod. "Guess so."

"That's unlike him."

"I know." I've ever seen him get attached or so much as care about any girl he's been with. Not about their feelings or well-being. What's his play here? One minute he's talking shit about her, and the next he's throwing blows my way because I want her? He's acting like a jealous ex.

A muscle ticks in his Julio's jaw. "We gonna punish him?"

I think about it for a minute, debating whether he deserves that level of attention. My eyes meet his and Holt flips me off from the sidelines when he thinks no one is looking. *Idiot.*

"Yeah, we're punishing him." Sometimes, lessons need to be learned. This one will be his.

"Shit. About time!" Felix says with a grin. "I can't stand that pretentious asshole. I don't even need a reason to throw down with you and work that *pendejo* over." *That fucker.*

I hold out my fist and he pounds it. I knew he'd be down. Felix loves a good fight. Especially when he can go in all covert. He's down for a face-to-face brawl too, but what he really enjoys is when he can get inside someone's head. He's a manipulative shit. Gets his rocks off by making dudes bigger than him scared. It's an endearing quality, if you ask me.

"Just today or for the foreseeable future," Julio asks.

"That's up to him."

He grunts and glares out across the field. "Yeah. Foreseeable future it is."

Holt has too much pride to do the smart thing and let this go. Doesn't matter that he started it. He's dumb enough to think he can finish it.

He's about to learn he's wrong.

13

CECILIA

"You and me, we need to talk about some things," Gabriel growls as soon as he's within earshot, and okay, yeah, he looks pissed. Can't say I blame him for the bad attitude. I mean, he and Austin really did a number on each other during practice.

It was hard to watch. Enjoyable at times, like when Austin's nose turned into a bloody faucet, but still rough. I don't know what all that was about. I thought they were friends. But Gabriel took a lot of hits, and I'm sure he's in pain.

He should probably see the campus nurse. Get his injuries checked out. But he doesn't look like he has any plans to head in that direction.

He looks pissed. And having all of Gabriel's anger directed at me now makes the urge to run far and fast really freaking strong. I remind myself it's the adrenaline talking.

He's still coming down from practice. He's fine. Everything is fine.

"About what?" My bottom lip quivers so I bite it to still the motion as I shove my book back into my bag and stand up. *It's okay. His adrenaline is high. He won't hurt you. Right?*

I give him an assessing look. Right. Gabriel is nice. He's not like Austin and his stupid frat buddies. Just an hour ago, he kissed me. And while it was unexpected, it wasn't unwelcome. My heart rate picks up.

Gabriel runs his fingers through his hair, shoving the sweat damp strands out of his face. He didn't shower after practice, stopping in the locker room just long enough to grab his things before coming right back out. I almost wish he would have.

Blood drips from the corner of his mouth where Austin landed a jab with his elbow. The asshole. And Gabriel's cheek is red, a bruise already blooming on his tan skin. The back of one calf is scraped nearly raw and I wince as I take in the blood that pools around his ankle, soaking his sock and staining it a deep red.

I swallow hard. That has to hurt. Do they always go at it like this during practice? Aren't there rules or something against that sort of thing? I thought Soccer was a contactless sport but what I saw today was definitely full contact behavior.

Gabriel gave as good as he got, and some of his friends joined in on it and threw a few of their own hits Austin's way toward the end, but ... why?

Is this because of me? Is that why he and Austin were at each other's throats like that?

I frown and immediately dismiss the idea. Gabriel doesn't know what Austin did to me. And besides, aren't they friends? This has to be about something else. Maybe testosterone was running too high on the field or something.

Gabriel takes my bag from me and slings it over his shoulder before taking my hand in his like it's the most natural thing to do. I scowl down at our entwined fingers but mutely follow behind him, still not sure what to expect right now as we make our way down the steps from the bleachers.

Two guys stand near the gate waiting for us. I recognize both from the field. They're Gabriel's teammates, so my mind wants to rationalize that they're safe. That his friends won't do anything to me. And if they try, Gabriel will stop them.

I want to believe that. Truly.

But the reminder does nothing for the anxiety running rampant inside me at the site of two unfamiliar faces.

What do I really know about Gabriel? Nothing. So what if he kissed me. That doesn't mean he all of a sudden cares about me. The real me. Not just his hero complex that makes him want to save a damsel in distress, but me as a person. For all I know it could all be a game. He could be just like Austin, and right now, I'm the lamb he's leading to slaughter.

Hell, Austin did a lot more than kiss me, and that didn't earn me an ounce of his loyalty or protection.

I shake my head, determined to dump the intrusive thoughts from my mind. *Don't go down that road, Cecilia. Not everyone is out to hurt you.*

The closer we get, the faster my heart hammers in my chest.

I'm going to be sick.

I tug my hand free from Gabriel's grip, my breaths coming faster and faster with each passing second. He turns to look over his shoulder at me with a frown but keeps walking, assuming I'll follow.

Loud voices reach my ears. I search for the sound and see Austin, Parker, and Gregory leaving the locker room with a few other players I don't recognize. But there's no mistaking them. They're laughing. Playfully shoving one another without a care in the world. Austin looks up, meeting my gaze, and a cruel sneer spreads across his face. He and his friends reach their cars but he's the last to get in, keeping his eyes locked on mine like he's issuing a warning. Someone calls his name and he gets into the car. One by one, the rest of the players leave. Everyone except Gabriel and his two two friends.

We're almost to them when it's suddenly too much.

I don't know them. I don't know what they're like. What they're capable of. I can't ... I can't do this.

What was I thinking? *Stupid. Cecilia. You're so stupid.*

"I'm gonna head out," I call to Gabriel's back and he stops. If I get out of here fast enough, maybe he won't notice my total freak out.

"I'll take you home." His voice is firm.

Yeah, no. "That's okay. I'll be fine. I just need my keys back." I hold out my hand, but don't move any closer. My eyes flick to the guys behind him, who watch us with open curiosity. The attention makes my skin itch.

"Cecilia?" Gabriel closes the distance between us, but so do his friends, deciding to come to us instead of continuing to wait. I take a step back, but as I do, Gabriel reaches out and cups the side of my face in one large, warm hand.

Concern lines his previously angry features.

"What's going on?"

My eyes flick from him to his friends and back again. "I want to go home." I add steel into my voice, hoping he'll give me what I'm silently asking for. An escape. A chance to slip away before I'm forced to face two large and unfamiliar men.

"And I'm going to take you home. The guys and I just had a few—"

"No." I suck in a sharp breath. "I need to go home now." I stomp my foot, knowing that it makes me look like a petulant child. I don't care. "My mom is probably already worried. Just, give me my keys. *Please.*"

He doesn't, and that small piece of trust that'd been forming between us shatters into a million pieces. Why won't he listen?

I retreat back another step.

Gabriel follows.

"What's going on right now?" There's genuine confusion in his voice, but I don't have it in me to explain it to him.

"Give me my keys," I demand once more.

His eyes narrow and something calculating enters his gaze. "Not until you explain what the hell is happening right now."

My mind races a mile a minute. I need to get out of here. If I can just make it past Gabriel and his friends, I can walk the few blocks to the bus stop and hop on that to get home. Dad has the spare key to my Jeep. I can come back for it tomorrow. It's not a big deal. I just need to—

Gabriel reaches out for me again and as soon as his hand closes around my arm, something inside of me snaps. All of the fear I felt that night comes crashing into me like ocean waves intent on dragging me out to sea.

"Get away from me!" I scream, stumbling back.

My legs collide with the bleachers behind me, and I fall on my ass before scrambling backwards in a makeshift crab crawl as I frantically climb back up the stands. My chest heaves up and down. My throat suddenly dry.

Gabriel is frozen, eyes wide in shock by my reaction, but I can't stop moving. Can't stop trying to get away. I scramble back until my back hits the wall at the back of the bleachers but it's still not enough. Not far enough. Not safe enough. *No. No. No.*

Tears fill my eyes and I blink hard, desperate to make them go away. "Don't fall apart. Do not fall apart," I whisper to myself.

My head is dizzy and my hands tremble as I fight to calm down, but nothing works. What is happening right now? It's been weeks since I've had a panic attack like this, but I can barely breathe right now. My heart pounds as though desperate to tear itself out of my chest. I scrub my hand over my face, fingers pressing deep into my skin.

Why is this happening right now? Just, fucking why?

"Cecilia?"

"Stop!" I snap, holding one hand in the air to ward him off as the other clings to my chest. I press against my racing heart, willing it to slow down, and everything around me slowly falls away.

My vision narrows and the edges blur. I can hear Gabriel's steps as he retreats, moving closer to his friends and further away from me.

Muffled voices reach me as he talks with his friends, but I can't make out their words. Not that I care. I'm sure it's about me. The crazy girl freaking out in front of them. I bet Gabriel's regretting that kiss now. I know I am.

No one comes any closer, and for that, I'm grateful. I suck in a deep breath through my mouth and exhale it as slowly as I can through my nose, focusing on the action like the internet suggested. I know I'm having a panic attack. They've happened enough times that I recognize the signs, but what I don't understand is why now? I'm back at school. I see people every day. I brush past men in the hallways. This shouldn't be happening to me. I had it under control.

I take another breath and close my eyes, straining my ears in case anyone decides to climb the bleachers toward me. I just need a minute. If I can just have a minute to catch my bearings, I'll be fine.

I wrack my brain for all the things I read about dealing with panic attacks and anxiety and the 3-3-3 rule comes to mind, so I cling to it. "Three, three, three," I whisper to myself.

"Name three sounds you can hear."

I take a deep breath and listen to the noise around me.

"The wind." Another breath. "Gabriel's voice. The sound of cars passing on the road."

Another deep breath.

"Move three parts of your body."

I open and close my fists. I bounce my knee. Deep breath. I roll my neck.

Another inhale before letting it out. I release a small piece of my panic on my next exhale.

"Point out three things you can see."

I open my eyes and let my surroundings come into focus. "Soccer field. Gabriel. Gabriel's friends."

I swallow hard. "I'm okay." I tell myself. "I'm okay."

14

GABRIEL

"Your girl okay?" Julio asks.

I shake my head and he grabs my arm right as I'm about to go after her, forcing me to stop.

"Give her a minute," he tells me in that zen *'I know fucking everything,'* tone of his. I love the man like a brother, but with the mood I'm in, we're gonna do more than have words if he doesn't let go of me right now.

"What'd you do, man?" Felix asks.

The urge to punch my friend in the face damn near overwhelms me. Why the hell does he assume I did anything? Let alone something that would cause this sort of reaction from her?

"I didn't do shit, asshole. But thanks for the vote of confidence." I turn back to Julio. "What do you mean, give her a minute?" I wave in her general direction as if he's blind to what's happening right now.

"Give her some space."

"Are you kidding me?" I shake him off and turn back toward her, but he stops me again, this time moving to stand in front of me.

"She's having a panic attack."

"No shit, bro. I have eyes." I move to sidestep past him, but the fucker shoves against my chest.

"She's having a panic attack because of *us*, asshole." That grabs my attention. "If you go over there now, you'll make it worse. Let her work through her shit. She doesn't need you hovering. Besides," he tilts his chin in her direction, "she's talking to herself, so it looks like she's trying to calm down. Give her a chance to accomplish that without you rushing over there hot and making shit worse for her."

I bristle at his words. "You don't know what you're talking about." I've been around her all day. I just fucking kissed her, and she was fine with it. Into it, even. She got weird at the pool the day I confronted her, but that was different. She didn't know me at the time, and it's not like I was being a ray of fucking sunshine, either.

Even then, she was cautious, but she wasn't freaking out the way she is right now. This feels wrong. She can't be freaking out because of me, right? We're good.

"Yeah, asshole. I do." Julio shoves me back a step and I knock into Felix when I shift to step around him. Fuck Julio and his bullshit. He doesn't know what she needs. He hasn't even met her. Neither of them have.

"Maybe you should listen to Julio, man. She doesn't look too hot." Felix rests his hand on my shoulder, his voice is laced with concern.

I want to punch something. Where the fuck is Holt's face when I actually want to see it?

"I know," I grind out. "Which is why I'm going to go talk to her if you two will get out of my fucking way." My nostrils flare, and I glance up to check on Cecilia. She hasn't moved from her seat but her head is in her hands, lips moving a mile a minute as she voices silent words to herself.

"What's her story?" Felix asks. "There a reason you're taking a special interest in the chick?"

I know he's trying to distract me, but I consider answering him anyway. The guys know about her. Not her name or even what she looks like, but we're family, we tell each other everything. And after finding her that night, wrists slit and sitting in a pool of her own blood, I was fucked up in a way I haven't been since losing my twin.

It brought back all the memories I've spent months trying to bury. Images of finding my brother—my other fucking half—in a similar position. Of the cuts that were so deep, I could see bone beneath the streaks of crimson blood. Of his head drooped to the side, his skin dull and lifeless and eyes at half mast, staring off at nothing.

I was a mess after that. And when I found her much the same, saw her pale skin and her self-inflicted wounds, all of those memories and feelings came rushing back, reminding me of everything I lost. Everything I could never get back.

Shit messed with my head for weeks, and if it hadn't been for Felix and Julio, I would be back in that dark place where I shut everything off and shove everyone out.

The guys know what finding her did to me. The memories it brought back. And after last week at the Pier, they know shit's still not okay.

They're not bad people, but I can already hear the lecture. All the reasons not to get involved. How I need to handle my own shit first before I can help anyone else with theirs. They wouldn't understand.

Cecilia needs me.

I didn't save my brother. And it eats at me every fucking day. But I can help her. And I don't know, maybe saving her, maybe it can help make up for failing my brother in some small way.

"Gabe?" Julio presses.

"She's been through a lot," I hedge, hoping he'll drop it, but of course he doesn't. Felix is too curious for that. He always has to know everyone else's damage.

"She was abused?" Felix guesses.

It's not a bad assumption, but she wasn't. Not that I know of, at least. Though now that I think about it ... I eye her curiously, an idea unfurling in my mind. Is that... I hesitate, not sure how to answer his question, but Julio shakes his head, his eyes contemplative as he says, "No. Not abused."

I frown. "You don't think so?" It would make sense. If she's been abused, beaten even, it would explain why she shrinks in on herself like that. Why guys in particular intimidate her, but I'm relieved to hear him disagree. I don't like the idea of anyone hurting her.

My relief is short-lived when he shakes his head again and says, "She's freaking out the way Allie did after you know what went down. If I had to guess, your girl's been raped."

Ice cold dread shoots through my veins and I snap my gaze toward him.

"You don't know that," I snap, rejecting the idea immediately. That can't be it. The thought alone makes bile rise in my throat.

A voice inside my head argues that maybe we do. I think back on everything I know about her. Everyone she's mentioned or had any interactions with that I can think of, and my mind zeroes in on one person in particular.

Austin Holt. That fucker. Who did he cover for?

My mind is reeling.

After what Allie went through— "Fuck!" I spin away from my friends, hands fisted at my sides. "Fucking fuck! That sonovabitch." I kick the pavement. How did I miss it? It was right there, standing in front of me this entire time. I know what slimy bastards the guys Holt hangs with can be, but this— "I swear to god, I'm going to—"

"Gabe!" Felix grips me by my shoulders and shakes me like he can knock some sense into me, but all it does is serve to piss me off more. "Calm the fuck down. What the hell are we missing here, man?"

How the fuck did I not see this? I asked him. Point blank. I asked the fucker if she was raped. I was joking. Sort of. But shit, the signs were all there. That asshole damn near spelled it out for me, but like the idiot I am, I ignored it.

He wanted me to doubt her. To think she was easy and asking for it. With all this #MeToo stuff in the media, it's made a lot of dudes paranoid. I've never really understood why. It's not hard to tell if a girl is into you or not, and if she says no, it's fucking no. Plain and simple.

Holt tried to make it sound like it was revenge. Like Cecilia threw around accusations to get guys in trouble when they didn't do anything wrong. He made her out to be a cleat chaser with a bruised ego.

But you can't fake the reaction she's having right now. Someone hurt her, and I'm betting Holt knows exactly who it is and he's protecting the fucker anyway.

Felix gets in my face again, but I shove him away, needing a minute to wrap my head around this revelation.

"What the hell, man?"

I grit my teeth and stare at my two best friends, concern and confusion filling their expressions.

They need to know. I'm not going to let that asshole get away with this. If Julio is right. If someone r...ra— *fuck*. I can't even say it. Goddammit. I'm so pissed with myself. I look to the girl who's been consuming my thoughts since we first spoke in the hallway, and all I can think about is what she must be going through.

Has she told anyone? Has she tried to get help? How has she been coping with all of this?

By the look of her current freak out, she hasn't been.

Shit.

I need Julio and Felix's help for what comes next. They've always had my back. Whatever needs to be done, I know I can count on them. We're ride or die. *Familia* to the bitter end.

"Holt knows." My words are strained, anger still riding me in lightening hot waves. "Holt said she threw around rape allegations this summer to get some of his buddies in trouble." I thought I had beef with him before when he acted like she was his, like he had a claim on her before practice today, but no. I pinch the bridge of my nose and count to ten. This isn't petty jealousy. What he did — "I'm going to kill him. I swear to god. If I find out he had anything—"

"What?!" Julio and Felix say in unison.

I clench my teeth. This is so fucked up.

Julio knows without me needing to say the words. "You think Holt knows who her rapist is? That he's protecting him? Assuming we're right in our assumption that that's why she's freaking out right now?" I can tell he doesn't want to believe it. Hell, I don't either. But it makes perfect fucking sense.

I nod. "Yeah. I do."

"Holt can be a royal prick sometimes, but to be that loyal to someone..."

He's not wrong. I love my boys. Would do anything for them and they'd do anything for me. But rape is a different story. Julio and Felix both have sisters. This kind of shit is inexcusable. I replay the entire conversation we had back in my head. He said she tried to get his buddies in trouble. But he also said she threw herself at him. He had her, too. Did he— The more I think about it, the more pieces start falling together.

A girl came forward a while back. I remember it being a big scandal for the Zeta Pi house. It was a few years ago and I don't think anything ever came of it. Was Holt involved back then?

"You remember freshman year?" I ask.

Julio frowns and shakes his head. "What do you mean?"

"One of the Delta Chi girls accused someone in Zeta Pi of drugging her drink at a party. I don't think it went anywhere, but I remember Holt and some of the others being pissed about it and spewing all sorts of shit back then in the locker room."

"Yeah, I remember that." Felix nods, pressing his thumb to his lips. "Holt was loud about it. He'd tell anyone who'd listen that she was lying."

"What the allegation against him?" It was so long ago, I don't remember.

"Nah. Chambers took the hit on the one I think." Felix says.

"You remember what came of it?" Julio asks.

Felix shrugs. "Last I heard, the girl retracted her statement and everyone involved was given the all clear. No one mentioned it after that."

Did she withdraw her statement because she was lying? Or because someone made her take it back?

I press my tongue to the back of my teeth.

"The first time I met her, the two of them were talking in the halls, and you know how chicks get when they're around Holt. All glassy eyed like he hangs the fucking stars."

Expressions grim, the guys nod. Anyone who plays ball is on the receiving end of extra attention here at PacNorth. Generally, unwanted attention. But Holt is also Zeta Pi on top of being a player. That fraternity is huge on campus, and unlike the rest of us outside of the Greeks, Zeta Pi enjoys the attention they receive.

"Cecilia wasn't like that. She was withdrawn. Eyes wide like she was ready to bolt. I remember thinking it was weird, but then I got a good look at her and realized who she was and—" I bite off my words. *Shit.* I switch directions hoping neither of them notice.

"I'll get her to confirm it before I do anything," I promise. "I might be pissed at the fucker after practice today, but I won't dive into this shit blind." No matter how bad I want to.

"Didn't you only just meet her then?" Julio asks, not missing a beat.

I huff out a breath and consider lying before thinking better of it. "Sort of," I hedge.

Felix's brows pull together. "What are you not telling us?"

Fuck. I stare out at the field, not seeing a way around this before scrubbing a hand over my face. "To the grave. You feel me?"

Both guys draw an X over their chest like we would do when we were kids. I know they're not the type to run their mouths, but telling them her business feels like a betrayal. One I hope she'll forgive me for.

"Cecilia is the girl I found. The one from the locker room." I wait for my words to sink in. "That's why I recognized her that day."

It only takes a few seconds for it all to click. Felix's eyes widen and Julio's jaw clenches tight, the veins on his tattooed neck standing out against his inked skin.

"Is that why she did it..." He trails off. There's no judgment in Julio's words, but his expression is visibly strained. His jaw is tight, eyes narrow. "Is that why you've been a mess lately?"

I decide to ignore the second half of his question.

I don't know if she tried to kill herself because of Holt and his buddies. For all I know, we're heading down a completely wrong train of thought. But if Holt or anyone else did touch her, or force themselves on her, it might be exactly the sort of thing to lead her to make the decision she made that day.

A sick feeling twists in my gut.

"When she walked away, Holt told me she was easy. That he and his buddies passed her around at some Zeta Pi party and she was bitter none of the guys were interested in more." I hang my head. "He fed me bullshit about her, planted all the right seeds that would normally keep me far away. But since ..." I grind my teeth together.

"You're invested because of the suicide?" Julio guesses. "That's why you gave her a second look instead of staying away?"

"I don't want her to end up like Carlos," I admit.

"You can't put that shit on yourself, man," Felix interjects. "You know it wasn't your fault." It doesn't matter how many times they say it. Shit never rings true for me.

"It doesn't matter anymore," I tell him. "I've gotten to know her. Cecilia doesn't fit the person Holt tries to paint her out to be." Old social media posts suggest she was outgoing before. Had more friends. But she didn't have a reputation for screwing around or attaching herself to players. Holt fed me his bullshit and I fell right into it.

Felix whistles and rocks back on his heels. "So, what's the plan?" There's a glint in his eyes and I can only imagine what's swirling around in that beautiful, twisted mind of his. Sometimes the shit he comes up with is scary. I'm not so sure I even want to know. With our luck, it's the sort of plan that will land our asses in hot water. Felix is always one for dramatics. In his head, the higher the risk, the better the reward. But I'm not going to fuck around here. We don't have time for games. Not when it comes to Cecilia. And none of our asses can afford to get caught. Something Felix rarely takes into consideration when plotting his schemes.

I turn to look over at Cecilia. She's still pale. Chest rising and falling faster than it should be. But she looks better than she did a few minutes ago.

"I don't know," I tell him. "But if Holt hurt her, or if he's protecting the asshole who did, I'm going to make them pay."

"I've got some ideas," he offers.

"We don't need to hear them," Julio deadpans.

"Come on. They're good ideas. At least hear me out." Felix complains.

Julio levels him with a glare. "I don't need to hear it to know it's not fucking happening. Whatever shit you've worked up, let it go."

Felix folds his arms over his chest, and I can see he wants to argue, but we both know it's a waste of breath. Julio is playing team leader right now. When he gets like this, we're better off biding our time and waiting for the right opening.

Satisfied Felix isn't going to interrupt him, Julio says, "You two head to the parking lot. Give me a few minutes to talk to her." I open my mouth to argue, but Julio cuts me off. "You're too close to this," he says, expression serious. "Too close to her. Let me see if I can get through to her so you can drive her home, alright?"

Not giving me a chance to argue, he brushes past me, but I grab him by the back of the shirt. He stops and throws me a scowl over his shoulder.

"She doesn't know you. What the hell makes you think you should be the one going up there right now?" The idea of anyone else consoling her makes my blood heat. It's an irrational feeling, but one I can't seem to shake.

Julio doesn't respond to my anger. He's always been the level-headed one of our group. He just shakes free from my hold and says, "Because I'm the one who helped Allie get through her shit. So, let me help your girl. Unless your pride is going to get in the way and you're cool with her suffering more?"

My jaw tightens because fuck no, I'm not okay with that.

Waiting a beat, I nod, and Julio takes that as permission to approach her.

Felix tugs my arm in encouragement and even though I fucking hate the thought of leaving her there, I do what Julio suggested and head to the parking lot to wait.

I hate fucking waiting.

15
CECILIA

Through my peripheral, I catch sight of Gabriel's friend as he climbs the steps of the bleachers. He moves slowly. Cautious. The way you would if you were approaching a caged animal. Like he knows one wrong move and I'll spook.

My shoulders are stiff, body wound tight in anticipation of what he wants. I clench my hands into fists, hating that his slow progression toward me makes my heart beat faster with each foot of distance he eliminates between us. It takes everything in me to stay in my seat. To not shove to my feet and race down the stairs to safety.

My knee bounces up and down. My breath quickens.

He pauses a few rows down from me and offers me a small wave. "Hey." I glance at him briefly before choosing to ignore him as he takes a seat. He faces me, placing his back to the field, and leans forward to rest his elbows on his knees while his hands hang loosely together.

"I'm Julio."

My gaze flicks over him and I take in his broad shoulders. The sweat-soaked shirt he wears. It clings to his chest, highlighting his muscular frame. The sheer strength he has in his tightly coiled body.

My knee bounces a little bit faster.

If I bolt and he gives chase, hands down, he will catch me. No question about it. This guy—Julio, he said his name is— is in peak physical form. I'm no scrub myself. I work out. And I swim. But I'm not a runner.

Julio's eyes watch me, tracking my movements, but he keeps his expression blank, making it difficult to tell what he's thinking.

I glance to the side, seeking out Gabriel, but I don't see him or the other guy anywhere close by. Without being too noticeable, I scan the soccer field before shifting to the locker room. Did he leave? Would he do that?

I shake away the feeling of being abandoned that threatens to sink into me and focus on the guy seated before me. He's who I need to worry about right now.

"If you're looking for Gabe, he's still here."

I ignore him, pretending I don't care while straining my ears in case he says anything else about Gabe's whereabouts.

"I suggested he go wait by the car. Give you and me a few minutes to talk."

My brows pull together. What do he and I have to talk about? I've never even met him before. Not that I know of, at least. I give him another casual once over, taking in the heavy ink tattooed into his skin. A lot of guys on campus have tattoos, but nothing like this.

A dark skull decorates the top of one hand, flanked by dark red roses. Black leaves peak out from behind the crimson petals to mix with a thick coil of thorn tipped vines that twist and tangle a path across his forearm.

On his other hand is a catholic rosary, the delicate beads wrapping around his wrist before falling over the top of his hand, leaving the cross to rest between his thumb and index finger. The details are meticulous. Even from here, I can see the level of artwork that went into the designs. The shading and highlighting that make each bead look as if they're a three-dimensional object resting atop his skin.

His neck is covered in ink, too. Colorful playing cards decorate the column of his throat, intermixed with traditional roses. They're not your standard deck. Each card is decorated with a different yet familiar image. One holds a moon. Another has a bleeding heart.

It takes me a moment to place the game, but when I do, a small smile curls the corners of my mouth. "Loteria," I whisper, not expecting him to hear me, but he does.

"You play?" He rubs the back of his neck and grins as if we're just two old friends catching up.

I chew on my bottom lip and shake my head. "Not since I was a kid." I admit.

"I sucker the guys into a game every now and again. Usually around the holidays, but it's been a while. Maybe you can join us next time?" He shrugs. "If you want to."

Right. That sounds like a terrific idea. Not. He did just see my massive meltdown, right? Why is he doing this? Talking to me? We don't know one another, so he has no reason to initiate a conversation with me right now.

Folding my arms across my chest, I wait for him to stop tiptoeing around whatever it is that he wants, because he wants something. Guys like him always do.

"You okay? This enough space for you?" He indicates the gap between us.

"Y..yeah. I'm good."

"Good. Good." He presses his lips together before releasing a huff of breath. He glances around us, like he's searching for the right words to say. And whatever they are, I need him to get on with it so I can get the hell out of here.

"Did you need something?" It comes out ruder than I intend, but I don't bother to apologize or take it back. I stopped trying to be polite and make other people comfortable a long time ago.

He sighs. "Look, I know we just met and it's not my place to pry into your business ..." he trails off and shakes his head. "Sorry. I'm fucking this up."

Julio rubs the back of his neck again. "You remind me of someone," he admits.

I lift a single brow and wait for him to elaborate.

"Is that a good or a bad thing?"

He cracks his knuckles. A nervous gesture if I had to guess. "Both depending on how you look at it. You remind me of my friend, Alejandra."

Okay. "Do I know her?" I ask, not really interested, but curious to see where he's going with this.

"Nah. We went to high school together, but she transferred senior year when she moved to Sun Valley."

"All Souls Academy?" I guess. It's the high school I graduated from, not that I remember Julio from my time there. He might be a year or two above me. We could have attended the same school and just never crossed paths. Or maybe he's an out-of-state transfer.

He chuckles. "Definitely not."

I bristle at his tone, and he immediately backpedals.

"I'm not judging," he adds. "But I didn't come from money, and I didn't have the grades for a scholarship to that kind of school. Allie and I went to Pacific Prep. Richland's public school. Gabe and Felix, too. We've been best friends since grade school."

"Mmm. Must be nice."

"It's good to have people you can lean on. Friends you know will have your back no matter what."

I swallow hard and look away. Lucky him. I think about Joelle and Kim. How we were once thick as thieves. Until last summer, that is.

"I'm happy you have that. It's good to have a support system," I tell him and push up on shaking legs. "But I need to go. It was nice meeting you."

"Don't you want to know why you remind me of Allie?"

Not really, I want to say. But I bite my tongue and wait, knowing he's going to tell me anyway.

He waves to my seat in a silent request. With a sigh, I sit back down and press my hands to my knees before giving him an expectant look.

His dark brown eyes soften, a sad smile curling the edges of his mouth. I look away. I don't like the way he looks at me. It's like he sees right through me. Into my soul. It's not creepy or uncomfortable, per se. He's not checking me out. But it's intimate in a way that says *I see you.* And I'm not sure I want anyone to really see me these days.

"Allie is one of my favorite people," he says. "She's kind and has this energy about her. There's something that draws people to her. I tell her it's her hobo mojo."

"Hobo mojo?"

His smile widens. "Yeah. She's one of those chicks that doesn't try to impress anyone. She's comfortable in her own skin. Sweatpants with one of those messy bun things on her head." He smirks. "She'll kick it with me and the guys, out eat us in pizza, and kick our asses in Call of Duty. She rubs that shit in, too." He shrugs. "She's easy to be around. There's never any pressure."

"She sounds great."

"She is." Julio licks his lips. "Thing is, senior year after she moved to Sun Valley, she was assaulted."

My head jerks toward him, and his smile dims.

"She was raped at a football game." The air grows heavy around us. "After that night, she wasn't the same carefree girl she used to be."

I swallow hard. "No. I imagine she wouldn't be."

"She's better now, though. She got help. Worked through her trauma."

"That's good." My chest tightens and I force myself to say, "I'm glad it all worked out for her."

He eyes me intently, seeing more than he should.

"The thing is, when it was fresh, before she got help, she'd have these panic attacks. She had a hard time being around guys. Even the ones she knew." He taps two fingers against his temple. "In here, she knew I was her friend. But here," he moves his hand to his chest, "here, I was a man. Someone bigger. Stronger. Someone who could hurt her if I wanted to."

My breath seizes in my lungs.

"Is that what happened earlier?" he asks, his voice soft, like he doesn't want to scare me away. "Have you been ... hurt?"

I blink back my tears, reigning in my emotions the best I can. "I'm sorry your friend was hurt. Something like that," I shake my head, shoving down the emotions trapped in my throat. "Nobody should ever have to go through what she did." I swipe at my face before masking the movement by running my hands through my hair.

"I get that you don't know me. In your shoes, I don't think I'd open up to me either. But I think you could use a friend. And it might sound conceited, but I have some pretty great ones."

"Are you offering them on loan or something?"

He chuckles. "I guess I am." He digs in his pocket and pulls out a crumpled piece of paper. "Do you have a pen?" he asks.

I unzip the front pouch on my bag and pull one out before tossing it to him. Bending at the waist, he uses his knee as a writing surface and scribbles something out over the page. Without standing, he holds his arm out as far as he can go and holds the pen and paper out for me. Hesitating for only a moment, I grab the offered items and take an immediate step back.

Unfolding the paper, I look at the name and phone number scrawled in neat writing.

Alejandra Ramirez 509-891-0004

"I'll let her know you might reach out," he offers. "No pressure. But I think she'd be someone who could help you."

"I don't—"

He raises a hand to stop me. "I don't need any sort of explanation. Your business is your own. I'm not here to judge. But if I'm right—and even if I'm not— but if I am, and you need someone to talk to who's been through a lot of shit and is good at listening, someone who might relate." He nods at the paper in my hand. "Give her a call. Allie's good people."

He rises to his feet and almost as an afterthought says, "Gabe's good people, too. I don't know what's between you two. The fucker is supposed to be focusing on *fútbol*, but I'll let it slide since you seem like a cool chick." He winks at me and I roll my eyes. "He cares, though," he says, expression suddenly solemn. "Gabe doesn't care about many people. He has his own wounds he's dealing with. So if you can, take it easy on the guy, will you?"

"Sure." I don't tell him I know about Gabe's brother. Or add that Gabe is the one who inserted himself into my life. I get the feeling he'd ask me to be careful with Gabe anyway.

"That's all I can ask for." He looks from me to the gate that leads to the parking lot. "I'd offer to walk you, but I'll save myself the rejection. Do you want me to head out first or would you like a head start?"

"You go ahead," I tell him, not wanting him, or any other guy for that matter, at my back.

"Cool. Can I tell Gabe you'll be down in a few? He's waiting by your car for you, and knowing him, he's probably pacing, worried I'll scare you off with stories from his childhood or some shit."

I snort. "Sure. You can tell him I'll be right there."

"Cool. I'll catch you later." He jogs down the bleachers with a wave before disappearing around the corner. When he's gone, I take a deep breath and look down at the wrinkled paper still in my hand.

Julio is right about one thing. Maybe this Allie girl and I do have something in common after all.

16

CECILIA

The tension is thick, and silence hangs heavy between us. I waited a few minutes after Julio left before grabbing my things and making my way down the bleachers.

Gabriel stood beside my car, keys in hand and a tight expression on his face. Neither of us said a word as we climbed inside, him in the driver's seat and me in the passenger side.

I could have argued. Told him I was fine to drive. But I'm not fine. And I'm too tired to argue with him for pride's sake. I'm exhausted and frustrated and humiliated. So, what's the point? My only priority at the moment is getting home so I can lock myself in my room and hide from the world for a while longer. Then I can go over what the fuck just happened and try to figure out how to make sure it never happens again.

We've been driving for ten minutes now and with each passing second, I wait for him to break the silence. For Gabriel to lash out over my behavior. To ask questions I don't have answers to. Or tell me he never wants to speak to me again.

I completely lost it back there, so that last one is probable. He might not say anything at this very moment. Or even today. He seems like a decent guy. Probably doesn't want to hurt my feelings after seeing me fall apart like that. But I can only imagine what's swirling around in that head of his.

He bit off way more than he could chew here. With any luck, he'll realize his mistake with this misguided hero complex of his and drop out of my classes and go about his life like I don't exist. That would be the right move. The smart move on his part.

My chest squeezes at the thought. I ignore it. I barely know him. There's zero reason for me to get attached. My head is just a mess. My emotions frazzled. He kissed me, and was kind to me, and it's just screwing with my head.

I do not care if Gabriel drops me like a hot sack of potatoes. Not one bit.

We're less than five minutes away from my parents' when Gabriel breaks his silence.

"Can we talk about what happened back there?" He keeps his eyes on the road, hands clenched around the steering wheel in a white-knuckled grip.

I suck in a shaky breath and chew on my lower lip. I'm not surprised by the question. I expected it. He deserves some sort of explanation. I know he does. If our roles were reversed, I'd want answers too. But... I don't want to answer his question. Or any others he might have. I want to pretend today never happened. That the past year of my life never happened. I just want to move on.

Maybe if I just ignore him, he'll get the hint and drop it.

"Cece?"

I bristle. "Don't call me that." My voice is brittle, and a rush of irrational tears stings the backs of my eyes. "Fuck," I mutter under my breath and press the backs of my hands to my eyes.

I hate that nickname. Hate it so much that I want to hurl myself into oncoming traffic anytime I hear it. Only Austin ever calls me that. It's not sweet or cute. It's a tool. A name he throws at me to remind me who's in control. I can't make him stop using it. I can't make Austin stop anything. And that's exactly why he does it. He revels in my discomfort. It makes me feel helpless.

I shiver and tuck my hands under my thighs.

"Yeah. Okay. My bad." Gabriel shakes his head. "I didn't mean to upset you."

He reaches out across the center console and I recoil.

"Shit." He sighs. "I'm really fucking this up here."
I don't say anything. We're almost to my street. Just a little further.

"I think we should talk about it." He tries again. "Cecilia?"

"I don't want to." My voice is a raw whisper.

His honey-brown eyes flick toward me before returning to the road. He navigates the car over, parking on a side street less than a block from my house. I eye the keys, still in the ignition. I don't want to fight with him. I just want to go home. But if I ask for my keys, I know he won't give them to me.

Screw it. I'll figure out how to get them tomorrow.

I reach for my seatbelt. I'll walk the rest of the way.

Gabriel shifts in his seat and places his hand over mine. His touch startles me and I jump just as the buckle unlatches, but he doesn't remove his hand.

"How about I talk? That okay?" When I don't immediately shove my door open and run for it, he continues. "I need to say some things. I'm going crazy trying to process all this shit and... I just need to say a few things. Okay?"

I hold back my snort. There's a whole mountain of shit I've been bottling up these past months. Things I'd love to get off my chest, so excuse me, but I'm a little short on sympathy at the moment.

He must see my response in my expression because he adds, "Please."

I purse my lips together. I should leave. I don't want to listen to whatever he has to say to me. But a small part of me wonders if maybe he'll leave me alone if I hear him out.

That's the only reason I stay. It has nothing to do with the sad puppy dog expression he has trained my way.

Look at me, finally looking at the glass half full for once. Silver linings. Assuming this works and he does back off after he gets whatever he needs off his chest.

When I don't object, he exhales a loud breath and turns to face me fully. Mimicking his position, I turn and press my back against the door, the cold from the window seeping through my shirt and chilling my skin.

"Okay. Good."

He considers me for a moment and I wait. Silence stretches between us. Seconds pass and he just stares at me, seemingly at a loss for words.

I blink. Wait. Blink again.

Another harsh exhale. He squares his shoulders and comes to some sort of decision. Opens his mouth.

Nothing.

His shoulders slump.

Gabriel runs his hands through his hair, tugging at the dark brown strands before staring out the windshield. Almost like it's too much just looking at me.

Welcome to the club. I hate looking at myself, too.

Still not looking at me, he says, "Back there," he waves in the general direction behind us, "that was a panic attack, yeah?"

I nod, but he doesn't see it.

Thinking I ignored him, he flicks his gaze toward me, and I nod again.

"Was that because of me? Did I set you off?"

I open my mouth. Close it. I consider the question more fully, but shake my head. I don't think it was him. I'd been around him all day. If he was going to set me off, it should have happened sooner.

"Julio and Felix?"

I shrug. I don't know. I mean, I guess it's a yes. But also no. My brows pull together and I close my eyes. It wasn't them specifically. At least, I don't think it was. They could have been any unfamiliar guys, and I probably would have had the same reaction. It didn't help seeing Austin today. Or his cronies on the team.

"Do you know them? Have you met either of them before today?"

I shake my head. "No."

"Good."

When I frown at his response, he explains. "I trust them with my life. They're like brothers to me, but," he gives me a sheepish look, "I wanted to be sure. You know?"

No. I don't know. What would my having met them before have to do with anything?

My confusion must be written across my face because Gabriel adds, "I think someone hurt you." I hold my breath, praying he stops there. I don't want him making the same assumptions his friend did. What if he told him? I silently curse. They're best fucking friends. Of course, he told him. Dammit. I should have asked. Or, at the very least, begged him to keep his suspicions to himself.

My chest rises and falls at a clipped pace, my breaths ragged and shallow. This can't get out. I can't become the topic of campus gossip. Not about that. It'll get back to Austin. I swallow hard. I can't let it get back to Austin.

"That's why you freaked out earlier, right? Because someone hurt you?"

"No." I vigorously shake my head. "No. No. No."

"Hey, it's okay." He reaches out for me and—shit. I can't. My hands fumble for the latch on the door and, getting it open, I fall back onto the sidewalk.

"Jesus—" Gabriel rounds the car before I even manage to scramble back to my feet. "Cecilia—"

I pick up my bag and make a beeline for my house.

"What just happened?"

Gabriel jogs to keep pace with me. The door to my car is wide open and I can't find it in me to care. I just need to get away.

"Cecilia, talk to me."

Gabriel puts himself in front of me, blocking my path, and grabs both of my shoulders. "Will you stop for one second?"

"No."

"No?"

I tear away from him. I can see my house. I'm almost there. My steps pick up. I'm nearly running, but Gabriel is right beside me.

"You can't just run away from this."

Watch me. I push past the front gate to my house and jog up the porch steps. Shoving my way inside, I slam the door behind me, but Gabriel is there to catch it. Without missing a beat, he follows me inside.

Mom and Dad are in the living room like they always are, waiting for me, but I can't deal with their shocked expressions right now.

I round on Gabriel. "Get out of my house!"

Gabriel's jaw tightens. He turns to my parents and in a respectful tone says, "Mrs. Russo. Mr. Russo. Hi." He nods in greeting.

"Don't talk to my parents." My vision goes red and the feeling of betrayal wraps vicious hands around my throat, reminding me they've already met. That they helped him invade my life. "Why are you saying hi to my parents? Get out!"

He keeps his eyes locked on me, but I'm not the one he speaks to.

"Is it alright if Cecilia and I speak in her room?"

Mom and Dad stare at him in stunned silence, but it's Dad who clears his throat and tugs a wide-eyed Mom to her feet. "We'll give you two some privacy." He grabs his keys from the hook by the door and tugs my mom out behind him. Neither one of them mutters so much as an apology to me before leaving.

I stare open mouthed at their backs. What the hell is happening? How could they do this? Just leave me here alone with him. They don't even know him.

The door closes behind them with a soft snick, leaving Gabriel and me alone in my house, and I just can't with him right now. I storm upstairs to my bedroom, ignoring the sound of his heavy steps on the carpet behind me.

I try and fail again to slam my door in his face. He kicks his foot out into the gap between the door and the frame before pushing his way into my space. My life. It's too much.

He has no right to do this. To insert himself into my life like this. I don't want him here.

"Get out."

"Not until we talk—"

"Get out!" I say again, my voice louder this time.

His eyes narrow, and a vein jumps out on his neck.

"You had a panic attack."

I spread my hands wide. "So what? They happen. It's over now. You can leave."

He stalks toward me, a tick forming along his jaw and a determined glint in his eyes.

I stumble back, but he follows, closing the distance between us despite my retreating steps. Gabriel doesn't stop until he backs me up against my dresser, leaving me nowhere to run as he cages me in, placing his hands either side of the dresser behind me.

My heart pounds in my chest, but not from panic. I cling to the anger swirling inside of me, but even it begins to recede when Gabriel's dark brown gaze pierces mine, and he says, "Someone hurt you." The way he says it, like it hurts him just knowing, makes my stomach flip inside out.

I swallow hard. "You don't know what you're talking about." My bottom lip trembles. He doesn't miss the motion and his eyes darken.

"Who hurt you, Cecilia?"

"No one."

"You're a liar."

"So what?" There's no point denying it. But it doesn't mean he deserves an explanation. This is my life. My trauma. Mine. I don't need to share that shit. Not with him. Not with anyone.

Gabriel cups the side of my face, his thumb stroking my cheek in a deceptively gentle caress. "Why are you fighting me? I want to help."

I shove against his chest, but pushing Gabriel is like trying to move a boulder. He barely shifts.

"I don't need your help." Angry, unshed tears fill my eyes. What I don't say aloud is that he *can't* help. Not really. I asked for help before and look at where it got me.

"You need to let it out."

I shake my head. No. If I do that, I'll never get it back inside again. I wouldn't be able to function. To go to classes. To be normal, or at least as normal as I am now. "Why won't you leave me alone?"

"Because you're hurting." He draws me close, pressing his lips to my temple. His touch is tender and for a moment, I find comfort in him when I know I shouldn't. Gabriel isn't someone I can afford to lean on.

I fist the material of his shirt between my fingers, but this time, I don't shove him away. I cling to him, dipping forward until my head presses beneath the hollow of his throat. He rests his chin on the crown of my head, his hands slipping to settle low on my hips.

"I'm fine." I force the words through gritted teeth.

His chin brushes along the top of my head, moving from left to right. "No. You're not."

"You can't know that."

He sighs. "Yeah. I can."

"How?" I demand, pulling back to gaze up at him.

His eyes land on mine and in them, I see my own feelings reflected back at me. Hurt. Anger. Pain. It sinks vicious claws into me.

"I see the hurt inside of you and it reminds me of my own. I can't walk away from that."

I suck in a breath and close my eyes.

"I'm tired of hurting."

Gabriel wraps his hands around my nape and presses me against his chest. The heavy drum of his heart beats against my ear and I fist my hands in his shirt, but I don't push him away.

"Me, too, baby. Me, too."

His words from before come back to me. About his brother. How he killed himself. How it tore his family apart. He's broken, too. Did anyone try to fix him the way he's trying to fix me? Is that why he's here? Because he wishes someone tried to put him back together?

My shoulders shake and I sniff as I struggle to bottle up my feelings. "Why do you care so much?" I whisper the words, almost afraid of his answer.

He's quiet for so long I wonder if he heard me, until he squeezes me tighter and says, "Maybe we can be broken together? It might make the pain hurt a little less."

I chew on my bottom lip, thinking for a moment before I nod against his chest. "Okay."

"Okay."

17

CECILIA

Silence stretches between us, but it's not the uncomfortable kind. I peer up into Gabriel's eyes and, for a moment, it's like he sees me. The real me. Not the mask I put on to go out into the world.

I don't know his motives. He says he wants to help, but I still don't understand why he even cares. But I realize none of it really matters. Not now.

We're staring at one another so intensely that I catch the second his frustration and anguish bleed from his gaze, quickly replaced with something else. Something more.

I swallow hard and my body immediately responds to the heat building behind his eyes, to the want reflected in his gaze.

My nipples pebble beneath my shirt and my heart races inside my chest, my body coming alive for him. I thought maybe the kiss on my Jeep was a fluke. But this only confirms what I questioned before. I like him. Okay, maybe like is too strong a word. But I'm attracted to him.

I haven't felt like this in months. Not since—before.

I wondered if I could feel like this about a guy again, and part of me doesn't want to second guess it.

"I'm going to kiss you," he warns.

Butterflies dance in my stomach and my tongue darts out to moisten my dry lips as anticipation builds inside me. He eyes me intently, holding himself entirely still until I give him a barely discernible nod. It's all the permission he needs, and he closes the distance between us, pressing his full lips to mine.

My eyes close on instinct and I sag against him as his hands hold me firmly to his chest. He presses his tongue to the seam of my lips and I respond to his silent question, opening for him and meeting his tongue with my own. Gabriel groans in the base of his throat and angles his head to deepen the kiss. A move I'm eager to reciprocate.

His lips are unhurried. Tender. I melt against him and, like in the school parking lot, he bends to grab the backs of my thighs, hoisting me up and into his arms.

My arms wind around his neck and I wrap my legs around his narrow waist, pressing myself against him. Gabriel moans into my mouth and carries me over to my bed, his lips never once leaving mine.

Dropping one knee on the mattress, he lays me back, all the while kissing me, caressing me. My body sinks into the comforter and I freeze, locking up at the feel of his strong, powerful frame hovering over mine.

I can't help my reaction. Squeezing my eyes closed, I count to ten in a desperate attempt to talk myself down. Gabriel doesn't notice at first. He continues to kiss me, trailing his lips across my cheek and along my jawline. One hand holds my hip, pressing me down, pinning me in place.

I can't... I open and close my mouth, struggling to breathe.

Panic rises in my chest and my breaths come out as heavy pants. Gabriel shifts his weight, moving his position to settle himself beside me.

He props himself up on one elbow while his other arm curls around my hip, tugging me close as he rolls me to my side to face him. "Hey," he whispers against my lips. "We're not going any further than this." His words are meant to reassure me, but I'm having a hard time getting enough air into my lungs. I swallow hard and open my eyes, peering up at him between my lashes. He lifts a hand and strokes his thumb along my jaw, eyes filled with concern.

"I'm sorry." My cheeks burn and I look away, but his hand cupping my jaw draws my attention back to him.

"Don't apologize," he says. "You have nothing to be sorry for. I'm not here to get in your pants. That's not what I'm after."

My brows furrow together. "It's not?"

He barks out a laugh and presses a quick kiss to my lips, unraveling the knot of tension inside me. "I mean, I won't lie and say I haven't thought about it." He waggles his brows and I can't help the smile that spreads across my face. "But we'll move at your pace. Whatever it might be. This, us, it's new," he tells me, reaching down to lace the fingers of his hand with mine. "We don't have to rush things. I'll be happy if you let me hold you." He presses another quick kiss to my lips. "And happier if I can kiss you."

I worry my bottom lip, looking down at our entwined hands. I don't want to over analyze what this means. He's kissed me twice now. But that doesn't mean this is a relationship. I've never done casual, but maybe casual is exactly what I need.

"We don't need to take anything further than that," Gabriel assures me.

"I—" His expression is tight, almost hopeful, as he waits for me to respond, but I don't know how to put words to what I want to say. Gabriel is infuriating, but there's no denying I'm attracted to him. That he brings out this side of me that I had buried away. He pushes me, gets under my skin. But more importantly, he makes me feel alive.

"What if I want to do more?" I ask.

His adam's apple bobs in his throat and he tucks a loose tendril of hair behind my ears. "I don't think—"

"Please." My eyes stay locked on his and electricity crackles between us as indecision plays out across his face.

I want to chase this feeling. To know I'm not broken beyond repair, and I think Gabriel can give me that.

"You said we could be broken together," I remind him.

His gaze rakes over my face, looking for any sign of indecision, but he won't find one. I'm sure about this, or at least as sure as I can be.

He licks his lips and his eyes flick to my mouth, a hungry look taking over his expression. "Are you sure?" His voice is husky and I squeeze my legs together as I nod in confirmation.

"Yes."

"We're not having sex."

I open my mouth to argue, but he raises one hand to stop me.

"I'm not saying I don't want to." He pulls me impossibly close, pressing the hard length of his erection against my abdomen to show me the extent of his desire. "But, you're not ready. And I'm not going to take advantage of you."

I chew on my bottom lip, feeling the sting of his rejection, but nod my head anyway, accepting defeat until he adds, "That doesn't mean I can't make you feel good."

My head jerks up and he grins.

"Would you like that?" he asks. "You want me to make you feel good?"

18

GABRIEL

Fuck, she's beautiful. My instinct is to roll her to her back, settle myself between her legs, and bury myself between her thighs, but doing that would be taking this—whatever it is—too far. I meant what I said to her. She's not ready. Not for sex. Maybe not even for what I have planned.

I'm flying blind here. Something obviously happened to her. I don't know how far to push her. What is and isn't okay. I'm letting instinct guide me and praying that if I fuck up, she lets me know and forgives me.

Biting her full bottom lip, she nods her head.

"I need words, Cecilia. Do you want me to make you feel good?"

"Yes." The word comes out breathy.

My smile widens. "You get uncomfortable, you tell me. Understand?"

Her brows pinch together.

"I mean it," I tell her and brush my fingers along her cheek. "Trust goes both ways. You need to trust that I'll make you feel good. And I need to trust that you're brave enough to tell me to stop if it becomes too much."

She swallows hard. "Okay."

"Okay?" She needs to be real fucking clear here. There's zero room for misunderstandings.

"If I get uncomfortable, I'll ask you to stop."

Not good enough. "No." She stiffens in my arms, but I don't let it deter me. "If you get uncomfortable, you'll *tell* me to stop. No asking, Cecilia. This is your show. Your rules. Got it?"

Another nod. Good.

Without any further fanfare, I lean in and capture her mouth. She responds to me immediately, her mouth opening beneath mine and granting me entry to slide my tongue into her mouth. God, she tastes good. Kissing her, I let my hands wander down her body until I'm cupping her ass. I give in to the impulse to squeeze it between my palms and she moans into my mouth. Fuck.

Releasing her, I trail my hand over her body, getting her familiar with my touch as we make out like teenagers for a full ten minutes. When she's boneless in my arms, I take a risk and push my hand beneath the hem of her shirt, shoving it up to expose her full, pert breasts. She sucks in a harsh breath as soon as the cool air hits her skin, but she doesn't push me away or tell me to stop. Her eyes are hooded, filled with a mix of desire and trepidation.

I make it a mission to ensure only the desire remains.

Tugging down the cup of her bra, I release her lips to trail kisses down her neck and collarbone. Her back arches, pressing her tits into my hands, and I use the movement to roll her onto her back as I tweak her nipples. They harden beneath my touch and she starts to squirm on the mattress. I know she wants more, but she's too shy to ask for it.

Careful not to spook her, I keep my body pressed to her side and lower my mouth to her breast as my hand goes on a downward descent. Grazing my teeth against her nipple, she whimpers and the sound alone gets me impossibly harder.

Popping the button on her jeans, I pause to see if she'll stop me. She doesn't. Lowering the zipper, I switch attention to her other breast and slip my hand beneath the fabric of her jeans.

Cecilia's tiny hands fly up to tangle in my hair right as my fingers brush against the lace of her panties and, not missing a beat, I tug them aside. She shudders in my arms and I release her nipple with a loud pop before capturing her lips again in a reverent kiss. She's so fucking sweet. So responsive.

Skimming my fingers along her folds, I take note of how wet she is for me and groan against her lips. "Do you like that?" I ask, pressing two fingers through the evidence of her desire before circling her clit with her wetness. Her hips buck forward, chasing my touch. "Do you want more?" I pull back enough to gauge her response and am greeted with eyes drunk on desire. Satisfaction thrums through me.

My dick throbs behind my zipper, straining to get free, but this right now, it isn't about me. It's about her. Her pleasure. Her release.

Flicking my wrist, it only takes a minute before Cecilia is close, body coiled tight and all but begging for release. Her chest heaves, making her pretty little tits bob with the motion. I don't know how long her parents will be gone so I need to speed this along and get her where I need her to be before we're interrupted.

Putting more pressure on her clit, I rub the little bundle of nerves until she's just about to sail over the edge and then I hold her there, on the precipice of her release. "Answer me." A dick move, but I need to know she's in this with me. That this need coursing through me isn't one sided. That I'm not imagining things.

"Yes. Yes. Yes." Little pants of pleasure escape her lips and her head rolls from side to side, making me chase her mouth for a kiss. Her entire body quivers and I bite her bottom lip, holding her in place before pinching her clit. She whimpers, and fuck does that sound do things to me.

I meet her gaze, watching as her orgasm takes over and her eyes roll into the back of her head. She moans with her release. Perfection. I continue to stroke her as she comes down, until her body spasms and she shoves my hand away.

"Too sensitive," she says.

"Mmm. For now."

She smiles. It's this cautious yet hopeful thing that I can't help but return. "I—" She hesitates, and something tells me whatever it is she's about to say, it's important, so I wait. "I didn't think it could feel like that."

"Amazing?" I quirk a single brow.

She smacks a hand to my chest. "I guess."

"Orgasms should always be good."

Cecilia snorts, tugging her shirt and bra back into place. "I know. It's just that it's been—" She cuts herself off.

"Are you ever going to tell me?" I ask, wanting her to open up.

Her eyes mist and I inwardly curse myself for fucking up this moment for her.

"You know whatever it is, you can tell me. I won't think of you any different."

A front door downstairs opens and closes and voices drift softly up the stairs. She swipes at the moisture on her face and points out the obvious. "Mom and Dad are home," she tells me. "You should probably go." Her words say one thing, but the look on her face says something else.

It begs me to stay.

Fuck. I'm not getting attached to this pint-sized brunette. I'm already attached. I may as well cut off my balls now and give them to her for safekeeping in her purse. Save both of us the trouble of denying what's going on right now.

"No can do," I tell her with a shake of my head. I lean back against her pillows and tug her across my chest. She comes willingly, curling into my side and resting a hand over my heart. Can she tell how fast it beats when I'm with her?

"I don't roll like that." Lies. I very much roll like that, but evidently, not with her. "You ordered the full meal deal, which comes with post orgasmic cuddling."

She giggles against me and I freeze, desperate to hear the sound from her again. "You're ridiculous," she tells me.

I jab my fingers into her ribs, tickling her side. She shrieks before squirming to get away.

"Did you just call me ridiculous?"

She laughs, this full-bellied sound. "What about it?" There's a dare in her voice, the playful side of her coming out, but before I can answer her, the door to her bedroom opens and Mrs. Russo pops her head in.

"We're back," she says, as though we didn't already know.

She eyes our position on the bed and Cecilia squirms to put space between us, but that shit is not happening. Tightening my grip on her, I shift just enough to hide the opening of her jeans and nod my head toward her mother. "Thank you for the time."

Her lips press together, and I can't help but be a little jealous by the guarded look in her eyes. She loves her daughter, that much is clear. Her protectiveness wants to kick me out of her daughter's room, but when she sees the look on Cecilia's face, her expression softens. She wants her daughter's happiness even more.

"We'll be downstairs if you two need anything," she tells us.

"Thanks, Mom."

"And leave this door open," she adds as an afterthought before she leaves.

Cecilia giggles again once her mother is gone. "Oh, my god," she groans.

"What?" I ask, enjoying the pretty blush on her cheeks.

"What do you mean, what? I'm pretty sure my mom knows exactly what we were doing?"

I shrug. "So. We're both adults. Save the embarrassment for when she walks in on us."

Cecilia's eyes bug out of her face. "When?"

I chuckle and capture her lips in a quick kiss. "Yes, Cecilia. When. Because I very much plan on making you come again and again. As many times as you'll let me."

She chews her bottom lip.

"Is that going to be a problem?" I ask.

She shakes her head.

"Good."

She opens her mouth to say something, but then closes it and looks away. Cupping the side of her face, I turn her gaze back to mine. "What is it?"

She shakes her head, but I'm like a dog with a bone.

"None of that. You don't have to share everything with me, but... I hate secrets," I confess. "I'm not saying you have to emo bare your soul to me but just, can we try not to have a mountain of secrets between us?"

"I don't want to go to your practices. We can hangout," she rushes to add. "But don't make me go to your practices."

I frown, wanting to reject the idea because I realize what she's really saying.

"He's on the team?"

She looks away.

"Cecilia—" I kiss her cheek. Her neck. "Is the person who hurt you on the team?"

Her lack of response isn't a denial.

"Okay. I won't ask you to come to my practices." But already my mind is spinning over the possibilities of who hurt my girl. My girl. Fuck. We made the jump to my girl real fucking quick.

Her body sags against her pillows and I hold her tight, pressing my lips to her temple.

"Thank you."

I hate that she feels like she has to thank me for something as simple as not forcing her to see her attacker. Is that what prompted the panic attack? Shit. It certainly didn't help.

"Whatever helps. Whatever makes you happy. We'll do that, okay? Just don't shut me out. Don't push me away."

"I'll try."

It's enough. For now.

19
CECILIA

Sitting on my desk the next day is a can of orange crush soda and next to said desk, in his own seat, is a very long, lean, and attractive Gabriel who I am adamantly trying not to gawk at but god, does he have to look so good?

It makes him impossible to ignore. Not that I'm trying to. Today, at least. But I don't want to stand here staring at him like a weirdo either. Already I can feel my cheeks heating as I think back to what we did yesterday. I cannot believe I let him do that to me. And more surprising, that I enjoyed every second of it.

Swallowing hard, I drop my bag beside my desk and pick up the can of soda. "Is this yours?" I hold it out to him and he shakes his head, a small smile playing on his lips.

"Nope. That's for you."

Huh? I'm more of a cherry cola girl, but I guess I could go for an orange soda every now and again.

"What's the occasion?"

Gabriel chuckles. It's this deep rumble in his chest that somehow vibrates through me. "Can't you just accept the gift?" he asks, flashing me his pearly whites.

"Sure. But why am I receiving said gift?" I eye the can curiously, wondering what he's playing at.

He shrugs. "It's a can of Crush for my crush. It seemed fitting."

"Awww…" That's insanely cheesy but also really sweet.

Gabriel smirks, and I realize I must have said that out loud. Whoops. If my cheeks weren't pink before, they certainly are now.

"I know," he tells me. "I'm pretty smooth when I want to be."

Rolling my eyes, I claim my seat and crack open the can, taking a sip. "I take it you do this with all the ladies?"

He scrunches his nose. "Hardly. I don't make it a habit of chasing after chicks."

"Only me?" I quip, unable to help myself.

"Only you," he confirms.

Warmth fills my chest and I chew on my bottom lip. I don't want to read too much into this. Gabriel is still a jock. Still someone who is most certainly not looking for a relationship and who cannot be trusted. Not with my heart.

Besides, I'm the girl who tried to kill herself. He's just being nice. That's all this is.

Thankfully, our teacher walks in, saving me from needing to come up with a response.

"How DO you feel about grabbing lunch with my boys since we have some free time?" Gabriel says on our way out of class. I got an email earlier this morning that my Diversity and Historical Oppression class was canceled. My instructor's wife is having a baby and I guess today is the lucky day. Gabriel must have received the same email.

"Your boys?"

He tugs my bag from my arm and slings it over his shoulder.

"I can carry that," I tell him.

"I know," he says, still not giving it back. I roll my eyes and give in to his chivalrous ways. It is sort of nice not having to lug the darn thing.

With his free hand, Gabriel threads his fingers through mine like it's the most natural thing in the world to do. Butterflies decide to take up residence in my stomach, which is bad. Really bad. I move to untangle my hand from his, but in response, Gabriel tightens his grip and scowls down at me.

"Is there a problem?" he asks.

"People are looking," I tell him, taking note of the curious looks we're now receiving. I might not be in the in crowd anymore, but I'm in no way ignorant to Gabriel's almost celebrity status at PacNorth University.

"So?"

"So!" What does he mean, so? "They're going to get the wrong idea."

He chuckles and shakes his head. "I'm hoping they get the right one."

"And what is that, exactly?" He's not saying what I think he's saying, right? I mean, there would be more of a conversation involved if he were, I would think. A question, at the very least. Like, will you be my girlfriend? Or can we go steady? Or whatever it is people call relationships these days. I'd say no. Obviously. But if that's what he was aiming for, he'd need to ask first, right? You can't just assume.

"That you're mine."

"What?!"

Gabriel stops in the middle of the hall, completely ignorant or, at the very least, uncaring of the fact that we're blocking traffic and people are having to move around us. Not that anyone seems to mind. They're all too happy to get out of Gabriel's way.

"Is there a problem?" he asks, irritation flicking across his features.

I untangle my hand from his and fold my arms protectively over my chest. Nostrils flaring, he matches my stance, folding his arms while leveling me with a deep scowl as he waits for an answer.

My body stiffens in defense and I shake my head, trying to shove back the urge to drop this and pretend it never happened. That I didn't bring it up. I don't want to fight with him. But I can't seem to find it in me to let this go.

"You can't just claim me all of a sudden because you feel like it," I tell him.

His nostrils flare again and his gaze sharpens as if I've wronged him somehow. "Why not?"

"That's not how things work."

Anger flashes in his gaze, but just as quickly, it's gone. He's good at that, I realize. Hiding his emotions when he wants to. Sucking on his front teeth, he prowls closer toward me and, feeling very much like prey, I do what any reasonable person would. I retreat. Taking several steps back, I try to create some distance, but Gabriel keeps pace with me until I have nowhere else to go and my back meets the smooth surface of the wall.

"How do things work then, Cecilia? Please," he growls the words in my ear, and I shiver. "Explain it to me." Pulling back just enough to once again meet my gaze, he quirks a single, arrogant brow.

"I—"

"Are you interested in someone else?" Based on the look on his face, he hates the idea of that just as much, if not more so, than I do.

"What? No!"

He nods his head. "Okay. Good."

I roll my eyes.

"What's the problem, then?"

"I—" I don't know, but I don't know how to tell him that without sounding like an idiot.

Cupping my cheek in his palm, Gabriel brushes his thumb across my bottom lip. "I like you," he says. "I know shit is complicated. I won't pretend it isn't, but I care. This isn't just about the suicide."

"It's not?"

He shakes his head. "No. It might have started that way, but," Gabriel sighs and presses his lips to my temple, "it's more, now. Let's see where this goes. No pressure. No expectations. I'm not trying to put labels on anything or make you uncomfortable. I just want to spend time with you. Can we do that?"

Chewing my lower lip, I nod.

"Cool. So, about lunch."

20

CECILIA

I assumed we'd eat on campus, but Gabriel has something else in mind as he leads me outside to one of the campus parking lots. The sun shines bright in the sky and a light breeze lifts my long hair around my shoulders. I rush to smooth it down, wishing I had a scrunchie or hair tie with me, but no such luck today.

I'm not really paying attention to where we're going, too focused on keeping my hair out of my face, when Gabriel comes to a stop at the edge of the lot closest to the main road and I nearly run into him. He steadies me with one hand on my shoulder, but releases me as soon as he's sure I won't fall.

Immediately, I miss the contact, which surprises me, and not for the first time. I like when Gabriel touches me.

There aren't many cars on this side of the parking lot, and I eye each of the ones I see curiously. None of them look like something Gabriel would drive. The first is a bright red convertible. Too flashy. The next is a minivan. Too domestic. And the last is a lifted truck with giant spinning rims. Whoever drives that clearly feels the need to compensate for something.

Call it a woman's intuition, but I doubt Gabriel needs to compensate for anything. So, I'm surprised when he angles his head toward the obnoxious thing on wheels.

Seriously?

Seeing the look on my face, he rolls his eyes and leads me around the monstrosity. Hidden behind the douchebag truck is a sleek, black on black motorcycle. *Damn.* He drives that? I lick my lips. I can absolutely see him riding it.

Me, on the other hand, not so much. Which is why my eyes bug out of my head when he raises one of two full-face helmets from the seat and offers it to me. I accept it, but instead of putting it on, I hold it at my side.

"This is yours?" He has the whole hot athlete thing already going for him. Does he really need to take his hotness to extreme levels by driving a freaking crotch rocket, too?

His responding grin is full of mischief. "It is." Taking the other helmet, he places it on his head, quickly securing the buckle beneath his chin. Meanwhile, I'm left staring at him like a moron.

Pushing up the visor on his helmet so I can see his honey-gold gaze, he asks, "Need some help?"

Swallowing hard, I hold out the helmet and shake my head. Nope. Just no. Getting on the back of that, with him, is a bad idea. "I'll follow you in my Jeep," I tell him.

"Why? This is much more fun." He winks, and even with his helmet covering most of his face, it's devastating.

"If you have a death wish." The helmet is heavy, so I let my arm fall back to my side.

"Is that really something you're worried about?" Gabriel asks, quirking a brow.

Ha. Ha. Point made. Swallowing down my apprehension, I give the bike one last long, considering look and take a deep breath. I can do this. It will be... fun.

I tug on the helmet and without me needing to ask, Gabriel reaches out, his nimble fingers making quick work of the loops and buckle beneath my chin. I ignore the way butterflies dance in my stomach when his fingertips brush my skin, keeping my gaze focused anywhere but on him. Why him? Why do I have to be attracted to him? I still don't understand it.

"There," he tells me, tapping my helmet. "All set." Picking up my backpack, he helps me slip my arms into the straps before securing his own bag to his chest, wearing it backwards. "Come on." Waving me forward, he gets onto the bike, slips in the key, and cranks the ignition.

It roars to life, drowning out the noise from the road. Gabriel pats the seat behind him and I eye it with a mix of curiosity and trepidation. *Here goes nothing.* Throwing my leg over, I settle myself behind him and wrap my arms around his narrow waist. The vibrations from the bike thrum through me and I squirm on the seat.

Gabriel gives me a moment to get adjusted before he kicks up the stand and guides us out of the parking lot.

We move slowly at first, weaving through the parking lot as we make our way out onto the main road. My body moves with his, tilting side to side as he takes tight corners and gradually increases our speed. I press myself firmer to his back, using his bulk to block out the wind while also hanging onto him for dear life. Being on the back of a motorcycle is... exhilarating. I'm not sure how else to describe it.

It's like being on a roller coaster as you crest the top of the peak and plummet down the ramp, only the drop never stops.

Gabriel reaches one hand back, grasping me right above my knee as we speed down the highway—definitely going faster than the posted speed limit. At first, I think he does it to comfort me, making sure I'm okay with how fast we're going. But he keeps his hand there for the remainder of the ride, only ever releasing me to shift gears or take a particularly sharp corner before returning his hand to my knee, like he can't not touch me.

It's only ten minutes later when we come to a stop in the driveway of a modest two-story house. Parking beside two other motorcycles, one a burnt orange and the other a deep indigo blue, Gabriel kills the engine and helps me off the bike. We leave our helmets on the seat and he takes my hand, leading me not to the front door but to a side gate.

"Who lives here?" I follow Gabriel into the backyard, but hesitate when I hear loud male voices coming from the back.

Gabriel pauses beside me. "I do," he tells me. "Felix, Julio, and I rent the place along with two other players from the team."

At the mention of other players, I visibly stiffen before Gabriel adds, "But it's just Felix and Julio chilling with us today. Hunt won't be here for another few weeks. He'll be a late transfer from Suncrest U. We offered him a room since we strong armed him into the move, but he's a good guy. You'll like him." I'll have to take his word for it, but the idea of being around anyone who isn't Gabriel makes my skin crawl. "Hunt's got a few more hoops to jump through before making things official, but he'll be around on weekends as he gets his stuff moved over."

I nod because that seems like the appropriate thing to do. "Who's your other roommate?"

"Atticus Bennett."

I relax, unfamiliar with the name, and when Gabriel starts walking again, I follow.

"He's a fraternity reject."

I come to a hard stop. "A what?"

Gabriel chuckles when he sees my expression. "I just mean he used to be a frat kid before he saw the light."

"The light?"

He tugs me into motion again. "Yeah. Bennett wasn't willing to play by their rules. Or, more accurately, break some very reasonable rules just because some frat jackasses told him to. Zeta Pi gave him an ultimatum. Get in line or get out. He decided to get out."

Oh. I like him already. "Good for him."

Gabriel's mouth curls into a smile. "I agree." He laces his fingers with mine. "You ready?"

"Yep," I say, with more confidence than I feel. He nods once, kisses my temple, and leads us the rest of the way.

In the yard, we find Felix and Julio chatting with one another beside a grill. "Hey, you made it," Julio says, holding his hand out for Gabriel. They do the handshake hug thing guys like to do and then all eyes turn to me.

"Didn't think you'd convince her to come." I've met Julio, so this one must be Felix.

"Hi." I wave.

"Don't be a dick," Gabriel growls, throwing his arm around my shoulder and tugging me close.

"Relax," Felix says, arms raised in surrender. To me says, "We're glad you came. Want something to drink?"

"Just water. Thanks."

Felix pulls a bottle of water from the cooler and tosses it to me, and we all fall into casual conversation. Little by little, I feel myself begin to relax. Julio mans the grill, turning over strips of carne asada and warming a handful of tortillas while the guys talk about practice and an upcoming game against Crown Point University they're confident they'll win.

"It's a home game," Felix says, giving me a look. "You going to come?" The question is casual enough, but when all eyes turn to me, I feel like a bug under a microscope.

"I—"

"Nah. She's not really into sports," Gabriel answers for me.

"Aw, but you've got to come," Felix complains. "Who else is going to cheer for us in the stands?"

Gabriel punches him in the arm.

"What the hell was that for?" Felix rubs his shoulder, wincing dramatically.

"She doesn't want to go. Drop it."

I'm about to interrupt. I don't want Gabriel fighting with his friend because of some misplaced need to protect me. I'm capable of telling Felix I'm not going myself, but then Felix gives me a conspiratorial wink, letting me know this is all a game to him. I bite my tongue, curious to see where this goes.

Julio catches my eye and takes a few steps back, silently suggesting I follow suit. I do, and we both watch as Gabriel and Felix advance on one another. "Relax, man. I'm just inviting your girl to hangout with us."

"She doesn't want to go," Gabriel grinds out.

In a low voice, Julio leans over and asks, "You doing okay?"

I nod. "Yeah. I'm just a little surprised."

He chuckles softly. "Gabriel is protective of the people he cares about. I get the feeling you're not a fan of crowds."

I shake my head in confirmation. "No. Not really."

"Bro, relax," Felix shouts.

"You relax." Gabriel shoves Felix in the chest.

I push away from the table, but Julio tugs on the hem of my shirt to stop me. "He needs this."

My brows furrow together. "They're going to start fighting," I tell him. "Like seriously fighting."

"Nah. They'll wrestle around some, but it won't come to blows. Gabriel's wound up and Felix can see that. He's egging him on, so he has an excuse to blow off some steam."

"How can you possibly know that?"

My head snaps toward Gabriel at the sound of a grunt, and the next thing I know, the two of them are rolling around on the ground like two overgrown teenagers.

"We're familia," Julio tells me. "We know one another inside and out. Don't worry." He takes a drink of his soda. "He'll be much more relaxed in a few minutes and you'll get to see a different side of Gabe."

"A different side?"

Julio chuckles. "Yeah. I get the feeling you only know the high-strung, protective, control freak side of him."

The ghost of a smile touches my lips. "You might be right."

"The relaxed, comfortable side of Gabriel is much more fun. You'll see."

LESS THAN TEN minutes after the fight begins, it comes to an abrupt stop when neither Gabriel nor Felix can hold on to their feigned anger any long. Both men lie flat on their backs in the middle of the yard, chests heaving as they laugh and playfully shove one another from their spots on the grass.

"Draw." Gabriel declares as he wipes the sweat from his face with his shirt, exposing the hard planes of his abs. I avert my gaze so I don't get caught staring, but when I search for something else to look at, my eyes connect with Julio's and he gives me a knowing look. Heat creeps up my face and I turn away.

"You good?" Julio asks. I can hear the smile in his voice, his tone teasing.

"Yep. Positively peachy."

He shifts closer and, leaning in, says, "If you need a fan or a bucket of cold water, just say the word. I'm happy to help in any way that I can."

Now it's my turn to shove him. "Very funny."

His smile widens, like pushing him away was somehow a gift. This is... I don't know how to describe it. Nice, I suppose. There's no attraction between Julio and I. Not that he isn't attractive. He is. I imagine the tattoos do wonders for him when he tries to pick up the ladies, but there's no spark between him and I the way there is with me and Gabriel. Being this close to Julio should make me uncomfortable or, at the very least, wary, but I'm neither of those things.

I imagine this is what it would be like if I had siblings. People I could joke around and be myself with. Even with my own friends—with Kim and Joelle—I don't think I ever had this. There were always expectations. Underlying worries that if I did or said the wrong thing, they'd think differently of me.

Given where I am now, those worries weren't unfounded. But, I don't see those kinds of concerns with these three. They're brothers, like Julio said. *Familia.*

Gabriel is the first to get up, climbing to his feet and closing the distance between him and his friend. He towers over Felix with a carefree smile on his face and you can see how relaxed his stance is. Julio was right. This is a different side of him. I've seen Gabriel smile before. Even joke and laugh. But there's always been this underlying strain to his features. A tension in his limbs. I didn't notice it before, but seeing him like this, happy and with his friends, people he's obviously comfortable with, it makes it more noticeable. I want him to be like that with me.

Reaching down, Gabriel holds out a hand, a silent offer to help Felix up.

Julio chuckles beside me and elbows me in the ribs to get my attention. "He knows better," he says, but before I can ask what he means, Felix slaps his hand into Gabriel's, but instead of pulling himself up, he kicks out a leg, knocking Gabriel's feet out from under him. Gabriel tries to catch himself, but Felix has hold of one of his hands and uses it to pull him down, forcing Gabriel back to the ground.

Almost in slow motion, Gabriel's expression morphs from a cocky grin to surprise as he stumbles forward, unable to stop his fall. Felix rolls himself clear and as soon as Gabriel's knees connect with the ground, he jumps to his feet and throws himself onto Gabriel's back, shoving him the rest of the way down.

With Gabriel flat on his stomach, Felix spins around and settles himself criss-cross-apple-sauce style in the center of Gabriel's back. A burst of laughter pours out of me.

Felix catches my eye and pumps his fist into the air. "To accept a draw is to admit defeat." Looking down at a struggling Gabriel, he adds, "I win!"

Gabriel growls beneath him and muscles straining, bucks Felix from his back. Without missing a beat, Felix jumps to his feet and, laughing out loud, runs toward me before circling around to my back. He uses me as a human shield between himself and Gabriel, bobbing left, then right, to keep himself out of Gabriel's direct path.

"Cecilia!" Felix runs out from behind me and jogs around the table. "Do something about your man. This face is too pretty for him to mess with." Felix caresses his own cheek and Julio chokes on a laugh beside me.

Rolling my eyes with a grin, I reach out when Gabriel moves as though to follow him. Grabbing the loop of his jeans, I tug him toward me and hop up onto the patio table. He comes willingly, pushing my knees out to position himself between my legs.

"You're going to let him get away with that?"

"Hell yeah, she is," Felix says. "She likes me."

Gabriel scowls at his friend and places a possessive hand on my thigh. "Mine," he declares, and the growl in his voice as he lays claim to me with that single word sends a shiver up my spine. I should laugh off the remark. Remind him I am not, in fact, his. But I don't. Instead, I tug him closer, telling myself I'm only helping to protect his friend. When Gabriel leans forward, gaze straying to my lips, I tilt my head up in open invitation. His eyes darken and he answers my silent request with the soft press of his lips. My eyes flutter closed, but all too quickly he pulls away.

"No hanky panky, you two" Felix admonishes.

Gabriel huffs out an exasperated breath.

"All right," Julio calls out, drawing all our attention. "Food is done. Come and eat."

21

GABRIEL

After taking Cecilia home, I return to find Julio and Felix inside, waiting for me. "Let's have it," I say, taking a seat on the couch opposite them. I know what's coming, and in a strange sort of way, I'm looking forward to it.

Bringing Cecilia here today didn't make sense. But at the same time, it made perfect sense. They didn't know she was coming, yet my boys took her presence in stride.

We don't bring casuals to the house. This is our home. Our haven. But despite what we've agreed, Cecilia isn't casual. Not even close. I don't know what she is to me yet, only that it's more. More than I expected. More than I deserve.

"She's good for you," Julio tells me.

"She is." If he's looking for an argument from me, he won't find one.

"Too good," Felix adds.

I grin. "She's that too."

"Don't fuck things up." Felix quirks a brow.

I throw a pillow at his face, but he dodges it.

"What? It's good advice."

Flipping him off, I settle back into my seat. "It's shit advice and I don't need it." The moment he looks away, I hurl another pillow at him. "I won't fuck this up." I connect with the left side of his face.

The fucker grins. "Good."

Julio ignores our exchange, rubbing the back of his tattooed neck. He's got that look on his face that lets me know he's contemplating something. Might as well give him the silence he needs to tell us what it is. Catching Felix's gaze, I dip my chin toward Julio.

He rolls his eyes and pretends to zip his mouth closed before tossing the imaginary key away.

"Has she told you what happened? Who hurt her?" Julio asks.

Well, that didn't last long. Sucking on my teeth, I shake my head. "No." Judging by the look on Julio's face, he's as frustrated by that as I am. "She doesn't trust me enough yet for that."

"You can't push her."

"I know." Doesn't mean I don't want to try. "Was it hard like this with Allie?" We don't talk about it much. What happened to her. Allie's business is her own to share, but we know the basics. I wish I could have been there for her when it happened. Helped her through it. She's like the sister I never had. But all of us at once would have been overwhelming for her and she's always been closest with Julio.

"Yes and no. It was different." I wait to see if he'll continue. If he doesn't, we move on. I won't ask him to share what he can't. "Everyone handles their shit differently. With Allie, it was fear that sank claws into her. Fear of being hurt. Of him coming back. Of not knowing who it was or what he looked like. In her mind, every man she came across could have been her attacker. There was nowhere safe."

I swallow hard, hating the idea of her living like that. Hanging with her now, you'd never guess at all the crap she's been through. "But she got over it," I hedge, because like I said, we don't talk about it. She knows we know, and that's that.

A cushion smacks me in the face.

"I don't think rape is the kind of thing you just get over." Felix dangles the other pillow I threw at him off the side of the sofa. A reminder he has one more.

"You know what I mean."

He shrugs.

Julio throws his own pillow at him. "Stop messing around." Turning back to me, he says, "Your girl doesn't seem to have an aversion to touch or to men. Not like Allie did."

"So maybe it wasn't as bad."

Felix snorts but says nothing.

"Don't assume that." Julio leans forward and laces his fingers together. "Like I said, everyone handles their shit differently. We haven't been around her enough to figure out her triggers, but she had a panic attack when the three of us approached that first day."

"So, groups might be an issue?" Felix questions.

I don't like the possibilities that leads to. "She was fine today."

"She felt safe." The way Julio says it, looking at me like I'm the reason for it, makes me sit taller in my seat. Until I remember one small detail.

"They're on the team." I've barely gotten the words out before Felix explodes to his feet.

"What!? Who?" he demands. "Benson? Was it him? I bet it was him. He's such a slimy little shit."

I need to head this off before Felix gets carried away. "I don't know if it was him." Though I can't say I'd put it past him. Felix is right. Benson is a slimy little shit. But we don't need Felix running off half cocked, beating the shit out of random players on the team. Coach would bench his ass, if not kick him off the team entirely. "It could be anyone on the team. She didn't say, which is why you two need to help me figure it out."

"You're sure?" Julio asks.

"I am."

"Then we check them all out," Felix suggests.

Julio presses his tongue to his cheek. "It's not Atticus."

"No. Not Atticus." I'm not inclined to rule anyone out without doing at least a little digging. That's how mistakes are made, and bad people continue to get away with more bad shit. But Atticus Bennet bats for the other team. No one outside of this house knows that. But it's enough to ease my own concerns and strike him from my list. He wouldn't try to fuck Cecilia because he has no interest in what's between her legs. But more than that, he's genuinely a good guy. Young, and still has a lot to learn, but he grew up with shitty parents and still gives a shit about other people's well-being. That kid wouldn't hurt a fly. He even saves the fucking spiders in the house and moves them outside instead of smashing them beneath his boot. He has my respect—not for the spiders. I hate those creepy little assholes and I don't care how harmless they are. All they'll get out of me is a view of the bottom of my shoe.

But despite his affection for the eight legged monsters, Atticus Bennett is good people. Compassionate. Trustworthy. Loyal.

Which is more than I can say for some guys on the team. Most are nothing more than overgrown toddlers.

They get the chance to play college ball. Have a shot at going pro—something Julio, Felix, and I work our hardest to achieve every fucking day—but most of the guys on the team waste their potential. They're blinded by parties and pissing contests.

They have four years here to carve the path for their futures. To be good enough for the MLS SuperDraft. To stand out. It's not what you do on the field that matters. It's everything you do leading up to it. Win or lose, your success is determined in the off season. In every minute and every hour you spend off the field and out of the gym.

"Who does that leave us with?" Felix paces the length of the living room. He doesn't do well with inaction. If there's a problem, he needs to fix it. Preferably with his fists. It's helpful most of the time, but not for sensitive things like this.

If we want to keep him out of trouble, we need a plan. Something clear and actionable so we can point him in one direction and cut him loose. I scrub my hands over my face. Why does this have to be so complicated?

"There are twenty-eight players on the team if we count Hunt." Julio's face is pensive and I can all but see the gears turning in his head. He grabs a notebook from the coffee table. A pen from behind Felix's ear—

"Hey!"

—and scribbles down everyone's name on the team, including ours. Thorough fucker.

"It's safe to assume Hunt wasn't involved, since he's a late transfer." He scratches the name from the list.

"Subtracting him, Atticus, and the three of us," he drags a line through our names next, "that leaves us with twenty-three possibilities if your assumption is right and he's on the team."

Cecilia didn't say it word for word, but she might as well have. She knew what I'd think when she made her request. And I'm sure she never would have made it if she knew I'd act on the information. But that's a problem for another day and I'm happy to pretend she let it slip, hoping I'd step in, figure it out, and save the day. Chicks believe in all that fairytale crap anyway, and this is my chance to ride in like Prince Charming and prove to her I can keep her safe.

"How many of our teammates are Greeks?" Holt is involved. I can feel it. Either he was there or he found out after the fact and helped cover it up. Either way, I'd put money on whoever hurt Cecilia being a Greek. She used to party with them. *Life is a party #ZetaPi...* that's what she posted on social before... before she tried to take her own life. *Fuck.* I hate thinking about that day.

"At least half."

That's more than I expected. "We start there. With the Greeks. If they're all innocent—"

Felix coughs into his fist. "How many pledged to Zeta Pi?"

Running his pen down the list, Julio places a check mark next to a handful of names. "Six."

"What are the odds it's one of them?" Felix cracks his knuckles and rolls his neck before shaking out his arms to loosen his limbs.

"No," I warn.

"He said six. Six is a reasonable number."

"Not for what you have in mind," Julio deadpans.

Felix wants to argue. It's written all over his face. "Your *machismo* is showing. Put that shit away."

"Fuck you." His nostrils flare.

"Knock it off," Julio growls. "And pay attention. The sooner we figure this out, the easier shit will be for Cecilia. No woman deserves to go through what she's been through and have the prick who hurt her still walking around free."

"Is there a reason we don't go straight to the source?" Felix asks. "We know Holt is involved, right? He knows who hurt her. Might even be protecting them?"

I nod.

"Then why aren't we knocking down the door of Zeta Pi and demanding some answers?"

"You know why," I grind out.

"Let me—"

"No!" Julio and I shout in unison.

"You two never let me have any fun."

"That's because your fun ends with bloodshed, followed by your ass in handcuffs."

Felix scoffs. "I don't get stuck wearing them for long."

"Have you given any thought to what comes next?" Julio asks.

Confusion draws my brows together. "What do you mean?"

"He means," Felix drawls, "let's say we find the bastard. We figure out who hurt your girl without any doubt. Then what?"

"We deal with them." Obviously.

Felix's dark brown eyes glimmer. "Yeah." He smiles, but not the normal carefree one he reserves for pretty girls and friends. This one has a vicious edge to it. "And how do you suppose we do that?" He leans back and spreads his arms wide across the back of the couch. Raising a single brow, he turns from me to Julio and back, meeting both of our gazes. "My ideas aren't so crazy now, are they?"

"You wanted to pummel answers out of innocent bystanders," I remind him.

"We don't know they're innocent."

"We don't know they're guilty either, dickhead. And if we're going to risk being benched, or hell, face expulsion, it better be because we beat the shit out of the right guy."

"But there will be ass kicking, right? You just want to make sure they're—" he uses air quotes, "not innocent."

Oh, my fucking god.

"I don't know. Okay. And until I do, you can't go messing around with guys on the team."

"You're fucking with Holt."

"That's different."

"How?"

"Enough!" Julio roars and stabs a finger toward me. "Pull the stick out of your ass and pay fucking attention." He turns to Felix. "And stop behaving like some blood thirsty chihuahua. It's embarrassing."

Felix's jaw goes slack. "Did you just compare me to a fucking rodent of a dog?"

"If it looks like a duck and talks like a duck—" Julio glares, daring Felix to argue. When he keeps his mouth closed, Julio looks back down at his notebook and gets back to the real problem at hand.

"If we find out who it is, step two will be to gather proof. Most people don't stop at one. Chances are whoever hurt her has hurt other women before her or has done it again since. Cecilia has her reasons for keeping quiet, but if another girl comes forward, that might be enough.

Tearing out a sheet of paper, Julio rewrites the six names he'd written a check mark next to and hands it to Felix. "You do not talk to the guys about any of this, got it?"

Felix shakes the list in his hand. "If I can't talk to the fuckers, why the hell are you giving me their names?"

"Because you're going to talk to their girlfriends. Their friends. Their roommates. Anyone those six are close to who might know the shit they get up to."

"Okay. Yeah. I'm down for that."

"We do this smart."

"Yeah. Yeah." Felix waves him away, already scrolling through the contacts on his phone. Even without hitting anyone, he's going to enjoy this.

"What do I do?"

"Nothing."

I jerk back in surprise. "Nothing? What the hell do you mean, nothing?"

Felix snickers and heads for the front door. "Sucks to be you." He grabs his helmet from the bench we keep by the door and throws back a wave. "I'll catch you boys later. I've got some undercover work to do."

"No fighting," Julio calls out, but Felix either doesn't hear or chooses to ignore him as he rushes out of the house, the door closing with a snick behind him.

Julio releases a sigh and steeples his fingers in front of him. "I swear he will be the reason I go gray in my twenties." He's not wrong. Felix will be the reason we all go gray. I don't know how his mother survived eighteen years of him under her roof. And she's got more still at home, just like him.

"Back to what you said. What do you mean, I do nothing?"

"You focus on your girl. Spend time with her. Help her feel safe. Let Felix and I figure this out."

Not happening. "No way, man. I can't just sit around—"

"You're not just sitting." Julio's eyes flash. He's not quick to anger. Most of the time at least. But looking at him now, I can tell he's riding that line. "You have the most important role to play here," he tells me.

My face tells him how I feel about that.

He covers his face with one hand, leaving me to stare at the skull and roses inked into the back of his hand. "Your girl is hurting."

Does he think I can't see that?

"So the best thing, the most important thing, for you to do, is to be there for her."

I will. I am. But that doesn't mean I can't do both. That I can't help with this, too. The words to argue are on the tip of my tongue, but Julio knows me better than anyone and doesn't give me even a second to voice them.

"There's a chance we figure out who hurt her and nothing comes of it."

I scoff. No way am I letting that happen.

"I'm serious, Gabe. You need to hear me."

I wave a hand for him to continue, but it doesn't matter what he says. I find out who hurt Cecilia and I make them pay. Enough said.

"Have you given any thought to her suicide attempt?" His expression is casual, like he's asking about the weather and not Cecilia trying to end her own life. But despite his tone, I don't miss the way his eyes track my expression, taking in every little detail as though he's cataloging my reaction to contemplate for later.

The answer to his question should be obvious. No. Cecilia's suicide attempt is not something I've given any thought to beyond making sure it doesn't happen again.

"What kind of question is that?"

He knows what my brother did. He showed up not long after the ambulance took Carlos's body away. Julio and Felix were the only people there for me. Allie had moved by then. Mom and Dad were both wrecked. And me, I was in fucking shock. Felix had to drag me into the shower and turn the water to cold before I snapped out of it enough to tear off my blood-stained clothes. He knows what Carlos's suicide did to me. To my family.

There is no good reason for me to dwell on Cecilia's failed attempt. If I have it my way, it was her first and last and we don't need to revisit what happened that night again.

"What if she tried to get help, came forward, named her attacker, and nothing came of it? We're assuming she wanted to take her own life because of the rape, but that's not what sends people over the edge."

"I think you need to drop your psych class. It's making you over analyze this shit."

"Hear me out. There's a timeline of things, right?"

My brows draw together. "Yeah. I guess."

"People commit suicide when they feel hopeless. I don't think rape alone made Cecilia feel that way. It's traumatic as fuck. But it's a single event." He pauses to make sure I'm following, and after I give him a short nod, he continues. "Rape, along with any form of assault, comes with baggage. Lifelong trauma for the victim to manage. But a person is at their lowest point when the assault occurs. That is when they feel hopeless, especially if no one intervenes."

"So something or someone made her feel more hopeless than when the assault went down?"

He nods. "I think so. I'm getting a B- in Psych this semester, so don't quote me, but I'm guessing she was assaulted and did try to get help. She came forward, told her story, but whoever it was that hurt her walked. If that was the case—"

I don't like where this is going.

"Then—"

"No. I don't accept that." No one gets a free pass to hurt women. I don't care who you are. The fucker deserves to go to prison. To have his life stripped away. He deserves to suffer just as much, no, more, than Cecilia has been made to suffer.

"You might have to."

"Bullshit. You want to tell me if Allie's attacker didn't end up in jail, if that sonovabitch walked after what he did to her, that the three of us wouldn't be rolling up to Sun Valley to handle it in our own way?"

A nerve ticks in his jaw. "He didn't get locked up because he raped her."

"No," I agree. "He didn't. But justice was served all the same. If the fucker who hurt Cecilia got off on the assault, we find another way to make him pay."

"That doesn't land our asses expelled or in jail."

"Sure," I tell him. We'll go with that.

CECILIA

My days blur together, but this time, in a good way. Before, time dragged on. Every second felt like a minute as I'd sit in my room, begging for it all—time, the world, everything—to just to stop.

I'm not desperate for the day to end anymore. I no longer dread each morning as it begins. It's such a mental mind shift, I'm still trying to wrap my head around it. I sorta forgot what it was like to... breathe, I guess. Getting out of bed doesn't feel like this herculean effort any more. I have something to look forward to. Things I want to do.

Most days, I catch myself watching the clock, eager for the moments when my path and Gabriel's cross. I look forward to seeing him, which makes it hard to resent the fact he's in two of my classes. Though I try anyway. Can't make it easy on him. Do that and I may as well shout out loud that I condone his behavior. His need to be with me all the time.

To know what I'm doing and where I'm at. Gabriel takes overprotectiveness to a whole new level, but he also makes life bearable.

Every morning, he greets me with a kiss on the cheek, and a can of Crush soda waits for me in the center of my desk. And after I take my seat, without fail, he grabs the legs of my desk and chair and drags me closer to him until he can throw his arm around my shoulder, where it remains for the duration of class. No matter where we're at or what the situation is, Gabriel always makes contact. His hand in mine. A hand on my thigh. His arm around my shoulder is the most common, but he always maintains physical contact between us somehow.

I keep waiting for this to get old. For him to forget about the soda or lose the motivation to drag over my chair, but two weeks into whatever this thing between us is, and he still does it. Every single day.

I already know I'll be more than a little disappointed when it inevitably comes to an end.

"You studying in the library after class today?"

We've developed a routine. During the week, we see each other during the two classes we share, and we always meet up with the guys for lunch. We usually stay on campus to save time before our next classes, but now and then, we go back to their place like we did before and Julio mans the grill while the rest of us hangout.

We've played cards a few times, which is fun, but usually we just sit around the table and talk about whatever is going on that day. I'm the quiet one of the group, but Felix has made it his mission to pull me out of my shell. I'd hate him for it if not for the fact I don't even realize it's happening. It's like he has strange voodoo powers that loosen my tongue and lull me into a false sense of familiarity. There's no proper way to explain it.

If Julio is what I imagine a big brother would be like, Felix is that annoying younger one you give in to just to get them to leave you alone and go away. Though it is also endearing in a way.

"No. Not today. I have an appointment after my last class."

The guys have practice every day of the week in the late afternoon and train most mornings and weekends. Since Gabriel still refuses to let me head straight home, insisting I get out and people more, we've come up with a sort of compromise. While he's at practice, I go for a swim or hangout in the library and study or work on my homework.

The library has been my more frequent stop with preseason training for swim starting. The pool is a lot more crowded in the afternoon now until dinnertime, so I try to get my laps in then, once most of the team has called it quits for the night.

"What appointment?" he asks.

Our professor walks in, which should save me from answering, but Gabriel isn't one to be deterred.

"It's nothing. I'll be busy for an hour and then you can go right back to hovering."

He scowls. "I don't hover."

I rub the furrow between his brows with my thumb until his face relaxes. "Sure you don't."

Grumbling something incoherent under his breath, he plays with my hair for the rest of class while I try to wrap my head around our professor's lecture. Fifty minutes later and with six pages of notes, my biggest takeaway from his lesson is, fuck the patriarchy.

I tell Gabriel and he laughs, tugging on my hair until I tilt up my chin. "Sounds like a plan, as long as I still get to kiss you."

Leaning in, he does exactly that, only this time, it's not a quick peck on the lips. The bell rang a few minutes ago, and the class has mostly cleared out, but we're not alone and our professor was most definitely still in the room. Not that it deters Gabriel in the least. He cups the side of my neck and angles his head to deepen the kiss. His tongue strokes against mine and he—or is it me?—groans.

Someone clears their throat. We ignore it. Whoever it is does it again, this time louder, and Gabriel reluctantly pulls away. I chase his lips before reigning myself in. Oops. Got a little carried away there.

Gabriel chuckles and, whispering against my hair, says, "I could kiss you all day." Mmm. That sounds nice. "Want to let me?"

"Have a good day Mr. Herrera. Ms. Russo."

"You too, Mr. Arndt." I force out the words with fake enthusiasm. "See you tomorrow."

Gabriel grabs my bag and, lacing his fingers with mine, leads the way out of class. "So, this appointment…"

"You won't let this go, will you?"

He stops in the hallway and tugs me into his arms. "Nope." Leaning in, he tugs on the neck of my oversized sweater before pressing his lips to my collarbone. The scruff on his jaw scrapes against my neck, causing me to shiver.

"What time is it at?"

I sigh as he kisses his way up my neck. "Two o'clock."

"I'll drive you."

"No."

He kisses my cheek. My chin. "I'll drive you." He still hasn't learned that repeating the same words twice won't make them true.

"You have practice. Besides, I can drive myself to one stupid appointment."

Gabriel draws back, a flash of concern washing over his face. "What's the appointment for? Is everything okay?"

"It's nothing. I'm fine."

He's not convinced. So much for privacy.

"It's a therapy session. There. Happy?"

He considers me for a moment, mulling over how he wants to respond. I'm not sure the revelation that I go to therapy—albeit reluctantly—deserves this much consideration, so being the avoider that I am, I slip out from beneath his arm and head off for my next class.

As expected, Gabriel falls into step beside me, his longer stride slowing to keep pace with my shorter legs. He wraps his arm around my shoulders and takes back the lead. *Boys.* But, whatever. I can follow.

"Your next class is clear across campus," I remind him, in case he's forgotten. If he doesn't go now, he's going to be late. Not that I think cares. He has some film class, if I remember right. Gabe calls it napping 101 since most of the movies he's seen already, so he uses the time to catch up on sleep.

"You never mentioned going to therapy before."

Great, so this is going to be a thing. "I didn't realize you'd have an issue with it." Not that it matters. I give Gabriel a lot of leeway where he and I are concerned. It's mostly because I don't care enough to fight with him about it, but I never got the memo stating I had to inform him about meetings and appointments. If I did, it would have made its way into the garbage. He might drag me out of the house and sucker me into peopling more than I would on my own, but he doesn't get to dictate every minute of my life.

"I don't. I think it's great you're seeing someone."

"You do?" It doesn't sound like he does.

Gabriel bobs his head, but the tension is still there around his eyes and mouth. "Sure. I'm guessing it helps?" He shrugs, coming to another stop, this time a few doors down from my next class. "It's good you're talking to someone."

I'm hearing his words, but they don't match the look on his face. "Why are you lying?"

Guilt flickers across his gaze, and his eyes widen. "I'm not lying." Yes, he is. One hundred percent this man is lying. Gabriel isn't that hard to read if you know what to look for, and these past weeks, I've spent close to every waking hour either with him or near him.

I know when he's lying. But this is such an insignificant thing to lie about. He's not a fan of therapists. What's the big deal?

"You are. It's weird. Why are you being weird?" Usually, I'm the one acting strange. Which makes his behavior extra weird, but also kind of nice for a change.

"It's nothing. Come on. Let's get you to class before you're late." I'm not the one who needs to worry about tardiness.

Gabriel's fingers skim across the waist of my jeans before hooking through one of the belt loops and tugging me forward. My skin heats at the contact, but he doesn't notice. It's his turn now to play the avoiding game.

"Nothing, like when you pushed me to tell you what my appointment was for?"

"Fair point."

A smile spreads across my face. I know. It's good he realizes it. Just beside the door, Gabriel pulls me to a stop.

"I think I'm jealous."

That surprises me. "Jealous that I go to therapy?" How does that make sense?

Gabriel creeps closer to me, a nervous look on his face. "Yes. No." He rubs the back of his neck. "I don't know." Kicking at the floor, he purses his lips. He's really worked up over this. Fascinating. This isn't the sort of jealousy a girl is usually after, but I wonder if Gabriel's ever even felt that sort of jealousy before? Doubtful. I don't know a single girl at this school who'd turn him down. I give him a minute to work out the thoughts in his head. Jealousy over me going to therapy makes zero sense. But he's welcome to my appointment if he wants it. I'd bet money Dr. Tabitha Walker would prefer his company to mine.

"It's stupid but..." He curses under his breath and I reach out, drawing his face toward me until his forehead rests against mine.

"What's going on?"

His chest heaves and he huffs out a loud breath. "It just bothers me that you, you know, talk to someone else."

My brows pull together. "I'm not following."

"You don't talk to me."

Yes, I do. "I'm talking to you right now."

He rolls his eyes. "Not about—" He looks around the hallway and lowers his voice. "—You know."

Ah. I get it. But really, that's what bothers him? A laugh bubbles out of me before I can stop it. "I don't talk to my therapist about any of that stuff, either."

His eyes widen a fraction of an inch. "You don't." I don't know if it's disappointment or relief I hear in his voice.

"No. I don't really talk at all."

Confusion has him frowning. "Then why go?"

"Because I have to. It keeps the parentals happy." I shrug. My parents and I made an agreement after *the incident*, as they like to call it. I live at home for one full semester. I attend classes. Get good grades. And I go to therapy twice a week. I tried to get out of that last one, but they were sticklers and I didn't care enough to fight them on it.

"Therapy is good, right? It helps?" The way he says it lets me know he himself isn't a fan. But it's sweet that he wants to be supportive.

"Not really. For therapy to work, you have to trust your therapist. Be willing to open up. Share your secrets. Bare your soul. All that jazz."

His eyes flick between mine, looking for something. "So get a different therapist."

"It's not that easy."

"Why not?"

Huh. I don't know. I never really gave much thought to it before now. "My parents picked this one."

"So? Do they go to the sessions with you?"

I shake my head. It's bad enough when I'm alone, I can only imagine how much worse it'd be if either of my parents joined me.

"Then it doesn't matter who they pick or who they want. If you're going to therapy, it's for you, not them. Find someone else." It's not a bad idea.

DID I mention I hate therapy?

"Cecilia?

Like really, really, whole bodily hate it.

"Cecilia?"

If I could climb under my covers, curl into a ball, and not wake up, I would, just so I never had to come here again.

"Cecilia?"

My eyes flick to hers before quickly looking away, but not before catching sight of the deep frown etched into her face. I smile to myself. Dr. Tabitha Walker used to wear this serene mask on her face during our sessions. I've dubbed it her *everything is sunshine and rainbows* expression.

No matter how long I ignored her, it never slipped. It was like remaining tranquil was her super power. I was sorta jealous of that. Of her ability to mask her frustration. Her impatience. Because she's not a robot and I'm not an idiot. I know when I'm being rude and annoying.

I'll give it to her, though. She made it longer than I thought she would. But all good things must come to an end, and six weeks into our sessions, her mask has slipped.

Dr. Walker taps her pen against her notebook. A sign of her growing impatience. "Cecilia, are you listening to me?" Her voice is filled with exasperation. I check the clock. Five more minutes and she'll call it, ending our session fifteen minutes early to put an end to the silence.

I sigh and look out the window. I can ignore her for five more minutes.

"Cecilia, I can't help you if you don't talk to me."

I don't want her help. I've said so before. She just doesn't listen.

"Wouldn't you like to get better?"

Unable to help myself, I snort. What kind of question is that? Of course I want to get better. Does she think I enjoy this? I don't. But, I've been coming here for six weeks and not once after an appointment do I ever feel better.

She can't fix me. I used to think no one could. But things are getting better. Gabriel and Felix and Julio, they make everything a little better.

"How's school going?"

It's an innocent enough question, but I know what this attempt at small talk is and I'm not falling for it.

"Are you enjoying your classes?"

My phone buzzes against my thigh and my therapist purses her lips. She's older than my mother. In her late fifties, with a very negative outlook regarding the use of cellphones in the office. She has at least three signs I can see from my seat that say, *Please silence your phone during your session.* Technically, I am following her rules. My ringer is off. Her signs say nothing about vibration.

Glancing at the screen, I read the message that came in.

GABRIEL: Evening swim? Coach suggested I try activities that utilize a full range of motion.

HECK YES! I type out a quick response, ignoring Dr. Walker's very pointed cough.

ME: Meet in 30?

GABRIEL: See you there.

CHECKING THE TIME ONCE MORE, I tuck my phone away and gather my keys to stand up. "School is fine. I'm passing all of my classes. I particularly enjoy my Diversity and

Historical Oppression class. Oh—" I point to the clock. "Our time is up. See you in two weeks." That should satisfy her for now. It's more than I've given before.

Rushing from her office, I jog down the stairs and escape outside. Gabriel is right. I need to find someone else. I suck in a deep breath of warm fall air and as I exhale, it's like a mountain of stress slides off me. Even coming to that one small decision is such a relief.

23

GABRIEL

"**E**verything good?" Julio asks.

"Yeah." I shove my phone in my bag and tear off my sweat-soaked T-shirt. Julio does the same, stripping down to his boxer briefs and rifling through his locker for clean clothes. "I'm meeting her at the pool. Gonna get some laps in."

"Since when do you know how to swim?" he asks.

"Since we were kids, asshole." I jab him in the chest as he pulls a fresh shirt over his head.

"Is that what you call it? I didn't realize the doggy paddle was an official stroke now."

"Hilarious." I close my locker, only to jerk back when I'm greeted to Felix's face only inches away from mine. "What the hell? Where the fuck did you come from?"

"I've got the story." He ignores the question, but after a response like that, I don't even care. It's been two weeks of trying to figure this shit out and my patience is thin.

Just then, Holt and a few of his lackies pass by, and both our groups go quiet. Holt's eyes lock with mine, flashing. Parker Benson, Logan Chambers, and Rion Pru follow alongside him, matching his *I smell shit* expression. My beef with Austin has the team divided. But the division is Holt's own doing and when Coach called us into his office last week to sort this all out, I told him as much. He's the one with the problem. If you ask his buddies why he and I have issues, they'll tell you it's because I stole his girl. It's bullshit and everyone here knows it. Cecilia was never his, not even for a second.

But that's the story he shovels to Coach and anyone else who'll listen. He plays the role of heartbroken suitor. Meanwhile, I know he's getting his dick wet every chance he gets, and the fucker isn't discreet about it. He's even hooking up with one of Cecilia's former friends, so why anybody would believe his story is a mystery. You don't pine for a chick only to fuck her best friend.

"Herrera—" he bites out. "I hear you've been poking your nose in my business."

Folding my arms over my chest, I lean back against my gym locker. "You heard wrong. What reason do I have for giving a shit about anything that has to do with you?"

His jaw tightens and a vein pulses in his forehead. Careful, pretty boy. Someone needs to get a tighter leash on those anger issues. Holt takes two steps forward, puffing out his chest.

Julio and Felix step in on either side of me. Austin's eyes narrow. "You're not the only one with friends," I remind him. In case it wasn't obvious.

Our team is split down the middle as far as taking sides is concerned, but only the boys with Zeta Pi are actively involved in our shit. Holt doesn't have as many allies as he thinks. Anyone with a half a brain knows it's not worth the risk just for this asshole's approval. A lot of the guys have scholarships to worry about. Futures to protect.

Austin steps into my space. "I don't know what she told you—"

With two hands, I shove him away from me. "Back up, man."

His nostrils flare. I can see it in his eyes. He wants to hit me. I wish he would. It'd give me the excuse I need to beat some sense into him. But Rion Pru has a firm grip on his arm and whatever he says, his voice low for only Austin to hear, does what it needs to. Shaking Rion off, Austin storms out of the locker room, Benson and Chambers hot behind him. Rion lingers, tracking his friends until they're out of the room.

"Have something to say?" Julio asks.

Rion sighs. "Yeah. A warning."

Felix scoffs. "We're not worried about that asshole."

"You should be," he says. "I don't know why he's so worked up over you," he dips his chin toward me, "but Holt is on a warpath. He already went to Coach and tried to get you kicked off the team."

My eyes widen. "What the fuck?"

"It didn't work." Julio shrugs and I whirl on him.

"You knew about this?"

Does he have the decency to show at least a little remorse? Of course not. He's too sure of himself for that.

"I'm team Captain. I see everything." He toys with the leather wolf bracelet on his wrist. We all have one. Allie bought them for us as an early graduation gift when we received our acceptance letters from PacNorth. Fucking friendship bracelets is what they are, not that you'll hear any of us complain about it. Like it's some unspoken rule, not a day goes by where we don't wear them. They come off for games and showers and that's about it. Julio claps my back. "You had other things to worry about." He gives me a knowing look. "And you know I've got your back. I'm not about to let Holt throw his weight around and fuck with my team."

"That might be true," Rion says. "But, don't think he's done. His parents are pretty powerful people in town and his mom serves on the board. He's not letting whatever is going on with you two go."

Good to know. "Appreciate the heads up." I hold out my hand and Rion accepts it. He's a sophomore and a Greek, so our paths don't cross off the field, but I won't forget the warning. I appreciate the solid he's doing me, putting his neck out for me when we both know Holt can just as quickly turn on him. In Holt's eyes, Pru warning me is a betrayal.

Rion heads for the exit and I turn back to grab my things when Felix calls after him. "You need to find new friends," he tells him.

"I like the ones I have."

Felix tsks. "You seem like a decent guy, so I'm gonna let you in on something. Do with it what you will."

Pru hesitates, his palm on the door.

"Over break, Holt, Benson, and Chambers raped a girl at a party." My head snaps toward him. The fuck? He's dead serious. I look at Julio, seeing the same surprise and anger reflected on his face. Pru, on the other hand, looks a little green.

"You need to ask yourself what kind of person you want to be," Felix tells him. "Because if it's anything like Holt— "

"It isn't," he assures us. "I'm not close with the guy, but he's in my fraternity. I can't do anything about that."

"You could clean house," Julio deadpans.

"I'm a sophomore. I don't have that kind of power."

"Then get it. You don't look surprised by what Felix said. Did you know?" I ask.

He violently shakes his head. "I didn't. I swear." For his sake, I hope he's not lying. To us or himself.

"What is it, then?" Felix pries. "If you know something, you need to tell us."

Pru's shoulders slump, and he hangs his head. "I didn't know," he begins. "But I'm not surprised. Holt and the guys he's close with, they brag a lot about the girls they hook up with. They pass around a lot of videos. Make a lot of jokes that aren't really jokes, if you know what I mean?"

Videos? My mind catches on that single word and a red haze drops over my vision. Rage threatens to drown me. I lunge forward, grabbing Rion by the neck and slamming him into the wall at his back. "He has videos and you're just now saying something about it?" I seethe.

Eyes wide, he doesn't even try to fight me off as he swallows hard, struggling to speak. "I've never watched them," he wheezes. "I swear. They were just sex tapes the guys liked to pass around. I assumed the girls were in on it."

I shove away from him in disgust.

Felix leans beside him, his expression casual, but I know him better than that. He's as pissed as I am. He's just better at hiding it. "Where do Holt and his buddies keep these videos?" he asks.

Rion rubs his neck. "I don't want to get involved in— "

"Too late," I snap.

"Here's what you're gonna do—" I walk away, leaving Felix to map out whatever plan he's got cooked up in that head of his. I don't care how crazy it is. If there's video footage of

Holt or anyone else fucking Cecilia, we'll do whatever it takes to find it and destroy it. Making sure it never sees the light of day again.

Something I plan to do to Holt.

I take a seat on a bench, head in my hands, and try to wrap my head around this shit. Holt, Benson, and Chambers raped her. It wasn't just one of them. They all had a go at her. My chest heaves, rage building inside of me. I fist my hands in my hair. I need to do something. Hit something.

Fuck.

"Take a breath." Julio drops a hand on my shoulder. "Don't think up worst-case scenarios just yet. Let's hear what Felix has to say."

"You heard what he said." I look up at my best friend, an ache blooming in my chest. "Three of them, Julio. Three!" I hold up three fingers.

A muscle ticks in his jaw. "I know. We'll take care of it."

The room gets quiet and I look over my shoulder to see Rion's left the room, leaving just Julio, Felix, and I. "Tell me," I demand.

He nods once and claims the bench across from me. "How much do you want to know?"

"All of it."

Felix winces. "I don't think—"

"All of it, Felix. I'm dead serious. I need to know what those fuckers did to my girl."

"Aren't you meeting up with her?" Julio asks.

We all turn to the clock above the door. "I've got ten minutes. Give me the quick version. You can tell me the rest back at the house."

Taking a deep breath, Felix fills the two of us in on what he's discovered. A fresh stab of pain arrows into me with every word he says. "They didn't believe her?"

Julio was right. She tried to get help, but the school turned their fucking backs on her.

"I think they did," Felix says. "I spoke with this chick who works in the title nine building. She felt for Cecilia. Acted like she cared."

"Then what happened?"

He shrugs. "Money. Politics. Power. Take your pick. The Holts leveraged all three. They came in on their high horses, threw enough money and threats around to scare the school into backing off."

"What about the police?"

He shakes his head. "I don't think it ever came to that."

I frown. "Why the hell not?"

"Look," he levels me with a look, one that says shut the hell up and let him talk, "I only know what I know. Okay. Do you have any idea how hard this shit was to figure out?"

Running a hand over my jaw, I wait.

"Thank you," he says. "Like I was saying, I don't think she went to the police. I talked to her old roommate—that girl is a spineless waste of space. Let me tell you."

Nostrils flaring, I'm seconds away from snapping at him to get to the point. I don't give a shit about her roommate or any of her former friends. None of them stuck around after what happened to her. I haven't heard a single word about anyone since we've been seeing each other. She's always with me and my boys or riding solo. Whatever their deal is, it's irrelevant.

"Felix—" Julio warns, waving for him to speed this up.

"Right. Sorry." He huffs out a breath. "So, according to the roommate. Cecilia said she was raped. Holt and those two ass wipes of his drugged her and..." His Adam's apple bobs. "Well, you can figure it out."

I nod. I don't need those details right now. They're for Cecilia to tell me whenever she's ready. What I need to know is why Benson, Chambers, and Holt are still walking around like fucking peacocks on campus after raping a girl. No way should they have gotten away with this. How the hell did we never hear about it? Guys gossip as much, if not more, than women, especially in the locker room. Something like this shouldn't have stayed under wraps for this long.

"What else?" Julio asks.

"I guess the roommate convinced her to go to the school first. She said something about Cecilia's dad being in politics."

"Yeah. I've met him. Nice guy. He's our mayor."

"No shit?" Felix asks.

I nod.

"Okay. That makes more sense. He's up for re-election. Holt tried blackmailing your girl into staying quiet for the sake of her father's campaign. The roommate suggested going to the school board. It was a smaller risk. The guys wouldn't serve jail time, but they'd be expelled. She wouldn't have to see them again."

Julio snorts. "It's less than he deserves."

"And he didn't even get that," I remind him. Not even a slap on the fucking wrist. What the hell is wrong with people?

"No. He didn't." Felix confirms. "Holt's mom is on the board, and both parents are criminal defense attorneys. They came in prepared. Threw their money and status around, threatened both Cecilia and the university with a lawsuit for defamation. From the sounds of it, it was brutal, and the school didn't want the trouble."

"So they gave up. Just like that?"

He nods. "They slapped her with a cease and desist after trying to bully her into signing an NDA. She refused."

Good for her. Those pretentious pricks don't deserve her silence. "After that, they withdrew their support from her dad's campaign. I think that's when shit fell apart for her. It's also the same time Holt started hooking up with her friend."

"The redhead?" I've seen her with him and recognize her from some of Cecilia's old social media posts.

"Yeah. Kim something. I didn't bother to get a last name." He shrugs. "I guess the roommate, Cecilia, and this Kim chick were best friends before, but Kim had a thing for Austin and he used that. Convinced her Cecilia was jealous and wanted to get back at him for choosing Kim over her. He fed her ego. Told her everything she wanted to hear."

"And she believed that garbage?" What the hell kind of friend is that?

"I doubt it. But she wants to, and that's enough. Getting the guy is more important to her than having her friend's back."

"The roommate too?"

"Joelle? No. She believes Cecilia. She's just too weak to do anything about it. She comes across as a decent person. Smart. Funny."

"You flirted with her, I take it?"

"How else did you expect me to get the scoop?" He rolls his eyes. "She's not all bad. But she's a follower and for too many years, she's been in the habit of following Kim. She tells her to jump, Joelle asks how high. It's sad. I'm pretty sure she regrets it."

"Did you fuck her?" Julio asks.

Felix's face fills with indignation. "Sleep with the enemy?" He makes a fist and pounds it where his heart sits in his chest. "Hell no. I'd never do Cecilia dirty like that."

Julio nods, but I don't miss the sudden gleam in Felix's eyes. "Hooking up with the wrong female falls into your department Remember, Julio? Not mine."

Releasing a groan, I shake my head. He just had to go there.

Julio clenches his fists. "It was one kiss." We've heard it before. Doesn't change what he did.

"Whatever helps you sleep at night." Felix gives him a mocking grin.

"Fuck you," he says. There's no heat in his words. Julio knows he messed up. And we'd be shitty friends if we didn't take the opportunity to remind him of his royal fuck up from time to time. It's what friends do. He's the one who kissed Allie's ex-friend drunk at a party. Just one more reason we all have to avoid that scene. Adriana used to kick it with us too. We were our own party of five. But she messed around with Allie's then boyfriend behind her back and you don't do that to your *familia*. Loyalty is everything. She proved she had none. Much like Cecilia's former friends.

"Pass, but I'll give Adriana your new number the next time I see her if you like?"

Julio growls in the back of his throat.

"Fight with each other another time. I need to meet up with Cecilia." I shoot her a text, telling her I'm going to be a few minutes late to buy myself some time.

"Right." He turns his attention to me. "Joelle believes her. But she's been friends with the Kim chick since grade school. She's only known Cecilia since freshman year. She picked the wrong side." He shrugs. "She made her bed and now she has to lie in it. Which sucks for Cecilia. Her friends should have been there for her. Parents are great and all but—"

"They don't know." If they did, they wouldn't care about the money or the campaign. They'd want her to get justice for what happened. There's no way they can know. They seem like good people. Parents who genuinely care about their daughter's wellbeing.

"The suicide they know about. There was no way to hide it. But I don't think they know about the rape. That's why they're so protective of her." It makes so much sense. "They don't know what made her take that path and they don't know what to do to make sure she doesn't slide down it again."

"Fuck. That's rough. She had to go through all that shit on her own," Felix whistles. "Your girl is tougher than she looks."

I know. It didn't take long to realize Cecilia is one of the strongest people I know, which is why I mean it when I say, "We can't let him get away with this."

"We won't." Felix agrees. "And I think I know someone who can help with that."

"Who?" Julio and I ask at the same time.

"Rumor is, Holt's been poking his nose around Gigi."

Gigi? I don't know any Gigi. Then it hits me. "Coach's kid?"

Felix nods. "Yep."

"No way is she legal." Julio adds. "Has she even graduated from high school?"

"Nope. And Holt knows that, but he's chasing her tail, anyway."

"So, what are you thinking? Use the girl to get to Holt? What about the others?" I ask.

"We're not setting her up. We can't put a kid at risk like that."

"I'm not suggesting we do," Felix says. "But if she's going to be an idiot kid regardless, I say we use it to our advantage."

"We should warn her. Tell Coach at least," I suggest. There are unspoken rules in place when you join any team, and at the top of the list is *you don't fuck the Coach's daughter*. They're always off limits.

"It won't matter," Felix tells us. "I tried getting a read on the girl. She spends a lot of time on campus because of her dad."

"And?"

"She's an idiot. She thinks Holt hangs the fucking stars. She's too obsessed with the idea of landing an older guy. I warned her what her dad would think, and she made it clear she doesn't care."

"Keep tabs on her. I'll dig into Benson and Chambers, see if I can find an angle for them," Julio tells Felix. "And you —" He turns to me. "Go see your girl and keep your shit together. Don't do anything stupid."

"I won't."

"Good. We'll handle this for now, like we've been doing, and pull you in when one of us has more."

I grind my molars. I fucking hate this.

"Gabe," he snaps.

"Yes. Got it."

Satisfied, he nods. "And watch your backs. Holt knows we're onto him. Today's little show didn't come out of nowhere. We need to be prepared."

I nod. Holt can throw whatever he wants at me. I'll be ready.

"And you need to fill Cecilia in."

What? No way. My eyes snap toward him. "Tell me you're kidding? She'll be pissed. It'll throw these last two weeks right down the drain. I'm not telling her."

"You have to."

I bark out a laugh. "I do not."

Julio gets to his feet. "She's going to figure it out and what do you think will hurt more, finding out now from you? Or hearing about it later because shit hit the fan and you're left standing there with egg on your face all because you wanted to keep secrets?"

My jaw clenches, lips pressing into a thin line. "I'll think about it."

"You do that." Julio leaves, and Felix grabs his things to follow. Moving at a slower pace, he pauses in the doorway and gives me a long look.

"You know he's right."

I nod. Because yeah, I do.

24

CECILIA

Dialing a phone number shouldn't be this difficult, but it is. I stare down at the crumpled piece of paper Julio gave me with Allie's phone number, trying to decide whether or not to call.

I don't want a new therapist or any therapist, really. But I need to talk to someone. I think when it all happened, I spent so much time and energy trying to keep myself together that I compartmentalized to the extreme. And when that failed, I shut down. Let myself go numb.

I'm not numb anymore, and though it hurts, I want to feel things. Experience the full range of my emotions. This girl, Allie, she's been through what I have. She'd get it.

Sinking my teeth into my bottom lip, I punch in her number. Taking a deep breath, I hit dial and bring the phone to my ear. It rings once and I panic. I end the call. Come on, Cecilia. You can do this. It's just a phone call.

You don't have to tell her anything you don't want to. She doesn't know. There is no way for it to get back to Austin.

I shake out my wrists and roll my neck back and forth. "Okay." Another deep breath. "You can do it."

I punch the number in again and hit send, but this time, before I have the chance to bring it to my ear, a flash of movement catches my attention and I turn in time to see Austin barreling toward me. *Shit.*

I hang up the phone and look around. I'm outside of the Aquatics building. There are people strolling down the pathways between buildings. I'm not alone. I repeat the last part again in my head. I'm not alone. Austin can't hurt me here. He can yell at me and bully me, but he can't *hurt* me like he did before.

"Are you stupid?" he snarls as soon as he's close.

I hunch my shoulders, making myself smaller, and wrap my arms around my waist. "Leave me alone, Austin." I step around him, but he mirrors my movements, blocking my escape.

"We had a deal." He shoves me back and I stumble into the building, my head smacking into the stone wall. *Ow!* My vision blurs and I blink hard to clear it. "I told you to keep your mouth shut. What the hell is wrong with you? It's like you have a fucking death wish."

I finger my scalp, wincing when I reach the crown of my head. Drawing my hand away, I look down to find blood coating my fingertips.

"You hurt me?" I can't take my eyes off the blood. He... my breath seesaws in and out. He hurt me. Here. Out in the open where anyone could see. He just shoved me, like he didn't even care. My hands shake.

"What did you say to him?"

I look up, meeting his furious gaze. If looks could kill, I'd be dead right now.

"What—" I shake my head to clear some of the fog. "What are you talking about?"

He crowds me, forcing me to press into the wall. Grabbing my chin, he squeezes until tears spring into my eyes. "Herrera and his friends are asking a lot of people a lot of fucking questions. So I'll ask one more time. What. Did. You. Say?"

"Nothing. I didn't tell him anything."

Shit. What did Gabriel do? He hasn't asked me any questions recently. Not anything serious. I assumed it meant he'd dropped it. I was wrong.

Tugging at Austin's grip, I try and fail to get him to release me. "You're hurting me," I tell him, as if it weren't obvious.

"I'm going to fucking destroy you," he threatens. "Last warning, Cece. Get your boy in line or it'll be your ass facing the consequences."

His hold loosens enough that I can tear myself away.

"And your family's." With that last threat hanging between us, he stalks away, leaving me reeling.

As soon as he's gone from sight, I drop to my knees and brace my hands on the ground. *Shit.* My breaths are ragged, invisible hands squeezing the air from my lungs. Tears fill my eyes and I'm powerless to keep them from falling as the reality of my situation crashes over me. I can't escape him. Austin always wins. He can do whatever he wants whenever he wants.

I can't live like this.

Someone shouts my name across the clearing and I look up to see Gabriel flat out running toward me.

"What happened?"

I shake my head, pushing his hands away when he tries to help me up. Wiping the tears from my eyes, I pull myself together.

He lifts my face to the sky, turning it side to side. I can't even look at him. If I do, I'll give in to the need to fall apart. To take the comfort I know he would offer.

"Where does it hurt?"

I point to my head. Words are beyond me right now. Taking the cue, Gabriel gingerly tilts my head down, his fingers probing along my skull. I wince when he hits a tender spot and he curses. "I'm going to probe a little more. I just want to make sure you don't need stitches. Is that okay?"

I nod, clenching my teeth when the motion sends a spear of pain into my skull. Breathing through my mouth, I hold still as Gabriel presses his fingers along the wound.

A hiss slips through my teeth, and Gabriel's hands fall away. "I don't think you need stitches." That's a relief. "But we should get you—"

"No." I don't want to go to the clinic or see a doctor. I just want to get the hell out of here.

"Cecilia?"

"I'm fine," I tell him, but the look on his face says he's not convinced.

Gabriel helps me up, his hands steadying me when I sway on my feet, but he says nothing else. He doesn't pry. Taking my bag from my arm, he slings it over his shoulder and leads me to the parking lot with a hand on the small of my back. A few people stop and stare, wondering why I'm such a mess. Gabriel fishes my keys out of my bag and, opening the passenger side door of my Jeep, helps me inside.

He stands in the open doorway, his eyes locked on me, and a storm of emotion burns inside his gaze. Reaching out, he tucks my hair behind my ear, presses his lips to my temple, and pulls the seat belt from beside me, reaching across my lap to secure the latch.

"Can I take you home?"

Swallowing hard, I nod.

"My home?"

Oh. "Okay."

Satisfied, he closes my door and jogs to the other side. He keeps a mask on his face and doesn't say any of the things I know are running through his mind.

Halfway there, his phone rings. Digging it from his pocket, he accepts the call, pressing his phone to his ear. I can only make out bits and pieces of the conversation. He keeps his answers short, but it's clear he's talking about me when he says things like, "She's okay." and, "I'm taking her home."

I try to muster up my frustration. Maybe even annoyance. But in the end, all I feel is tired and dejected. Hanging up, he squeezes my hand across the center console and offers me a careful smile.

"You still good? Vision blurry? Are you in pain?"

"I'm okay," I tell him, leaving out that my vision is fuzzy around the edges and there is definitely some pain. No point in making him worry more.

In the driveway, Gabriel helps me out and leads me inside to the living room. Julio and Felix are there and I get a glimpse of a guy I assume is one of their other roommates. He doesn't introduce himself and I don't take the time to ask.

Julio grabs a first aid kit from the kitchen and takes one look at Gabriel, who's pacing the room before dropping beside me. He pulls out some antiseptic and cleans the cut on my head before sitting back and eyeing me with worry. "You going to tell us what happened before Gabe wears down a permanent path on the floors?" He chuckles, but it's forced.

"Had a brief run in with an asshole. Nothing I can't handle."

"Fuck!" Gabriel explodes into action, slamming his fist into the drywall beside him. It disappears into the wall, only for him to tear it back out. Bits of dust and debris fall to the floor, and I stare open mouthed at the hole he made. I knew he was upset, but I didn't realize he was this angry, and I'm terrified to ask if any of his anger is directed at me.

Chest heaving, he opens and closes his fist, staring down at his now bleeding knuckles.

"Get it together." There's a warning in Julio's voice. "She's been through enough, and your tantrum isn't helping."

Gabriel's mouth twists in disgust. Out of habit, I curl in on myself, sinking deeper into the cushions of the sofa. Gabriel catches my reaction and the color drains from his face.

"Shit." He exhales a few colorful curses and drops to his knees in front of me. "I didn't think. I'm sorry. I—" He cups my face in his bruised hand and holds my gaze. "I'm so fucking angry," he confesses.

"With me?" Sinking my teeth into my bottom lip I try to turn away, but he crawls closer,, cradling my face in both his hands.

"Never." He uses his thumbs to wipe beneath my eyes and presses his lips to my forehead. "I'm not mad at you. I'm mad at myself for not being there to protect you." And there lies the problem. I'm not Gabriel's responsibility to protect.

"You couldn't have known—"

"That Holt would come after you?" His words take me by surprise.

"Gabe, you didn't—" Julio begins.

"I should have," Gabriel cuts him off. "We know how guys like Holt operate. If I paid attention, I would have seen this coming. Cecilia would have been safe." He sits back on his heels and runs his fingers through his hair, tugging at the dark brown strands in frustration.

"What did you do?" My voice shakes and I hate the look of guilt that flashes across both their faces. Pulling away, I straighten in my seat, tucking my legs beneath me. I need some separation between us. Gabriel and Julio stare at one another, some silent communication passing between them.

That's fine. I can wait. A dull throb takes up residence in my head, and both sides of my jaw where Austin grabbed me are sore. Probably bruised.

Felix steps into the room, registers the look on our faces and clears his throat, signaling for Julio to follow. I'd laugh at how quickly those two run to avoid confrontation, but it'd hurt my face too much.

Once we're alone, Gabriel gets up from the floor and claims the spot on the sofa beside me. His fingers flex along his thigh and he drums his fingers across his leg. The bleeding has stopped, but his hand has to hurt. I consider taking his hand and cleaning it. Julio left the first aid kit behind when he left. But then Gabriel makes a fist and says, "I know about Holt, Benson, and Chambers."

It's like the ground is torn out from under me.

"I know they hurt you this summer. That you went to the school board. And that PacNorth did nothing about it."

My bottom lip quivers. He doesn't look at me as he unearths my secrets. As he flays me open to bleed out on the floor. He knows. I sniff and stare off at an empty spot on the wall, fighting back my tears. He isn't supposed to know. Not all the awful details surrounding it. It's bad enough he suspected. Worse that he's who found me on the locker room floor. *God*. What must he think of me?

"How?" I choke on my words and Gabriel hangs his head, still refusing to look at me. It's like a knife to my chest.

"We asked around. Felix talked to your old roommate— "

"Joelle?"

He nods.

I can't sit. Shoving to my feet, I move to stand beside the window. Pressing my fingers to the cold glass, I look at him through its reflection, unsure what to say. He crossed so many lines. All of them, in fact. And for what? To assuage some morbid curiosity? "Why?" I need an answer. What was so important that he'd betray me like this?

Gabriel looks up. "I needed to know." His stricken gaze meets mine in the glass and I almost choose to bite my tongue. But I can't. Not about this. This is my business.

Mine. Not his. I don't care if he needs to know. He hasn't earned that right.

I whirl on him, making my head spin. "Why?" His answer isn't good enough. Everything was fine before. But this — I replay Austin's warnings. This changes everything. It's not fair. Everything I care about keeps getting taken from me.

"I needed to do something. To help— "

"You were helping. Don't you see that?" I throw my arm out. "This," I tell him, "Being here. Spending time with you. That's how you help. You gave me comfort and security. A safe space where I could find myself again."

His eyes soften. I know he cares about me. He treats me like a princess. Cared for. Cherished. Which is why I feel like the biggest bitch when I say, "And then you took it away."

Eyes flooding with panic, he closes the distance between us. "No." He furiously shakes his head. "That's not what I wanted to do." His eyes plead with me to understand. To see things his way. But I can't. "Holt and Chambers and Benson, they can't get away with what they did to you."

"They already did," I remind him. "You can't change what's already done. Promise you'll stay out of this." What I don't say is that he'll only make things worse if he doesn't. I don't want to hurt him, and being the reason I'm hurt will do exactly that. But this isn't only about me. Maybe if it was, I'd stand in the line of fire. But Austin will ruin my family. He won't settle for just ruining me.

I won't go up against him when I already know I'll lose.

"If I can't?" He reaches for me and I step away. Hurt flashes across his face.

"Then I can't do this."

Nostrils flaring, he fists his hands at his side, ensuring he doesn't reach for me again. "What's that supposed to mean?"

"This." I wave at the space between us. "Us."

"You don't mean that."

Standing tall, I look him straight in the eyes. "Yes. I do."

We stare off against one another, each of us refusing to give so much as an inch of ground. "You'd throw me away? Just like that?" I don't miss the hurt in his voice.

"I'm not throwing you away."

"Sure feels like it."

I shake my head, wishing he understood, but he can't. He doesn't know everything. And despite my feelings for him, I don't trust him enough to tell him.

"Austin has the power to ruin me. To ruin my family." He's got to understand that. They've been on the team together for at least a year or two. He'd know Austin has money. Know what family he comes from.

"He uses that as a threat because he knows you can just as easily ruin him."

I want to laugh. "No. I can't."

"Don't you want to at least try?"

I consider his questions before answering. But even in my wildest dreams, I've never let myself think of that. "No. I don't."

"I don't believe you."

"You don't have to." Gabriel is going to believe what he wants, but I'm not lying to him. "Julio said you guys have a friend. Allie?"

He nods.

"She went through something like this?"

Another dip of his head.

"Ask her." This might backfire on me, but I'm praying it doesn't. "Ask her what it's like. How long it follows you around. Ask her how much worse it gets when your darkest secrets and deepest fears go public. When people know what happened and either pity you, or label you a liar and a whore."

"You're not a— "

I hold up a hand to stop him. "I know I'm not. What happened wasn't my fault. I didn't ask for it and all of the fault lies with my attackers. You and I, we know that. But none of it matters. Everyone will have their own opinions and I'll have to face them. I lost my best friends," I tell him. "I thought we were like you three. Ride or die. Like family.

But they both turned their backs on me, and I did nothing wrong."

He pulls me against his chest. I fight him at first, refusing to accept the comfort he offers, but after a minute or two, exhaustion settles into my limbs and I slump in his embrace. Minutes later, I wrap my arms around his waist, close my eyes, and take what feels like my first deep breath in hours.

"I'm sorry you have shit taste in friends."

A choked laugh spills out of me.

"I can help with that. I have excellent taste in friends. And I'll always have your back. Julio and Felix too."

Smiling against him, I listen to the steady thrum of his heart. Gabriel means well and I don't doubt that he and the others would stand beside me, but I don't want to be in a position where they have to. "I don't want another fight with Austin." I won't survive it. I almost didn't the first go around.

Gabriel says nothing to that. Instead, he rubs circles on my back and peppers kisses along my temple. When my eyes grow heavy, he leads me upstairs and I follow him down the hallway to his room, not once feeling even an ounce of reservation.

His room boasts a black, king-size bed. It takes up most of the room, positioned in the center as the focal point. To the left, he has a small bookcase. The shelves are double stacked with well worn paperbacks, and there are several pillows on the floor beside it. Like he curls up on the ground to read instead of lying in bed. I can almost picture him like that—sprawled out on the floor with a paperback in his hand. I'd bet he folds his page corners instead of using a bookmark when he comes to a stopping point. The heathen.

My face softens, thinking about him in the room. It's sparse, but there are small elements like the picture of him and the others on his nightstand, that highlight the person he is. I move closer to the image, carefully picking it up. It's housed in a wooden frame and painted in primary colors. Macaroni noodles are glued to its sides. A gift from a child would be my guess.

There's a threadbare blanket thrown over a chair in the corner. It's crocheted with a mismatched assortment of yarn and has holes big enough for my hand to fit through, but still, he keeps it. It means something to him even in the condition it's in.

"Do you want to shower? I have clothes you can—"

Turning to face him, I cut off his words with a kiss. His body responds and he groans against my lips. The sound sends a spear of need straight to my center. Hands gliding up my body, he cradles the base of my head, but makes no move to deepen the kiss.

Tomorrow I'll have to think about today. About Gabriel and I. About Austin and his threats. But for the rest of today, I can pretend none of it matters. I can pretend things are still better. That I'm okay.

"We can't—" Gabriel pulls away, but I follow him, refusing to let the events of today take this moment from me. "Cecilia," he groans, and the fingers of one hand flex against my hip.

"Please," I whisper against his lips.

"You're hurt."

"Then help me feel better."

25

GABRIEL

Fuck. I shouldn't agree to this. What the hell am I thinking? This is wrong. She's hurt and vulnerable. Shit. But I don't know if I have it in me to deny her.

Cecilia rises up on her tiptoes and hovers her lips over mine. "Please," her words whisper along my lips.

Do you think I can get my mouth to voice the words, very reasonable words, that suggest we pump the brakes? Slow down, at least until she feels better?

Of course not.

I'm lost when it comes to this girl. I want her, more than I've ever wanted anyone or anything in my life before.

I've kissed her lips. Stroked her body. Brought her to the height of pleasure with nothing more than my hand. But it's not enough. I want more. Everything she has to give, and it takes every single molecule of self-control I have to keep myself from taking it. From grabbing her face, devouring her mouth with mine, and claiming her in a way that makes her and I more than casual.

I want fucking permanent.

But she's scared. I want to take what she offers, but it'd destroy me if she later regretted it. I can't lose her. Seeing her on the ground today shook me to my core. But fear isn't reason enough to let those assholes get away with what they did to her.

Cecilia's lips mold against mine. My control slips. Cradling her head in my hand, I wait, giving her the chance to take the lead. To be in control. That's what she needs right now. Control. I feel it in her kiss. In the tight line of her neck and shoulders. She's trying to reclaim some of her power back.

And I'll be damned if I take it away from her. Cecilia's tongue peaks out, and I groan as she leans in and explores my mouth. She's shy at first. Almost timid like she worries any moment I will reject her.

I could never.

Pulling her closer, Cecilia presses against me, her breast mashing into my chest. I feel the exact moment her confidence rises. This is only the beginning, I want to tell her. There's no rush. She can take all the time that she needs.

I release her face, running my hands down her arms before briefly squeezing her waist. Releasing her, I keep my eyes locked with hers and step backwards until the backs of my shins meet the small pullout couch in my room. I sink into my seat and motion her forward.

A small smile curls her lips, and she follows after me. Legs spread wide, I run my hands over my jean clad thighs and wait to see what she'll do next. Cecilia hesitates for only a second before lowering herself to straddle my lap.

I fight the urge to shift in my seat. To thrust my already hard length against the warmth of her pussy. She settles her weight on me, her small hands pressing against my chest.

Her heat seeps through the thin material of her leggings. And I squeeze my eyes closed, envisioning her bare and spread out for me, like a feast, ready to be savored and enjoyed. Is she wet for me? Does her pussy ache to be filled the way my cock aches to fill her? I bite back a groan and kiss her again, craving the feel of her skin against mine.

Cecilia's mouth tastes like cherry and cola, the flavor sinking into my taste buds as I chase after her lips. We kiss for what feels like an eternity but also not nearly long enough. It will never be enough with her. Like before, I feel the moment she gets restless. When kissing and licking and touching is no longer enough.

Her teeth nip at my bottom lip and against my control, my hips thrust up against her center.

Cecilia gasps into my mouth and I silently curse myself for my reaction, but fuck, I love it when she bites. I lick the corner of her mouth before biting her full bottom lip and she blesses me with the most incredible feeling.

Pressing down, Cecilia grinds herself against me. I groan, my fingers tightening around her hips. Fuck. I tear my mouth from hers and try to catch my breath.

"Is that—I'm sorry."

What? No. She should not be apologizing right now.

Cecilia worriedly chews her bottom lip, cheeks flushed, and looks away. I pull her eyes back to me.

"What are you apologizing for?"

She opens her mouth, but no words come out.

"Do you think I didn't like it?" I ask.

Her cheeks turn a darker shade of pink and I smirk. Fuck, she's cute.

Careful. So fucking careful, I thrust my cock against her center while pulling down on her hips.

Her lips part and her lashes flutter. "Oh," she gasps. "That feels..."

"Good?" I ask.

She nods, and I do it again. I'm rewarded with a breathy moan falling from her lips.

Cecilia grinding down on my dick is a mixture of pure pleasure and agony. Something I've never felt quite like this before.

The hard length of my cock is aligned with her pussy and her thighs cage me in, resting on either side of my waist, but it's a cage of my own making. And one I have zero desire to escape.

For the next several minutes we dry hump like teenagers on the sofa, her tiny nails digging into my shoulders as she chases her release. Her eyes are glazed and her hair is a mess, but she's never been more beautiful than she is right now. Needy. Desperate. Determined to take her pleasure.

I'm all but fucking her through our clothes, my dick shoving its way through the fabric of her pants and the thin material of my soccer shorts, but it's not enough. I want more.

Releasing her, I fist my hands at my sides and shove them back against the cushions.

I refuse to fuck this up. Her hands move from digging into my skin to clawing at the fabric of my shirt as her throat makes this soft mewling sound that drives me absolutely insane. I swear this girl will be the death of me.

Following her lead, I help her tug my shirt over my head, leaving my chest bare. Her eyes darken with lust and she licks her lips in clear appreciation.

Fingers itching, I slip them beneath the hem of her shirt before meeting her gaze. A silent question passes between us and she nods.

Fucking yes.

Swallowing hard, I push up the fabric of her shirt and she obediently raises her arms for me. Peeling it from her skin,

I take in every inch of perfectly tanned skin I expose before tossing the shirt aside.

I eye her reverently. *"Es un sueña."*

"What does that mean?" I can hear the worry in her voice. The insecurities.

Leaning forward, I kiss the tops of each of her breasts before tilting my head up and meeting her gaze. "You're a dream."

A small smile curls the corners of her lips.

"I don't deserve you," I tell her, and it's true. I don't. Cecilia Russo is cut from a different cloth. An angel walking amongst us mere mortals. She is stronger and braver than anyone I know and I was an idiot to ever believe her selfish or a coward for trying to take her own life. She is the complete opposite of those things and she is quickly becoming my everything.

"I'm too selfish to let you go," I confess. "I want you, Cecilia." I smile and shake my head. "No. I don't want you," I tell her. "I need you."

I hope she knows that. Believes it down to the very marrow of her bones. She's upset with me now. Hurt because I want to protect her. But there is no one else for me. Already, without even having her, she's ruined me for anyone else. Only she will do.

Her eyes widen and her throat bobs as she swallows hard. I see her doubts reflected in her eyes. The fear. But with me, there is nothing to be afraid of. I would sooner carve my bleeding heart from my chest than do anything to hurt her.

I grab her by the back of the neck and press my forehead to hers. "You are the only woman I want." I wait for my words to sink in, but instead of answering my declaration with words of her own, Cecilia boldly reaches behind herself and unclasps her bra, letting the thin material fall to her waist.

I jerk my gaze down and crush the lace fabric in my hands, knowing that all it will take is one look and I'm done for. My control will snap.

"Then for tonight, take me."

Did I hear that right? Cecilia takes the bra from my hands and sets it aside before taking my larger hand in hers and guiding it to her breast.

Shit. Swallowing hard, I stare at her chest and my other hand follows suit to cup her other breast.

"I want this," she says and rocks into me. "I want you."

I knead her breasts in my palms, stroking my thumbs over her nipples. She whimpers so I do it again, paying close attention to how her body responds.

She makes these breathy, needy sounds as I play with her tits, and the sounds alone are enough to have precum leaking from my dick. Fuck. I'll cum in my shorts if we keep going like this.

"What do you need?" I ask, needing her to advance this along, but I don't want to push her. To take more than she's willing to give. If I fuck this up, I'll never forgive myself.

Cecilia pushes to her feet, and it takes everything in me to drop my hands to my sides instead of pulling her back. With a coy look on her face, she surprises me again as she lowers her pants, taking her underwear with them until she stands before me, completely bare.

Leaning forward, I brace my forearms on my knees. "Fuck me." My words are hoarse and I fight to remain in my seat.

"I want you inside of me."

Hallelujah. Hearing her words is heaven to my ears, but I still have to ask.

"Are you sure?"

She nods.

"Words, baby. I need words."

"Yes. I'm sure."

Taking her word that she's ready for what comes next, I lift my hips and shove my shorts down, kicking them free as soon as they hit the ground. My dick bobs to attention, proud and eager to be of use.

Cecilia's eyes widen, gaze locked on my cock. Her tongue peeks out to wet her lips, and I give her a moment to take me in.

Fisting myself, I lean back and stroke my length, watching her face for any sign of hesitancy. There is none.

"Come here."

She climbs back onto my lap, her bare pussy brushing along my length. I hiss and release my dick to slide my hand between us. She's like satin beneath my fingertips and my brain momentarily goes haywire.

"Look at you, wet and so fucking ready for me."

She kisses my lips and moans against my mouth as I slip two fingers between her thighs to play with her clit. She shudders, grinding against my hand in short, jerky movements.

I tease her, building her orgasm gradually so I can watch every second as she slowly unravels.

She throws her head back, the tendons in her neck straining, and I know I'm getting close. "Please," she begs. "I'm close."

"Do you want to come on my fingers or my cock?" I wordlessly beg for her to say my cock. If she wants to come on my fingers, I'll give her that, and after she comes, I'll slap a smile on my face and tuck my raging hard on back into my shorts. Whatever she wants. But god, do I want to be inside her.

"Inside me." She releases another breathy moan. Thank fuck. I move my hand out of my way and guide her over to me.

"Sink down on me," I demand, not trusting myself to go slow. I'm wound too tight. Too desperate.

I drag my lips over her neck, her collarbone, and slowly, so fucking slowly, she sinks her pussy down on my cock.

Perfect fucking fit. My heart races in my chest and I watch her pupils dilate as she takes in every inch of me.

Her lips create a small O, and I lean forward to capture her mouth.

"Ride me."

I'm not sure if it's a demand or a plea, and to be perfectly honest, I don't care, as long as she moves against me. She's careful at first, giving herself time to adjust to my size, but after only a couple of minutes, she picks up the pace, her hips slamming against mine, and she once again chases her release.

"That's it. Just like that. Take what you need."

Her breasts bounce between us, drawing my attention to her nipples. I lean in, sucking one into my mouth. She moans, her hips thrusting faster.

Gripping her ass, I help to pick up the pace, finally giving in the urge to thrust up into her.

We find a rhythm, neither too fast nor too slow. It's perfect. Her pussy clenches around me, and I know I'm close. Hell, I'm surprised I've made it this long. But she has to come first. This isn't about me. It's about her. She has to come first.

I find her clit again with my fingers and work the tight bundle of nerves over as my other hand digs into her ass.

"Oh god."

Fuck. Right there.

"Come for me," I demand. She's right there. "That's it. Good girl. Do you like that?"

I shift my hips, and she sinks down onto me at a deeper angle. *Fuck.* I won't make it much longer.

Squeezing her eyes closed, Cecilia nods. "Yes. Yes. Yes." Her legs shake. Almost there.

I slam up into her three more times and am gifted the sound of her release. Cecilia cries out, choking on her own breaths as her pussy convulses around me. I pull her down to my chest, wrapping my arms around her as I pump into her two more times before finding my release.

"Fuck!" I groan, seeing goddamn stars behind my eyes.

Breathing heavily, I stroke Cecilia's back and ease the tangled strands of her hair from her face.

Her skin is damp with sweat, and I can feel the erratic beat of her heart against my chest, which wouldn't be a problem except her shoulders are shaking and I feel moisture in the crook of my neck where her face is currently buried.

"Cecilia?" Shit. Did I hurt her? I try to draw her back, but she just burrows herself deeper against me.

"Baby, are you okay?"

"I'm... I'm fine." She chokes on her words. Fuck. What did I do?

I wrap my arms around her, trying to give her the comfort she needs. But I did this. How can I expect to be the one to make her feel better if I'm the reason she's falling apart in the first place?

Dammit. I should have waited. She wasn't ready. I should have known that. Seen the signs. Shame washes over me and I swallow the lump in my throat. "I didn't mean to hurt you. I wasn't thinking— "

She jerks back. "What?"

Her eyes are red, the skin of her cheeks splotchy. I stoke her face, wiping an errant tear away and pray she can she how fucking sorry I am. "I'm sor— "

"Why?"

She sniffs and her nose scrunchies as she looks down on me with a confused expression. I don't know what's happening. But I'm not a complete moron. Chicks don't cry after sex because it's good.

"You're crying."

Cecilia covers her face with her hands. "Not because of you!"

My brows pull together, and I tug her hands from her face.

"I'm not following."

She exhales a breath and wipes the last bit of moisture from her eyes. "I'm sorry," she tells me. "I'm not upset. I swear."

My mouth opens to argue. I don't need her to spare my feelings. I need her to be okay.

"Really. I'm not."

I frown, still not convinced. "No more secrets."

"I know," she says and kisses me. "I was a little overwhelmed. That's all."

"Did I do something wrong? Did I hurt you?"

She shakes her head and a flush creeps up her neck. "I didn't know what to expect. If I'd like it or if I'd freak out. If it would remind me of..." She shrugs. "You know." Cecilia sinks her teeth into her lower lip.

"And?"

A hesitant smile lights up her face. "It was good."

A weight lifts from my chest. "Yeah?"

"Yeah." Her smile spreads and she leans in to kiss me again. "I'm sorry. I mean, to make you think something was wrong. It was perfect. All of it."

I nip at her lips before giving her a dubious look. "Perfect, huh?"

"Don't let it go to your head," she warns.

I kiss her again. "Promise you're okay?"

She kisses me back. "Promise. I think everything just hit me at once," she admits. "But all good things." Cecilia shifts her weight and the evidence of both our releases drips out of her once I pull my cock free.

Without thinking, I press my hand to her core and dip two fingers inside, pushing my cum back inside her. *What am I doing?*

"We should clean up," I suggest, making no effort to move.

"We should." Cecilia lays down against my chest, pressing her lips to my collarbone.

"We're okay?"

She sighs, her body falling lax against me. "Mmm. Better than okay."

I want to believe her. To revel in the feeling of her in my arms, but a voice in my head screams I'm missing something. And the same voice worries this is somehow the beginning of goodbye.

26

CECILIA

It hits me the next morning, just like I knew it would. I try to pretend nothing's changed. To convince myself we can get past this. But the longer the day goes on, the heavier the weight in my chest grows. He's incapable of letting this thing with Austin go.

I wait for Gabriel on the bleachers near the soccer field. I know what has to be done and already, I grieve the loss of what I am willfully giving up. They say if you love someone, then let them go.

I'm in love with Gabriel Herrera. And giving him up is one of the hardest things I will do, but I have to. I'm not okay. I wish I was. I really do. But I'm not, and I can't fix what's broken inside of me overnight. He deserves better. So much better than the broken and jagged pieces I have to offer him.

I take a deep breath and steel myself, catching sight of him across the field. His smile lights up when he sees me and he jogs the few yards between us, his sure steps leading him straight toward me.

"Hey." He swoops down and kisses my cheek before dropping his gear on the empty bench behind him. Honey-gold eyes meet mine, but when I don't respond, his brows furrow and his smile dims. He cocks his head in silent question and I hang mine, not sure where to even begin.

"Everything okay?" he asks. "Did Holt—"

"No." I don't want him to worry about that.

Gabriel drops down into a crouch in front of me, making us eye level. He tilts my chin up, bringing my gaze to his.

Concern lines his face when he asks, "What's going on? You know you can tell me anything."

I open my mouth, but nothing comes out. Biting down hard, I look away, forcing myself to breathe. *Come on, Cecilia. Spit it out. Just get it over with already.*

His hands drop to his sides, eyes searching mine for clues to my shift in behavior. He reaches for my hand, but I pull away. He can't touch me. Not if I'm going to go through with this.

A flash of hurt passes over his face before he schools his expression and laces his fingers together. He waits, but he's no fool. He knows what I'm trying to do. It's written across his face.

"I can't see you anymore." I force the words past my lips before clamping them tight to keep myself from taking them back. I want to. More than anything. But I wait.

As the seconds tick by, the silence stretches between us, and the urge to take them back grows stronger. But I don't. I can't. Tension weighs heavy between us and I peer through my lashes, gauging his reaction to my admission.

His brows are furrowed and confusion spreads across his face, but what I don't see is acceptance. "What are you talking about?" His voice is filled with disbelief.

I swallow down the lump in my throat and square my shoulders. This is the right call. It might not feel that way right now, but it is, and I need to believe it.

"I think it would be better if we spent some time apart. Did our own thing for a while." It's a lame explanation, even for me, but I can't seem to get my mouth to speak all the words I'd rehearsed earlier today. I should break this off. Make it a clean cut. But a part of me wants to leave the door open. To leave us some semblance of a chance.

Color fills his face and the heavy set of his shoulders stiffens. "Where is this coming from? Did Holt or someone else put you up to this?" A muscle ticks in his jaw as his confusion quickly morphs into anger. "Did he— "

"No," I rush to tell him. "No one put me up to this. This is all me. I..." I bite my bottom lip. "I need space."

He shakes his head, his doubt evident, and it makes me fall for him more. Even now, he refuses to give up on me. On us. But he has to.

"I'll back off," he says. "I'll stop. All of us will stop. You want me to leave Holt be, fine. Consider it done."

We both know he doesn't mean it. It would never last.

"I can't be with you," I tell him, imploring him to understand. "We're not right for each other— "

"The hell we're not." He shoves to his feet. "You and me," he points back and forth between us, towering over me, "we fit. You know we do."

I swallow hard, looking up at him. "We fit because I'm broken. Because you fill my cracks—" I choke on my words. Dammit. Why is this so hard? "I don't want to be broken anymore."

Gabriel draws me to my feet and cups my face in his palms. There's a desperate glint in his eyes. Like he's on the verge of unraveling. "You're not broken. You're perfect. You're— "

"No." I shake my head and pull away. "As long as we're together, I'll only ever be broken."

He flinches. "I—That's—" His jaw clenches. He knows I'm right. He knows he's become something of a crutch for me, even if that was never his intention.

"It's too easy to lean on you. To stay like this. Fractured. Un-whole." My confrontation with Austin the other day is enough to confirm that.

"Don't do this." His voice is ragged. "Don't throw what we have away." He bares his teeth and I can tell he's biting back his words. Holding himself in check. It's the unshed tears in his eyes that almost undo me. The last thing I want is to hurt him.

But I can't pretend any longer.

"I don't want to be with you." The lie falls from my lips, my words little more than a whisper, but he hears them, and they hit their intended mark.

Gabriel flinches as though my words are a physical blow.

Rearing back, he shakes his head in denial. It's written all over his face. He wants to fight me on this. But he isn't sure. There's an inkling of doubt in his gaze. It's the same one inside of me that wonders if I'm enough. Could I ever be enough for someone like him?

Tears sting the backs of my eyes and I furiously blink them away. If I fall apart now, all of this will be for nothing. He has to believe me.

I wait for him to storm off or lash out, throwing hurtful words my way.

He does neither of those things. Instead, he grinds out one single word. "Bullshit."

My eyes widen.

"What?"

He runs his tongue over his teeth and glares down at me. "We were fine yesterday. We fucked. I held you. Everything was perfect leading up to this morning. Something happened."

I shake my head. Nothing happened. Not anything he doesn't already know.

"Stop lying to me!" he demands. "What changed? This kind of shit doesn't come out of nowhere, Cecilia." Frustration rolls off of him in waves, but instead of comforting him, reassuring him of my feelings, I allow the tension between us to thicken. I let it grow more and more uncomfortable with each second I refuse to answer him. There is no easy answer. Not one that will satisfy him.

"Fuck." He doesn't know what to do with himself and paces the narrow space between the bleachers. "Lay it out for me. What happened? What did I do?"

I hate that he blames himself. This isn't his fault. We just... "We're not good for each other. Not now." Maybe later. Some time in the future when I'm strong again. No longer in need of saving.

He jerks to a stop and stabs a finger toward me. "Stop lying."

"I'm not."

He huffs out a breath, his chest rising and falling at a rapid clip. He looks like he's battling with himself. Struggling to figure out what to do next. I can see the wheels in his head spinning. Gabriel wants to fix this. Just like he wants to fix me. But he needs to realize he can't.

I am not his burden to bear.

Tugging the sleeves of my hoodie down, I fold my chilled hands across my chest and tuck them under my arms. "I'm not trying to hurt you," I tell him. "This will never work, Gabriel. Not now at least."

He shakes his head, expression locking down. "I don't believe you," he tells me, but I hear the defeat in his voice. Because a part of him does. A part of him knows that no matter how much we care for each other, this isn't healthy for either of us. I can't be his absolution. Saving me doesn't bring his brother back. It doesn't replace everything he's lost. And being with him allows me to ignore my own trauma. The things that were done to me. He's my crutch.

I need to know I can walk on my own two feet without him. That I'm strong enough to face Austin on my own should I have to.

I can't be with Gabriel and constantly worry he only wants me because I'm broken and in need of saving.

If we stay together, if we work through this right now, I will always wonder. That doubt will be there, lingering in the recesses of my mind, and it will fester until it can no longer be ignored. Until it destroys what we have and by then, it'll be too late to recover.

We need time to work on ourselves. To become who we're meant to be, outside of one another. We won't stand a chance until then.

"Calling me a liar doesn't change things. You can't force me to be in a relationship with you. I'm asking you to respect my decision. To give me space."

He rubs the back of his neck and grimaces. Without looking at me, he asks, "Why are you lying to me? To yourself? The least you can do is give me the fucking truth if you're going to call shit off and blindside me like this."

A single tear slips past my defenses and I swipe it away, not answering him.

"This is bullshit." He stabs a finger at the ground between us. "I know I fucked up. I didn't protect you from Holt—"

"I don't want your protection!"

His eyes plead with me to help him understand, but I can't. I don't know what else there is to say.

Gabriel reaches for me, but when he sees me tense up, he draws his hand back, dropping it to his side. "You need to give me something here. Because I can't accept this bullshit, baby. Give me something."

"I can't."

His nostrils flare. "So this is it? You're pushing me away?"

"I'm not pushing you away—"

"The fuck you're not, Cecilia."

"That's not what I'm doing. You're not listening— "

"I heard you loud and clear. You don't want me to look out for you. You don't want me to go after Holt and the others who hurt you, but I'm going to level with you here, since you're not willing to do the same for me." He waits until I meet his gaze. "I love you."

My heart stutters in my chest, and I look away.

"I love you so much that hearing you say you want to do your own thing, that you don't want to be with me anymore, it fucking guts me. Even though I know you're

340

lying to my face." I open my mouth to argue, but he doesn't give me the chance to. "And that, that shit hurts, too. We don't lie to each other." He scrubs a hand over his face, frustration coiling his body tight. "I want all your truths. The good and the bad. The beautiful, the ugly, and even your twisted broken truths. Everything you have to offer. Because I'm a greedy bastard and you are *mine*."

"Gabriel— "

"You're delusional if you think pushing me away helps either of us." He doesn't wait for me to respond. "I was a mess before you. After Carlos's death, I compartmentalized my shit and faked it as best I could. I was dead inside. But you..." He sucks in a breath. "Cecilia, you make me feel, and yeah, sometimes feelings hurt. I won't pretend they don't. But I see the way you look at me. Even now. The idea of us not being together isn't any more appealing to you than it is to me.

Whatever is going on in that head of yours, spell it out for me. We can get through it. I know we can."

I've never had someone outside of my parents care about me this much. No one has ever fought for me like this. But it doesn't change things. No matter how much I wish it did.

Tears fill my vision to slip silently down my cheeks.

Gabriel presses his forehead to mine and I close my eyes, letting my tears continue to fall. His thumbs swipe at my cheeks and I breathe in the smell of his cologne, taking comfort in the familiar scent for longer than I should.

"I know I'm not perfect," he whispers. "But don't ask me to give you up."

I open my mouth and he stills, bracing himself as I hammer in the final nail.

"You have to."

———————

GABRIEL AND CECILIA'S STORY CONTINUES IN THE STRIKER Available Now—> https://amzn.to/3QCKHgO

———————

Turn the Page for a sneak peek!

GABRIEL

"**G**abe, man. You gotta talk about this," Felix says, concern creasing his forehead as he lingers in my doorway.

"I'm fine," I grunt, shoulders hunched without looking up. No way in hell am I about to rehash how Cecilia ripped my heart out and stomped on the pieces.

Sharing my fucking feelings isn't going to make what I'm dealing with any better. In fact, I'm ninety-nine-point-nine-percent positive it will only make things worse.

Felix steps further into my room, persistent bastard that he is. "You've been a ghost for weeks. I know something happened with you and Cecilia, but when any of us so much as says her name, you either bite our heads off or you shut down. What gives?"

I rake both hands through my hair, emotions churning violently in my gut. *That's because she ended things.* What a fucking joke. I don't even know why I'm so torn up about this. About her. It doesn't make any sense. But nothing about my feelings for Cecilia made sense. They didn't need to.

She was just ... fuck. I don't even know. She was her, and I was me, and together, we fit. We just fucking fit.

I told her I loved her. Me. I said those three fucking words. Words I've never said to any other girl before. I handed her my still-beating heart and let her carve it up as she saw fit, trusting that she felt the same way I did.

Idiot.

I don't know what I was thinking. I trusted the girl who snuck beneath my armor when no one else could. And when I laid myself bare at her feet, she told me to walk away. Like severing this connection between us is so damn easy.

Maybe for her, it is. But it's not like that for me.

I can't stop caring about her with the flip of a switch. If it was that easy, I wouldn't feel like this. Like my fucking soul is cannibalizing itself, leaving behind a gaping wound in my chest.

I fucking hate it.

I rub at the ache beneath my ribs, desperate to ease some of the pain.

We weren't dating. She wasn't my girlfriend. We were just ... *fuck.*

Even now, I don't know how to describe what we were.

And a part of me thinks I never needed to.

I didn't need a label to know it was special. That what was going on between us was different. More than anything I'd ever had before with another woman. But for some irrational reason, it sort of pisses me off that I can't even call her my ex. As far as anyone else can tell, we were never anything.

"Just leave it alone," I snap, hands clenching at my sides to hide their faint tremor. I can't keep reliving the worst day of my goddamn life. Not if I want to keep what's left of my sanity.

Heavy footfalls sound down the hall before Julio—another of my roommates—fills the doorway just behind Felix, brow furrowed. The combined weight of their stares makes my skin prickle uncomfortably.

Christ. They're turning into mother fucking hens.

"For fuck's sake," I mutter under my breath, shoulders tensing. There goes any chance at privacy. I'm trying to sort through the tangled mess in my head, and I don't need a goddamn audience for it.

The weekends are the only reprieve I get from seeing her, and this weekend came and went too goddamn fast.

I'm trying to amp myself up for today—Monday—and these assholes won't leave me the hell alone.

"You've been moping around for weeks," Julio says bluntly, always one to cut right to the chase. The guy doesn't even start off with a good morning. "You're not the only one who lives here, cabrón." —*fucker*— "So, spill. Why have you been an absolute dick, lately?"

I flip my best friends off, jaw tight. I don't care if I'm being a moody bastard right now. I think I've earned the right to work through this on my own terms, without either of them scrutinizing my every move.

Julio's dark eyes flash with frustration, clearly not on the same page. "Can you at least pretend to be a functioning human long enough to welcome Deacon? The guy *you* invited to move into nuestra casita." —*our home*— "He's going to be here any minute and you need to get whatever stick you have up your ass, out."

Shit.

I forgot he was moving in today. I scrub my hand over my face and try like hell to shove my feelings back into their box.

Deacon's a freshman transfer from Suncrest U. We met when he helped friends of ours fork our soccer field.

A prank in retaliation for one of Julio's fuck ups. I silently eye the fucker. Maybe I should remind him of how not so long ago he was dealing with a mess of his own, too. And what did he do when Felix and I suggested we hash it out?

He told us to back the fuck off.

And we did.

I'd love to give the asshole a reminder, but knowing Julio the way that I do, it would just make him dig deeper. He's a stubborn bastard like that. Always wanting to peel back everyone's fucking trauma, except for his own.

I sigh. The Deacon thing can't be avoided. I made a bet with the guy after he helped Allie, Bibiana, and Kasey fork our field. If he scored a goal against me, we'd clean up their mess. If he missed, they were cleaning up after themselves.

Long story short, he scored. Talk about a blow to my fucking ego. But after seeing the guy's kick, we recruited him onto our team. Who knew the cocky footballer would be a legit *fútboler*.

Convincing him to change sports and switch schools seemed like a good idea at the time. Now I'm not so sure. The timing is absolute shit if you ask me.

The idea of slapping on a polite smile as I make stilted small talk makes my insides twist up even more. I can't handle this shit. Not today. Not when I have to see her in less than an hour.

Low voices drift down the hall as the front door opens. It's Atticus—roommate number three—giving Deacon the grand tour. I should make an effort to welcome the guy. I know that. But the mere idea of exchanging pleasantries and pretending I'm not imploding on the inside feels fucking impossible right now.

Fuck. When did I become such a little bitch?

I've been through tough shit before. Carlos's suicide. My parents divorce. Real shit.

So why the hell is it so goddamn hard to function now?

I stare out my bedroom window. The sun is shining. The autumn leaves have turned from green to a multitude of yellows, reds, and oranges.

By all accounts it's a beautiful day.

And it's a lie.

How can I act like everything's fine when it fucking isn't? When every word out of Cecilia's mouth echoes endlessly inside of my head?

"And this is Gabe's room," Atticus tells him once they reach my door. "Hey, man," Atticus greets me, hand raised in the air.

Breathe, I tell myself. Say hello. It's not that hard. Only … it is.

My molars grind together, jaw locked tight.

Felix jumps to the rescue, playing the gracious host while I avoid eye contact and remain stubbornly silent. *Fuck this shit.*

"Hey! Atticus giving you the grand tour?" Felix asks. "Has he shown you the garage? No?"

Deacon responds, but I can't make out his words over the ringing in my ears. I don't want to do this. I'm not ready to see her again. I need more time.

"Bro, it's perfection. We always kick it in there. Come on, I'll—" Their voices fade as Felix steers Deacon and Atticus down the hallway and toward the back door, granting me a temporary reprieve.

A second later, the door clicks shut, leaving me alone with Julio's scrutinizing stare once more. He stays propped just inside my doorway, the wooden door closed at his back and his tattooed arms crossed over his chest.

The weight of his gaze bores into me as the silence stretches tight.

I grit my teeth, resentment simmering beneath my skin. It's not that much to ask to be left alone.

"Get your shit together, man," Julio says, tone harsh with judgment.

I bristle, hands clenched into fists at my sides. "You don't know what I'm dealing with, J," I fire back.

Julio has no goddamn idea what it's like to put yourself out there. To lay your feelings bare, only to have them stomped on and dismissed without a second thought. How could he? The guy hasn't been in a serious relationship in ... well, ever. And whatever spark he did have with a certain someone—she who will not be named—he snuffed out.

It was his call. His choice.

I wasn't afforded that luxury.

Julio steps further into the room, eyes searching mine for answers I don't have. "Then talk to me. I've always had your back, but I can't do anything if you shut me and everyone else out."

I scrub both hands roughly down my face, throat tightening around all the things I want to say, but can't seem to voice.

He's not wrong. I've been pushing him and the others away when I know all they want is to help me. Problem is, I don't want their help. I don't want to deal with any of this.

"I don't even know how to process this myself right now," I force out hoarsely, unable to meet his gaze. "Let alone talk through it. What Cecilia said ..." I trail off, shaking my head as the echo of her words threatens to drag me back down into the abyss.

Fuck.

What is wrong with me? I don't get like this. Not over a girl. I'm not this guy. Never have been. So why the fuck is this shit hitting me so goddamn hard?

Julio grips my shoulder, his palm rough and warm. Grounding. "Tell me what happened, man. Start there."

Sucking in a sharp breath, I shake my head.

"Come on, man. Try." Knowing Julio, he's going to keep poking until I cave. May as well get it over with now and just tear off the damn band-aid.

"She ended things. Said she didn't want this. Didn't want me." I repeat Cecilia's speech aloud for the first time, and with each word I say, I watch as Julio's expression sinks more and more into one of pity.

I don't want his pity. Though it's obvious I have it.

I force out the last of my words, making sure to get it all out. If pushed again, I won't be able to rehash this shit a second time. Just voicing her rejection aloud leaves me raw. Wounded.

But there it is. All of it. I don't leave a single detail out.

My pathetic confession hangs heavy between us. Admitting it out loud doesn't grant the respite I think either of us hoped for. It only intensifies the crushing weight on my chest. Why do people think talking about this kind of shit will make them feel better? It doesn't.

Fuck.

I rub a hand over my chest.

It hurts. This feeling. It fucking hurts, and I need to figure out some way to make it go away.

Julio squeezes my shoulder, tone softening. "Damn. I'm sorry, man. I know how much she meant to you."

Does he, though? My throat tightens around the bitter lump expanding inside my throat. Cecilia isn't some casual fling I can move on from overnight. She's so much more than that. She's ... everything.

"I thought we had something real. Something that could go the distance." My voice cracks on the admission. But I saw a future with this girl. "I know she has shit to deal with. Of course, I know that. But ..." I hang my head. "It felt real. It felt like more than just ... I don't know." I rub the back of my neck. "Guess it was all one-sided. Whatever it was. She made it crystal clear where she stands."

Julio nods, eyes shining with sympathy. "I know it's hard to hear, but maybe this is a good thing. I hate to see you hurting like this. We all do. But you said it yourself, she's got her own shit to work through. Letting her go sounds like the right call."

I jerk sharply out of his grasp. "Letting her go?" I repeat incredulously. As if my feelings for Cecilia can be boxed up and set aside like this week's trash. "Are you fucking with me right now?"

His dark brows draw together.

I'm not letting her go. Julio's one of my best friends. He's not supposed to tell me to move on. He's supposed to, I don't know, give me advice or some shit on how to get her back.

"You're an asshole," I tell him.

Resentment simmers in my veins. I know why Cecilia is pushing me away. She's scared of needing someone. Scared of relying on me too much to keep her demons at bay.

But she shouldn't be. And yeah, she ended shit, but I'm not giving up on us that easily. Right?

Right.

The more and more I think about it, the more determination settles in my bones. I'm not going to just lie down and let her push me out of her life. Not when she's shut out everyone else around her.

She doesn't get to dictate my feelings.

This is bullshit.

I refuse to be just another person who's abandoned her when things get too hard. I'm not about to be added to the growing list of people she can't depend on or open up to. Nah. Not happening.

Cecilia's let me in before.

An idea forms in my mind.

She'll let me in again. This is only a setback. Cecilia needs to know I won't bail. That I'll put in the work. That I'll be there when she needs me, no matter what.

"You don't get it." If anyone could understand, I thought it'd be Julio. "She needs me right now, even if she won't admit it. I can break through her walls again if I try hard enough. I can fix this. Fix … us."

My voice trails off as I realize how weak and desperate I sound.

I don't care.

Cecilia is worth fighting for. What we have, it's worth going all in on. I have to believe that. Because, fuck, I don't know how I'm supposed to go on myself if I don't.

Julio's shoulders slump in defeat, and he walks back to the door with a heavy sigh. "I know you love her," he tells me.

If he knew what I felt for her, he wouldn't tell me to let her go.

"But don't let this destroy you, too. Not after how much *you've* been through. How far *you've* come."

My jaw flexes.

He hesitates by the door, turning back to face me. Doubt shadows his dark brown eyes and I can see how much he's weighing his words. "I know it doesn't feel like it right now, but moving on is for the best. I truly believe that. You've already been through hell yourself. With your brother. And then all the bullshit with your parents. Taking on Cecilia's trauma too—" He shakes his head. "That's a lot for anyone to handle. Even you. You're not invincible, Gabriel. You bleed red just like the rest of us."

My jaw clenches, teeth grinding together hard enough that pain shoots up behind my eyes. But I remain silent. I let him speak his mind, as misguided as he is. Julio needs to get it out of his system.

He runs a hand through his short-cropped hair. "I'm just saying, sometimes love means knowing when to walk away. Cecilia has a mountain of issues to work out alone before she can handle being in a relationship again. Sometimes it's just ..." He hesitates. "The right girl and the wrong time." I get the feeling we're not only talking about my relationship now.

"She doesn't have to go through it alone. Not when she has me."

He nods his head and gives me a sympathetic look. "You're my best friend. My brother. I don't want to see you wrecked when you win her back, only for her to break it off again later on down the road. It'll hurt that much more. We both know that girl isn't ready for anything serious right now."

I stare back at him, anger simmering beneath my skin even as I fight to keep my expression carefully blank. I don't want him to know how much this hurts—his lack of support. How it fucking guts me. Because yeah, he is my best friend. My brother. We're ride or die. *Familia* to the bitter end. Which is what makes all of this that much worse.

After a painfully long moment, Julio turns back to the door with a disappointed shake of his head. "Just think it over," he says quietly. "Sometimes it's better to make a clean break now than to drag it out. It'll save both of you a lot of pain in the end."

CECILIA

"**Y**ou can do this," I remind myself, clutching my books tighter to my chest. The bell is going to ring any minute, which means if I don't walk inside right now, I'm going to be late.

I can do this. Deep breaths. Things are going to get better.

I know they will.

Right? I mean. They have to. Gabriel can't hate me forever, right?

God, I hope not.

Sucking in a lungful of air, I walk toward my first class, eyes glued to my feet.

I bump into a hard body, and my heartbeat stutters. An involuntary reaction.

A knot forms in the pit of my stomach.

Before I can react, large hands grip my upper arms to steady me. Revulsion spirals through me at the unwanted touch, and I wrench myself away, skin crawling.

Breathe. I remind myself. You're at school. It's fine. Just breathe.

"Sorry. Excuse me," I choke out, trying not to let this frazzle me, but when I look up to see who I ran into, I recoil.

Austin Holt leers down at me, blocking my path. I jump, barely stifling a shriek as he looms over me, his hulking frame casting me in shadow. I can't breathe with the heavy weight of his stare dragging over me.

No.

What does he want from me now?

I cross my arms, hugging myself tight as I retreat further into the corner in a vain attempt to make myself smaller.

Invisible.

Anything to avoid notice.

But I'm never that lucky.

Nausea and panic rise like twin tides set to drown me. I squeeze my eyes shut, fighting to stay afloat amidst the waves. His cologne assails my senses. It's thick and cloying. Like an Axe body spray commercial gone wrong.

Memories flicker across my closed eyelids.

Hands pulling at my clothes. A heavy weight pinning me down to the bed.

No. No. No.

Do not go there. You're not there. You're here. At school. You're safe. Austin can't hurt you here.

Except, he already has.

Just a few weeks ago, Austin slammed my head into the wall outside the campus pool. Both in retaliation and warning.

He doesn't care where he is when he hurts me or who might see it. An audience doesn't stop Austin. It never has. In fact, I'm almost certain he craves the attention. The impunity.

I can't breathe. I can't—

"Cece," he drops his voice low in an almost seductive drawl. "Fancy seeing you here." An arrogant smirk twists his mouth, and I tighten my arms around myself, fighting off a shiver.

He reaches a hand toward me, and I take an involuntary step back, sinking into the nearby wall. My heart pounds in my chest. Why won't he just leave me alone? I can't— I shake my head. I just can't. Not today. Not ever.

Fuck.

I avoid his probing gaze.

Austin scrutinizes me like I'm a butterfly pinned to the wall.

Maybe if I refuse to engage, he'll get bored and move on. That's it. I just have to keep it together long enough for him to get bored. Austin wants a reaction out of me.

I won't give him one.

"Aw, don't be like that," he croons, planting one muscular arm on the wall beside my head. He leans in close enough for me to get another whiff of his cologne. To see the blond stubble lining his jaw.

I clench my teeth to keep them from chattering and stare at the stupid puka shell necklace around his neck.

Austin presses into me until my back is flush with the wall, caging me in place as students rush by, oblivious. Their voices fade into the background noise beneath the roaring of blood in my ears.

They see us. Of course they do. But with the way we're positioned, Austin and I look like secret lovers. They don't see him as the monster and me, his unwilling victim. But that's exactly what we are. Austin Holt will never be anything but the monster in my nightmares, and I hate him for it. I hate him for breaking me. For stealing bits and pieces of who I am. For turning me into this ... this shell of a person. He ruined everything.

I swallow down my scream.

He ruined me.

The urge to cry for help overwhelms me, but fear locks up my throat, leaving me mute and trembling.

Austin's smile twists cruelly as he places a fingertip beneath my chin and forces my eyes up to meet the arctic chill of his pale blue gaze.

"Wha... wha... what do you want?" I stumble over the words.

Dammit. I'm stronger than this.

Don't show him your fear. Don't give him what he wants.

Austin's fingers shift until he's cupping my jaw, but the hold isn't gentle. It's possessive. Controlling. Bile rises in my throat.

"I've been thinking about you," he says. "Have you been thinking about me, too? About our night together?"

Tears well in my eyes.

"I've been thinking about that night a lot lately. Especially since you've needed near constant reminders about our little ..." he pauses until my eyes flicker to his, fingers digging painfully into my skin, "arrangement."

His breath ghosts over my cheek as he leans in to whisper near my ear, "I'd hate to resort to more extreme measures to keep this pretty little mouth shut, Cece. So tell me, are you behaving yourself? Or should we revisit our night together? You know, for old times' sake."

Tears blur my vision, but I blink them back, refusing to show any more weakness in front of this monster than I already have.

His finger trails from my chin down my throat in a perverse caress.

Revulsion and nausea roil inside me.

"I'm doing what you asked," I choke out in a ragged whisper. "I've kept my mouth shut. I haven't said a word since ..." I trail off, unable to get the words out, but he knows what I mean. He knows I haven't said a word about the assault since the morning after it happened. Not since I realized no one was going to believe me. Not the school. Not my friends.

And if they don't believe me, why bother going to the police?

Austin knew before he ever laid a hand on me that he'd get away with it. But it took me losing everything to come to that same realization.

Statistics for rape victims are deplorable in the United States. Richland is no exception.

One in every six women in the U.S. has been a victim of sexual assault. I'm not special here. Just a member of a club I wish I'd never been a part of.

Suncrest U did a study a while back that found less than six percent of reported rapes in the United States lead to an arrest. Less than one percent lead to a conviction. And only half a percent of those convictions result in jail time.

And that's not even including the over sixty percent of rapes that aren't even reported. Ones like mine.

It shouldn't surprise me that Austin and his friends got away with what they did to me. I'm just another statistic. A silent, forgotten number that society couldn't care less about.

Austin clicks his tongue, straightening as his smile sharpens with cruelty. "Keep it that way. Your boy is sniffing around my business. Get him to stop or—" He lets the threat hang in the air between us.

"I broke things off," I tell him, hating the way that admission tastes on my tongue. My heart squeezes. Just thinking about Gabriel, about the look on his face when he told me he loved me, it twists something inside of me.

I look down at my chest, searching for the blood I know should be pouring out of my heart. It feels like someone's stabbed a blade deep in my chest. There's nothing there. But the pain is real. This ache. Austin found a way to take yet another thing from me.

He tilts his head, a curious glimmer in his eyes. "Trouble in paradise? Lover boy unable to—" He makes a crude motion with his hips, grinding into me. "—satisfy you?"

"Get off of me," I shriek. Bracing both hands against Austin's chest, I push with all my might.

He doesn't even sway.

My breath seizes in my lungs. He's too close. He's going to ... no. He can't. He—Urgh!

A mocking chuckle pours out of him.

Fear skitters down my spine. I need to get out of here. But I can't move. I can't breathe. And I'm trapped between the wall and Austin's body. My breathing grows labored, the sound loud in the near-empty hallways.

Where did everyone go? There were more people before. Did the bell ring and I somehow missed it?

"Is that what happened, Cece? Did you realize you need a real man to—"

"Get the fuck away from her," an all too familiar voice bites out. The next thing I know, Austin is thrown back away from me and slammed into the wall across from me. His body bounces off the wall, a small grunt hissing past his lips.

My eyes jerk to familiar pools of amber right before Gabriel tears his furious gaze away from mine, only to shove his face into Austin's. "I told you to stay the fuck away from her," Gabriel snarls, fists twisting into the collar of Austin's polo shirt.

Gabriel looks two seconds away from punching Austin in the face, but he can't.

Not here.

There's too much at stake for him.

"Gabe—" I start.

"Or what?" Austin bites back. "Last I heard, she dumped your ass. So, why don't you mind your own business?"

Gabriel's nostrils flare and he draws his fist back, but before he can swing, I lunge for it. Wrapping my hands around his wrist, I pull down on his arm, praying he won't shrug me off.

"He isn't worth it," I tell him, my voice pleading.

Austin's grin widens. "You sure about that?" His eyes rake me up and down with clear interest as bile scorches the back of my throat.

The first bell rings, a shrill alarm reminding me to get to class. Only I can't just walk away from this. Not knowing that as soon as I turn my back, Gabriel will punch Austin in the face. He'd happily be the one to deliver the first blow.

It's what Austin wants. I can see it in his eyes. He wants Gabriel to punch him, which means he already knows the repercussions Gabriel will face.

I can't let Gabriel throw his future down the drain. Austin's parents are lawyers. They'll go straight to the Dean's office—guns blazing—and have Gabriel expelled.

Screw him.

Austin doesn't deserve that satisfaction. He's ruined enough lives as it is. I won't let him destroy Gabriel's.

"What's it gonna be, Hererra?" Austin taunts. "You gonna defend your girl, or are you gonna walk away like a scared little bitch?"

Gabe bares his teeth but eases back, his entire body vibrating with barely tempered restraint.

Austin's hands raise in mock surrender even as his smile remains cold and satisfied. He tips an imaginary hat my way. "The bitch route it is. Good thing you cut this one loose." He chuckles. "See you around, Cece. Enjoy class." He turns to saunter down the now empty hall and disappears around the corner just as the late bell rings, his jaunty whistle echoing back to Gabriel and me where we stand.

I slump against the wall, shaking and fighting back irrational tears. I'm going to be sick. Or pass out. Or both. Now that the adrenaline is leaving my system, I'm falling apart fast.

Fuck.

Why won't Austin just leave me alone? What is it going to take? I've done everything he's asked. There's nothing left for me to give. No further concession I can make.

Pulling in one gasping breath after another, I close my eyes, counting down from one hundred to quell the rising panic threatening to choke me. If Gabriel hadn't been here … No. I can't think about that right now.

I'm fine. Austin is gone. I'm going to be fine.

Deep breath in. *Exhale.* Deep breath out.

My hands tremble as I smooth back my long brown hair, my fingers unsteady.

I avoid Gabriel's searching gaze, instead staring down at the Volcom graphic on my oversized T-shirt. It hangs off one shoulder, exposing more bare skin than I'd like. Should have stuck with a sweater.

I cross my arms over my chest and try to stop shaking.

Gentle fingers under my chin tilt my head up. I nearly flinch away but remind myself this isn't Austin. It's Gabe. And Gabriel is safe. He won't hurt me. Even though when we last spoke, I was the one to hurt him.

His honey-gold eyes bore into mine, his jaw clenched. "Are you okay?"

I open my mouth but can't find any words. I manage a slight nod. A lie. But denying that I'm all right won't help either of us right now.

Gabriel's nostrils flare, a muscle in his cheek feathering. I can see the effort it takes to rein in his anger. He doesn't like my response. He doesn't believe me.

His thumb brushes my cheek. A barely there caress before dropping away. My heart plummets, and already I mourn the loss of his touch.

"Come on," he says roughly. "Let's get you to class."

He turns on his heel, shoulders rigid, but keeps his steps short. A way to ensure I'm able to keep up with his longer stride.

I trail after him. My legs are unsteady, and my gut churns with all the words left unsaid between us. Gabriel isn't supposed to save me. I'm not his responsibility. Not anymore.

I just wish I was strong enough to save myself.

CECILIA

T he day drags on at a snail's pace. Sitting through my first class of the week with Gabriel is uncomfortable, to say the least. There's this heavy tension hanging between us, and despite the weeks that have passed, it never seems to abate.

He still sits beside me, just like before—when he bothers to show up to class at least. And I know the classes he's missed lately are because of me. But even when he's here, he doesn't look at me. Doesn't flash me that crooked smile of his. He doesn't try to pull me into conversation.

I used to hate that. Hated that he wanted to be friends. That he tried to pull me out of my shell. But this ... this is so much worse.

It's a painful, suffocating silence.

The weight of unspoken words fill the space where casual banter used to flow, and by the time the bell rings signaling the end of class, I'm desperate for a reprieve from it.

Only there isn't one. Gabriel and I have two classes together today, and I get the feeling that the next one will be even worse. I don't know how to fix this. And if I'm honest, I'm not entirely sure I want to.

He isn't supposed to be my friend. He isn't supposed to be my anything.

Mom used to say, *time heals all wounds*.

Time hasn't helped me recover from what Austin did to me, but maybe with enough time, I can heal from this. From losing Gabriel.

The semester will end soon enough and with us no longer seeing each other, there's no reason for him to be in any more of my classes. He won't need to insert himself into my life. He won't drag me to his practices or drop in at my parents' house unannounced.

We won't cross paths every day. There's a good chance we can go an entire semester without even seeing one another.

Maybe then it will hurt less. That's all I can hope for these days.

After I gather my things, Gabriel walks beside me in silence, keeping pace with my shorter steps. I don't know why. He isn't talking to me, so why walk with me to class when he can easily outpace me?

But this has become a routine of sorts.

He shadows me but doesn't talk to me. He sits by me but never looks at me.

It's infuriating. Meanwhile, I can't help but steal glances at the hard line of his jaw, the furrow between his dark brows.

What is he thinking?

Is he angry? He looks it. But whether his anger is directed at me or someone else, I don't know. He might still be pissed about Austin. Though that was an hour ago. Maybe someone or something else is on his mind right now?

We've drifted apart in such a short span of time that I don't know how to read him anymore.

But I miss him. And I hate that I miss him because I have no right to. Not when I'm the one who pushed him away.

Part of me wishes I could slip my hand into his like I used to, and have things go back to the way they were before I opened my mouth and ruined everything.

But I can't. Life doesn't work that way. And it wouldn't be fair to him.

I told myself I wouldn't be selfish. Not when it comes to him.

We walk into our next class, and just like before, Gabriel claims the seat beside me. Our second class goes by much like the first, our professor droning on about this week's lecture. I'm barely paying attention, too caught up in watching Gabriel from the corner of my eye.

He looks as miserable as I feel. Is he sleeping okay? Are those dark circles or just shadows under his eyes?

Is this what it'll be like from now on? Gabriel spoke to me earlier in the hall when he defended me against Austin. A part of me thought it would continue. That this strange silent treatment thing going on between us would finally come to an end.

At least, I hoped it would.

Gabriel takes methodical notes beside me, his attention locked on the front of the room.

It's like I don't even exist.

Of my three classes, two of them are with him, and while I can't stand this weird limbo we're stuck in, I still dread when class comes to an end. Gabriel will go off to soccer practice, and I'll drag myself back home, where I know I'll overthink and second-guess my decision to break things off between us for the hundredth time.

I need a distraction. Some way to quiet my racing thoughts before I completely lose it. A swim, or maybe a run? It's days like this when I'm reminded of the fact I no longer have friends.

Joelle and Kim dropped me as soon as Austin drew battle lines in the sand. They were shitty friends. But they were the only ones I had and an irrational part of me misses them. Misses having someone to call and confide in.

The bell rings, jolting me from my thoughts. Our professor announces what chapters we'll need to have read by tomorrow, and everyone begins shuffling their things into their backpacks, eager for freedom.

I shove my own books haphazardly into my bag, refusing to let my eyes drift back to Gabriel. I can't stomach seeing that closed-off look of his aimed my way. Maybe I should make an appointment with my counselor. See if I can make some changes to my schedule before the semester ends.

I might have to take a zero since the withdrawal date has already passed, but it might be worth it. It's not like I'm in a rush to graduate or anything.

My phone chimes, and I look down at the screen, seeing the email alert from another of my professors.

Dear Students,

Class is canceled today and tomorrow due to an unforeseen personal matter. Please read up on last week's assignments. We will have a quiz on Wednesday on the materials we've been covering. It is weighted at 15% of your final grade. I encourage you to study in an effort to be prepared.

Regards, Professor Bowman.

My shoulders slump. *Great.*

Gabriel hovers beside me, his movements slow as though he's waiting for me. I try not to read into it. He's always walked me to my last class of the day when he's here, regardless of how tense things are between us, but it's canceled today.

Do I tell him?

No.

It's presumptuous to assume he'll want to walk me to class today, isn't it?

It is.

I'll just head to my Jeep and see what he does. Maybe he'll go the opposite direction as soon as we exit the classroom.

I don't know. And I hate not knowing.

We exit the building side by side, silence stretching between us. He's still following me, but we're not going in the direction of my class, and he hasn't asked me why. He also hasn't moved to head for the locker rooms, which are on the opposite end of our campus.

He just wordlessly walks beside me.

I want to bridge this gaping chasm between us, but I don't know how.

Or if he even wants me to try.

Lost in my thoughts, I don't see Felix bounding up to us, or the guy trailing close behind him. But I do notice when Gabriel stiffens beside me, coming to a stop. My footsteps falter beside him.

"Cecilia!" Felix greets me with a grin. "Long time no see. Have you met our new roomie?"

He tugs Deacon forward, and on instinct, I take a reflexive step back.

Gabriel all but growls beside me as he quickly tucks me behind his back.

"Shit, my bad." Felix offers me a chagrined grin. "I forgot about ..." He shrugs. "You know."

My aversion to strange men? Nearly all men, really. There are very few exceptions. Gabriel being one of them. I've gotten used to Julio and Felix, but only enough to be near them. Not to hug them or be any sort of touchy-feely with them. In a strictly platonic way, obviously. But you know what I mean. We've been friendly. But I don't know. I guess I really only count Gabriel as a friend.

Before, I mean. We're not friends now. We're not ... anything.

I swallow down the lump in my throat, reminding myself that it's fine. I'm fine. Felix is safe. And if this guy lives with Gabriel, I'll assume they're friends, which means he's probably an alright guy.

Taking a deep breath, I force myself to take one cautious step forward, enough for me to see the new guy while still keeping myself shielded by Gabriel's back.

"No worries," I force out a smile, tamping down my anxiety. "New roommate?" I ask, my gaze flicking from Felix to Gabriel and then to the other guy. I take in his visible ink, both forearms decorated with intricate designs. He has light brown, almost hazel eyes framed with dark brows. Medium brown skin. Full lips.

There's a cross tattoo on the left side of his neck. A scroll design filled with script on the right. He's attractive, I guess. If you're into the whole athletically built, tattooed god sort of thing. But he's also ... imposing. A formidable player.

Is he on the soccer team? I don't remember seeing him on the field when I used to go to Gabriel's practices. And he's not the sort of guy you'd easily miss.

Gabriel likes to keep his circle tight.

I wonder how they know each other. And why I've never seen him around before.

"Yeah. Hey. I'm Deacon." The new guy shoots me a cocky smile, soft brown eyes scanning my face with interest. "Cecilia, right? Pretty name for a pretty girl."

Heat climbs up my neck, and not in a good way. I don't want him to notice me. To look at me like that. Like he finds me attractive. My breathing shutters, and Gabriel shifts abruptly, blocking me from Deacon's view. He glances over his shoulder once, looking down at me with concern flashing across his handsome face before turning back to the guys.

"You two should get to the field." His voice is hard. Cold. "Practice is going to be grueling today."

Felix's smile falters.

Silent communication passes between him and Gabriel before he nods, subtly drawing Deacon away. "Right. So, uh we'll see you out there. Later, Cecilia."

"Bye." I mutter, giving him a half-hearted wave.

I'm not sure he hears me.

As soon as they're gone from view, Gabriel turns halfway back towards me, then pauses, some of the tension seeming to drain from his broad shoulders.

He sucks on his teeth for a moment.

"You good?" His tone softens a fraction. This is Gabriel trying.

My chest squeezes and I nod. "Yeah. I'm good."

He nods his head, and the silence stretches between us again.

"Did you forget something in your car?"

My eyes snap up to his. "What?" The question slips out on autopilot before I put two and two together and correct my response. "Oh, no."

He tilts his head toward the doors. "You were heading to the parking lot ..." he trails off.

"My last class is canceled." I shrug. "Guess I'm all done for the day."

He dips his chin once before tilting his face up to the ceiling, almost like he's searching for the right words to say. Seconds tick past before he huffs out a sigh and god, I didn't know there could be so many words unsaid in a sound.

"I don't know where we go from here." There's defeat in his voice.

Neither do I, I want to tell him. But I don't know if that's the right thing to say or if I should say anything at all, so I stay quiet and wait for him to decide what to do. How we should move forward. I took Gabriel's choices away when I broke things off. This—allowing him to decide how we move forward—it's the least I can do.

"Do you want to come watch our practice?" Before I can respond, he adds, "I know the guys would like to see you. Julio asked about you this morning."

Oh. I find that hard to believe, and I don't really need the pity invite. He shouldn't have to see me at practice if he doesn't want to.

"No. That's okay. I ... uh ..." Julio is great. All the guys are. But they're not my friends, no matter how welcoming they've been to me. They're Gabriel's friends. His best friends.

And I'm the girl who broke their friend's heart.

I doubt any of them really want to be around me, though I appreciate that Felix was kind just now and said hello.

"You have other plans?" He knows I don't. I never do. I go to school. I go home. I hit the campus pool if I need a swim.

Rinse and repeat.

"Yeah." The lie rolls off my tongue. "I'll uh, see you around."

• • •

GABRIEL AND CECILIA'S STORY CONTINUES IN THE STRIKER Available Now—> https://amzn.to/3QCKH9O

www.ingramcontent.com/pod-product-compliance
Lightning Source LLC
Chambersburg PA
CBHW010839190726
48286CB00012BA/2913

* 9 7 8 1 9 5 3 2 6 4 2 0 6 *